ALSO BY BLAKE NELSON

BLAKE NELSON

BOY

a novel

SIMON PULSE

NEW YORK • LONDON • TORONTO • SYDNEY • NEW DELHI

SIMON PULSE

An imprint of Simon & Schuster Children's Publishing Division
1230 Avenue of the Americas, New York, New York 10020
First Simon Pulse hardcover edition June 2017
Text copyright © 2017 by Blake Nelson
Jacket design and illustration by Regina Flath copyright © 2017 by Simon & Schuster, Inc.
All rights reserved, including the right of reproduction in whole or in part in any form.
SIMON PULSE and colophon are registered trademarks of Simon & Schuster, Inc.
For information about special discounts for bulk purchases, please contact
Simon & Schuster Special Sales at 1-866-506-1949 or business@simonandschuster.com.
The Simon & Schuster Speakers Bureau can bring authors to your live event.
For more information or to book an event contact the Simon & Schuster
Speakers Bureau at 1-866-248-3049 or visit our website at www.simonspeakers.com.
Interior designed by Steve Scott
The text of this book was set in Palatino.
Manufactured in the United States of America
2 4 6 8 10 9 7 5 3 1
Library of Congress Cataloging-in-Publication Data
Names: Nelson, Blake, 1960- author.
Title: Boy / Blake Nelson.
Description: Simon Pulse hardcover edition. | New York : Simon Pulse, [2017] |
Summary: Popular sixteen-year-old Gavin is happy spending his time with friends,
dating, and playing tennis, until a mysterious girl named Antoinette transfers to his school
and influences the way he views himself, his friends, and his relationships.
Identifiers: LCCN 2016033311 (print) | LCCN 2017006338 (eBook) |
ISBN 9781481488136 (hc) | ISBN 9781481488150 (eBook)
Subjects: | CYAC: High schools—Fiction. | Schools—Fiction. | Dating (Social customs)—
Fiction. | Friendship—Fiction. | Popularity—Fiction. | Cliques (Sociology)—Fiction.
Classification: LCC PZ7.N4328 Bo 2017 (print) | LCC PZ7.N4328 (eBook) |
DDC [Fic]—dc23
LC record available at https://lccn.loc.gov/2016033311

FOR PENNY

SOPHOMORE YEAR

Stare. It is the way to educate your eye.
—*Walker Evans*

Just having the camera, being able to pull back from
situations and be an observer, it saved my life. . . .
—*Ryan McGinley*

I remember the morning Antoinette became a "known" person at our school. I was in Mr. Miller's geometry class. It was first period and everyone was half asleep. Kaitlyn Becker was scribbling in her math book, her head sideways on her desk. Someone was whispering in the back row. I was sitting by the window, staring out at the courtyard. A thick fog had settled in, which made the trees look ghostly and mysterious. The benches and walkways looked like they were from another time. What made it do that? The moisture in the air? The blurriness of the light? Fog made things look *sad*, I thought. Like a *memory*. Like something that had happened a long time ago and could never be undone.

There was an announcement, which I didn't quite hear, and when I turned back toward the room, our teacher was gone.

"Hey," I said to the boy next to me. "What happened to Mr. Miller?"

"He went to the office."

"What for?"

"I dunno."

I looked around. The whole class had been left sitting at

our desks, with no one in charge. That was unusual.

Then we heard adult shoes clacking down the hall. An adult voice called out. One of the kids stuck his head out the door to see what was going on. A teacher yelled for him to go back in, sit down, and close the door.

Something was definitely up. We sat in our seats, looking at each other, wondering what had happened.

In the hallway after class, everyone was buzzing about a girl named Antoinette Renwick. She had been taken to the office by the principal. A police car had been seen in the parking lot. People weren't sure what had happened. Had she done something wrong? Was she under arrest?

I vaguely knew who Antoinette Renwick was. She was one of the new kids that year. She had black hair and thick dark eyebrows. She also wore weird clothes: old sweaters and skirts and non-Nike tennis shoes.

Like everyone else, I spent the rest of the day wondering about Antoinette. Had she brought drugs to school? Maybe she'd stolen something. I didn't know where she came from. Texas, someone said, but they weren't sure. Maybe she was poor or came from a messed-up family.

After school, the news went around that Antoinette's older brother had jumped off the Vista Bridge and died. A suicide. Everyone was stunned by that. Nobody knew this older brother, Marcus Renwick. He was nineteen, someone said.

Everyone felt bad for Antoinette, but there wasn't much they could do, since nobody really knew her. And anyway, she was long gone by now, since the cops had come and taken her that morning.

Before I left, I heard some girls mention the street she lived on. It wasn't that far from my house. When I got home, I decided to ride my bike over there and see what was going on.

I found her street. I didn't have the actual address, but it was obvious which house it was. A police car was in the driveway, and a bunch of other cars were parked around it. I rode up on the sidewalk across the street and stopped and stood there, straddling my bike.

I couldn't see anything, really. Everyone was inside. The house looked pretty normal: two stories, a small yard, a tree, a garage.

Then a taxicab came around the corner. I tried to look inconspicuous. The taxi stopped in the street. An older woman holding a wadded Kleenex got out. She was crying and trying to talk on her phone at the same time. She nearly dropped her bag as she went inside.

I felt a little weird then, like if the neighbors saw me it might seem strange that I was standing there, spying on the Renwick house.

Then the front door opened again. This time Antoinette came out. I thought about taking off, but she didn't see me. She didn't even look up. She was wearing one of those oversize arctic parkas. She sat down on the front step. She pulled her knees up into her chest, tucked her hair behind one ear, and stared straight down at her feet.

After a minute she checked behind her, and when she saw no one was watching, she pulled a cigarette from her pocket and slipped it in her mouth. She lit the end. That was pretty weird. Nobody at our school smoked. And definitely no sophomores did. Maybe kids smoked in Texas. She took a drag and blew out the smoke. She flicked the ash.

Then she suddenly looked up. Her eyes went straight to me. She must have sensed she was being watched.

I was busted. I didn't know what to do. I gripped my bike handles and swallowed.

"Hello?" she said. "Can I help you?"

I shook my head no.

She studied me for a moment. "You go to my school," she said.

I nodded.

"What? You can't talk?"

"I can talk," I said.

"What's your name?"

"Gavin."

She took another drag of her cigarette and squinted at me. "My brother died today," she said.

"I know."

Antoinette stared in my direction. But she wasn't seeing me anymore. She was seeing something else. I don't know

4

what, the harshness of life, maybe. She took another drag from her cigarette. Her hand was shaking now. Her lower lip began to tremble. Her face seemed about to collapse.

I felt my heart nearly leap out of my chest for her.

Then the door made a noise. Someone was trying to open it. Antoinette quickly slipped the cigarette under her shoe and ground it out. She tossed the butt into the bushes. The door opened and a woman's head appeared. She said something I couldn't hear. Antoinette stood up and went inside.

It was almost dinnertime when I got back to my own house. My mother asked me where I'd been. I told her the whole story, about the cops coming to school and the new girl and how her brother had killed himself. And how I rode my bike to her house to see what was happening.

"So you know this girl?" asked my mom.

"No," I said. "I just wanted to see the house."

"What for?"

"To see what it looked like."

"What did it look like?"

"Like the house of someone who died."

My mother gave me one of her looks. Then she told me to get ready for dinner.

I also had an older brother: Russell Meeks. He was seventeen, a senior at my same school, Evergreen High. He was working on his college applications, so that's what we talked about at dinner that night. Russell was very smart and ambitious. He wanted to be a lawyer, like my dad, so there was a lot of focus on what college he would go to. The Ivy Leagues were what everyone was thinking, since they're supposedly the best.

I ate and listened. My brother had recently started talking in a new way. It was a very clear and careful way of speaking, but it also had this special nasal quality to it, like he was smarter than you, like you probably wouldn't understand what he was talking about, that's how smart he was. Nobody else in my family mentioned this new tone. Maybe they didn't notice it. Or maybe they accepted it as part of Russell's gradual changing from normal kid into Ivy League college student.

It was mostly him and my dad talking. My dad had gone to college back East. And then to New York City for law school. He always brought this up when he talked about his past. What New York was like. How different it was from

Portland, Oregon. How you didn't know how the world worked until you'd lived back there, where the important people were, where the real stuff happened.

Anyway, Russell was saying something about a friend of his who was applying to Cornell. So then my dad had to give his opinion on that. They got in a big debate about which was better, Harvard or Stanford or Cornell. That's when I realized Russell had learned his new tone of voice from my dad. It wasn't the exact same style of talking, but it conveyed the same basic message of *I'm a douche bag.*

As she cleared the table, my mother brought up the news about Antoinette. So then I had to talk. I told about the suicide in my mumbling way, which, as usual, drove my father crazy. "Speak up, Gavin!" he said. "Nobody can hear you!"

"I said," I repeated. "That a girl in my grade got taken out of class because her brother killed himself."

"Was that the jumper?" said Russell. "I heard about that. The guy who jumped off the Vista Bridge?"

I nodded that it was.

"Do you know this girl?" said my dad.

"No," I said.

"Who's she friends with?" asked my mother.

"Nobody, really. Her family just moved here."

"That's so sad," said my mother.

"Who are his parents?" asked my dad. "What do they do?"

"What difference does that make?" I mumbled into my plate.

My dad didn't bother to answer. This was the kind of thing he hated to talk about. Suicidal teenagers. People who had problems. People who weren't achieving and succeeding and going to top colleges and New York law schools. Russell, too. They would much rather go drink brandy in the den and talk about whether Cornell was better than Stanford.

After dinner I went upstairs to my room. Tennis was my thing. That was where I'd achieved and succeeded. I'd won a bunch of local tournaments in the twelve and unders, so my room was like that: a bunch of trophies lined up on a shelf and my walls covered with posters of my favorite tennis stars. Roger Federer. Andy Roddick. Rafael Nadal. There were lots of Nike swooshes everywhere. Sometimes at night I'd practice my serving motion in my room, while I listened to music. Sometimes I would bounce a tennis ball on my racquet face. I had once done that 1,217 times in a row, which was still a record at my tennis camp.

But that's not what I did that night. A couple weeks before, my mother had bought some old art books at a rummage sale. One was a book of landscape paintings from the 1700s. These showed scenes of cows and fields and little valleys. I'd brought this book up to my room and cut out one of the pictures and thumbtacked it to the wall above my desk. I did this as a joke, really. I wasn't into art. I just felt like looking at something different for a change.

But that night, after the encounter outside Antoinette's house, I found myself looking through the art book again. And then I decided to take down my Roger Federer poster. I was bored with it. I unstuck it from the wall and went through the art book and found two more paintings that I liked, one of a road going past a farm, with a huge sky and clouds above, and another of a harbor, which also had clouds and a big sky. I cut them both out, trying to keep the cut line as straight and neat as I could. Then I thumbtacked them to the wall where the Roger Federer poster had been, one on top of the other, keeping them just the right distance apart.

Once I'd done that, I started looking at my other posters. One of my oldest ones showed the history of tennis in the United States. It was pretty lame, with all these old dudes and their old-style shorts. So I went back to the art book with my scissors and slowly turned the pages, looking for something to replace it.

I was listening to the college radio station while I did this. They were playing good electronic stuff, like they do at night. So I had this fun night of redoing my room and listening to music and cutting these pictures out of this art book. The other thing was: I kept thinking about Antoinette. Not like anything in particular, just having her in the back of my mind. As the night went on, I realized I was doing this for her. I was making my room into something she would like.

It took a couple days for Antoinette to come back to school. She showed up on a Friday morning and a hush fell over the frosh/sophomore wing. People wanted to talk about her and gossip, you could tell. But nobody really knew her. Nobody knew what had happened exactly.

The teachers tried to act like everything was normal. During first period, Mrs. Hennings was teaching her class, but then Olivia Goldstein asked her point-blank what was the best thing to say to someone if a family member had committed suicide. So then there was a big discussion about that. According to Mrs. Hennings, the proper thing to say was, "I'm sorry for your loss," just like you'd say if someone died some other way, like getting hit by a bus. For some reason that was the example people kept using, "getting hit by a bus," as if that were the most normal way to die.

Other people didn't need to be told what to say. They went right up to Antoinette and said how sorry they were and offered to help in any way they could. These were the weirder, less popular girls. They were eager to be part of something so serious and dramatic. Like finally someone needed their help, finally they had a role to play at their school.

I had my own feelings about the situation. Mainly that it might seem weird to people that I went to Antoinette's house that day. People might talk. I decided I should say something to Antoinette to make her see it wasn't a big deal.

I waited a couple days for things to calm down. Then I saw Antoinette waiting after school for her ride. She was sitting on a bench, by herself, which was rare, since she now had this little group of girls following her around. These were those same girls who had offered their condolences the week before. They were like a gang all of a sudden. Antoinette's "suicide friends," people called them.

I walked up to her, making sure to be extra polite. "Hi," I said, without sitting down.

Antoinette glanced up at me once, then looked away.

"My name's Gavin. I don't know if you remember me—"

"I remember you," she said.

I very slowly sat down beside her. Not too close. For a moment we didn't speak. We watched the other students, freshmen mostly, walking out to their parents' cars.

"How's it going?" I said.

Antoinette did a little shrug.

I nodded my head a few times. "I know it must have seemed weird," I said. "Me showing up at your house the other day."

"Yeah," she said. "It did."

"What happened was . . . well . . . I heard about your

brother . . . and I felt bad, of course . . . and I was in the neighborhood anyway and I decided to swing by . . . not for any reason, you know . . . and then you happened to come outside at the exact moment—"

"How did you know where I lived?"

"Someone said the street," I told her.

That seemed to satisfy her. A silence fell between us. I felt like it was a good silence, a positive silence. "I'm sorry for your loss," I said.

"That's what everyone says."

Some of Antoinette's new friends were standing nearby. They were watching me talk to her. They were trying to decide if they should come to her rescue or not.

I figured I'd said enough. It was time to go.

"Anyway . . . ," I said, getting to my feet.

"Thanks for stopping by, Gavin," said Antoinette.

I nodded once and walked away. Behind me, I could hear Antoinette's friends hurrying to her aid, questioning her about me.

"Do you know who that is?"

"That's Gavin Meeks!"

"Do you know him?"

"What did he want?"

"Oh my God, Antoinette, he was totally talking to you!"

That's probably another thing I should mention: I was one of the popular kids at Evergreen. This was partly because Claude Leon, my best friend and tennis partner, was the *most* popular person in my class and had been since fourth grade. And also, it was just how things worked out. I was good at sports. I dressed a certain way. I lived in a certain neighborhood. So those were the people I naturally hung out with.

Once the shock of her brother's suicide wore off, my friends forgot about Antoinette. She was far away from us socially, being new and unknown and not being friends with anyone we were friends with. I never did tell anyone about going to her house the day of the suicide.

When things returned to normal, our group went back to our usual business of goofing around, having fun, and thinking up new ways to hook up with each other. In terms of romance, I had lagged behind my other friends. Plenty of girls liked me, or would have liked me if I liked them, but I was shy about these things. I hadn't figured out how to close the deal and get an actual girlfriend.

Claude, who had been with super-hot Petra Roberts

most of freshman year, had recently paired up with Hanna Sloan, who was the other great beauty of our grade. Maybe that was what held me back: watching my best friend work his way through *all* the most desirable girls in our school.

Now, though, as we were getting further into sophomore year, people began plotting to get me a girlfriend. "It's a waste of a cute guy to have Gavin not be with someone," Hanna told people.

After a lot of discussions, it was decided Grace Anderson was the girl I should be with. Grace was perfect for me, they said, never mind that we'd known each other since kindergarten and had barely spoken. That didn't matter. Grace was getting more into boys now, and she was very cute, and also certain parts of her had "grown" recently. Most important: she and Hanna were practically best friends. And since Claude and I were best friends, it made for a logical match.

It was Claude who first brought it up. "Hey, Gavin," he said, one day in the cafeteria. "What do you think of Grace?"

"Grace Anderson?" I said. "She's okay."

"Just okay?" said Claude. "Dude, she's *hot*."

Some of our other guy friends were sitting with us. They agreed. There was much murmuring about the hotness of Grace.

"I'm not sure she's my type," I said.

"What's your type?" said someone else.

That was the thing. I was a sophomore. I didn't really have a type. Not that I knew of.

"You should go out with her," said Claude.

"With Grace?"

"Yeah," he said. "She likes you."

"How do you know?"

"Hanna told me."

I shrugged.

"You should like her," repeated Claude. "She's cute. She's nice. She's got a hot body. What else do you want?"

The other guys agreed. I looked around at them. They were all nodding. They had talked about it. The girls had talked about it.

So that was that: Grace and I would be together. I was tall and blond and good at tennis. Grace was cute and was friends with Hanna. Riding my bike home, I resolved to make it happen. I would ask Grace out on a date. And then I would ask her to be my girlfriend.

But that night, in my room, I found myself thinking about Antoinette. She wasn't nearly as good-looking as Grace. And it wasn't like I really knew her. But she'd stuck in my head. It had been a month since her brother died. And several weeks since our conversation in the breezeway. But I'd never stopped thinking about her.

If I had to have a girlfriend, why not Antoinette? I began flipping through my cut-up book of landscape paintings.

Was she my type? Could we do stuff together? Could I kiss her? Talking to her had been *thrilling* in some way. Talking to Grace, well, I had known her practically my whole life and I couldn't remember a single thing she had ever said.

In bed it got worse. I would turn one way and think about Antoinette and then turn the other way and think about her some more. I thought about her weird clothes. I didn't know if I could deal with that. Why couldn't she just wear Nikes and jeans like everyone else? But in another way, I could respect it. She was being herself. She was making a statement. I'd never been friends with anyone like that. It made me curious. It made me want to talk to her more.

But the next morning, in the cold light of day, I felt differently. I saw the absurdity of thinking I could be with Antoinette. I barely knew her. She had weird friends. She *smoked*. She obviously didn't snowboard or play tennis or do any of the things I did. Plus, her brother had committed suicide. What did that mean about the rest of her family? Probably nothing good.

No. It would never work. It was impossible. Grace was a much better fit. Grace and I had real things in common: friends, activities, history. She dressed right. She looked good. It just made more sense. It would be so much easier.

We still had to do it, though, Grace and I. We still had to officially get together. Our first attempt was at a basketball game. Several of us guys went, including Claude and Logan Hewitt. Grace and some other girls sat behind us in the bleachers. Claude elbowed me to move up to the girls' bench and sit beside Grace, but I thought that would be awkward. There wasn't room. And she was right behind me anyway. Her knees were touching my back. Wasn't that being together, in a way?

After the game, I stood next to her outside while people waited for their rides. I had this idea that I would kiss her good-bye when her ride came. But when her mom's car pulled up, I saw the stupidity of my plan. I couldn't kiss her in front of her mother. So that didn't work.

Then the next weekend, some of us went to Hanna's to watch *The Godfather*. Grace and I sat together on the couch. This seemed like the perfect place to kiss her, but I waited too long and then Hanna's little sister came in, and then someone ordered a pizza and I never got a chance.

Back at school, Claude pulled me aside. "Dude, what's going on?" he said.

"What do you mean?"

"You gotta put the moves on Grace. You like her, right?"

"Of course I like her."

"So put the moves on her."

"I am. I mean, I'm trying."

"Girls can only take so much hesitation. She's admitted she likes you. And you've admitted you like her. So what's stopping you?"

"Nothing. I know."

Fortunately, the next Friday, Logan Hewitt's older sister had a party and a few of us sophomores were allowed to come. We were in the basement when Hanna decided that we should play spin the bottle. We were too old for this, but Hanna turned it into a joke, which made it acceptable. Plus, people were feeling sorry for Grace and me. Mostly for Grace because she was doing what she was supposed to, less for me, since I was the one holding things up.

Hanna made us form a circle. Then she took a Coke bottle, placed it in the middle, and gave it a spin. When it stopped, it was pointing at me.

"I got Gavin!" she said. "That's perfect. Gavin, I pass you on to Grace."

"What?" said someone.

"I said I'm passing Gavin on to Grace. Which means I get to go again." Hanna snatched the bottle back.

"Can you do that?" said someone else.

"Of course you can do that!" said Hanna. "It's a rule. You can pass your spin to someone else, but only once per game."

Nobody had heard of this rule. But Hanna wanted Grace and me to get on with it, and this was the easiest way.

"And because that was the first spin," continued Hanna, flashing everyone a sexy grin, "you guys have to go in the bedroom for *extended minutes*."

There was more grumbling about Hanna's made-up

rules. But I stood up. Grace stood up too. We barely looked at each other as we slowly marched into the Hewitts' basement bedroom, which was more like a storage room but did have a bed in it. I knew I couldn't hesitate now, so I didn't. As soon as I'd shut the door, I turned to Grace and kissed her. The main thing was to get it done, to seal the deal.

We made out for a solid five minutes, standing next to the door. After that Grace opened her eyes and smiled at me with relief. She made a gushy girly face and kissed me again. She began to touch my neck and run her hands through my hair.

After we made out standing up, we lay on the bed. Grace began to giggle, and at one point she rolled on top of me and pecked at my face, kissing me all over with her thin lips. As she did, I unfastened the buttons of her shirt. She had a fancy silk bra on. "Nice bra," I whispered.

"Victoria's Secret," she whispered back.

We didn't go any further than that. The important thing was that we stayed in the bedroom for nearly twenty minutes. Mostly kissing and rolling around on the bed. We didn't talk much. It didn't seem necessary. We were together now. We were a couple. I think we both wanted to think about that and get used to it. It was a pretty big change in your life.

So what was it like to have a girlfriend? The first thing I noticed: There was a lot of texting. Grace updated me every few minutes on what she was doing:

I'm eating an orange.

Bio homework. Forgot it in my locker!

Hanna says tennis players have cute buns.

I did my best to text back. It was easier if she asked me questions. Then I could answer. Other times I'd write whatever was happening.

Logan just nailed Thomas in the balls.

Mr. Miller "disappointed" by Algebra quizzes.

NOT talking about you guys, talking about the Seahawks!

The best part was the making out. Grace was a great kisser, one of the best in the school, people said. That, combined with her natural cuteness, her silky soft hair, and her general girlish enthusiasm, made sitting around French kissing pretty much all we wanted to do.

Another fun thing: Our status at school changed dramatically. Being a couple, and being so closely associated with Claude and Hanna, we were suddenly very important sophomores. Sometimes I'd catch people staring at me in a certain way, like if only *they* could have a super-cute girlfriend and be in love and be having sex. (We weren't actually having sex, but everyone assumed we were or would be soon.)

And then there was the sharing your life with another person. Every day, Grace and I checked in with each other to see what we were doing after school. The fact that we were an official couple overrode small problems like we didn't like the same music or she didn't get my jokes. I thought about Grace all the time. When we were apart, I wondered where she was and what she was doing. Other people, other girls, quickly faded from my mind. If I did think of someone else—like Antoinette—it was only to realize how ridiculous it was to think we could have been happy together.

That year the Valentine's Dance became an extra-big deal. Several couples of my friends were having anniversaries. Logan Hewitt had been with Olivia Goldstein for one month. Grace and I had been together two months. Claude and Hanna would be celebrating almost five months. People seemed very excited, and not just about the dance but about love and relationships in general.

There was one small problem brewing. It involved Claude and Petra. They had been together freshman year, but now, after a short time with Logan Hewitt over the summer, Petra wasn't with anyone. Since Petra and Claude were still friends, she and Claude still talked occasionally. Hanna didn't like this.

Then one day Hanna looked through Claude's phone and saw that Petra was calling Claude all the time. Claude claimed this was just to comfort Petra after she broke up with Logan. But most of the calls were more recent than that. Many were late at night. The truth was: Petra still loved Claude and couldn't let him go.

Hanna had tried to be nice to Petra. Now she started saying how pathetic she was and making fun of her practically to her face. She didn't have to do this. No one in their right mind thought Claude would pick Petra over Hanna. Hanna was the hottest girl in our whole school by now, and Petra had just got dumped by Logan for Olivia Goldstein. But Hanna was like that. Not a drama queen exactly, but definitely a little crazy. As Grace said: "If there's blood in the water, Hanna's gonna smell it."

So then the dance came. All the couples went and lots of other people too. Petra was super dressed up, with eye makeup and a new haircut. She got a lot of attention that night, from a bunch of different guys.

Unfortunately, halfway through the dance, Claude and Petra got left on the dance floor together. This was an accident: A bunch of people had been dancing randomly, but then most of them walked off at the same time. This left Claude and Petra by themselves in the middle of the song. Claude, being stubborn and feeling it was in his rights, finished the dance with Petra.

Hanna saw this and was furious. She retreated to a corner and fumed. Claude went over to her, to reassure her, which only made things worse. So then all of Hanna's girlfriends had to go commiserate and offer support. This included Grace, who owed Hanna big-time for getting her a boyfriend.

The guys gathered around Claude, but we weren't as good at giving support as the girls. We mostly stood there, frowning to ourselves and scratching our heads. Claude thought it was ridiculous that Hanna was creating such a scene. Of course he would never cheat on Hanna. He loved her more than anything.

After a while I saw there was nothing to be done and wandered off. I got a cup of punch and took a seat on the side and watched the DJ, who was now playing to an empty dance floor. Glancing back to see how Claude was doing, I realized I had sat down next to Antoinette Renwick.

I hadn't even noticed she was there. She was with another girl, one of her "suicide friends." I glanced down at Antoinette's knee and foot. She was wearing a strange brand of shoes I'd never seen before.

After a while, the other girl got out her phone. Antoinette, who was holding a red plastic cup of punch, turned and saw me.

I also had a red plastic cup of punch. I lifted it toward her in a salute. "Hey," I said, over the music. "What's up?"

"Nothing," she said.

"I'm Gavin," I said, since it had been months since we spoke.

"I know who you are."

The song ended. I watched the DJ. I tried to think of something to say to Antoinette. "What kind of shoes are those?" I asked.

"You wouldn't know," she said.

"Try me."

"They're French."

"Seems like a long way to go for a pair of shoes," I joked.

"Don't be an asshole," she said.

"I'm not being an asshole."

"Yes you are."

"How do you figure that?"

"Why are you even talking to me?" said Antoinette. "Hanna Sloan is over there having a meltdown. Doesn't she need your *immediate attention*?"

I took a slow sip of my punch. "That has nothing to do with me."

"I don't think so. Whatever Hanna does affects you a lot. You're one of her minions."

I felt my cheeks burn for a moment. "How do you figure I'm a *minion*?" I asked.

"What are you, then? You do whatever she says. You're going out with that idiot Grace Anderson."

I kept my cool. "I happen to like Grace Anderson."

"Sure you do."

"How would you know anything about Grace and me?"

"I know plenty."

"You think you know."

"I *do* know," said Antoinette, sneering into her cup. "You guys . . . you and Claude and Hanna and the rest of them . . ."

I wanted to respond. I wanted to put her in her place. But I couldn't think of how. Maybe it was best to disengage. And to think I'd considered going out with this girl!

Antoinette snorted with disgust and stood up. She stomped off toward the back of the room, her black mop of hair bouncing slightly as she walked.

At that moment Grace saw me from across the room. She came skipping over. She gave me a big hug and whispered in my ear: "I think Hanna and Claude have patched things up!"

"Thank God," I said.

It was later that spring that Hanna decided smoking weed was cool. Lots of people smoked weed, of course, but in our group it wasn't the center of things, like with some people. But that was before Hanna and Claude got high, listened to music, and made out for three heavenly hours.

Since Hanna and Claude loved it so much, Grace and I had to do it too. We all went to the Westgate Pavilion one Friday and smoked a joint in Hanna's car in the underground parking lot. Hanna was very funny when she was high. She was cracking us up. I don't know how she did it; weed made me so stupid I could barely talk. Grace, on the other hand, couldn't *stop* talking, rambling on about whatever popped into her head. It got so bad Hanna finally said, "Grace, I love you, but I can't listen to you for another second."

After that the four of us wandered the mall. Then Hanna and Claude disappeared. Eventually Grace and I realized they had gone back to the car for some alone time. So then Grace and I were stuck walking around by ourselves. We ran into Petra and another girl. Petra thought we were laughing at her, since we were giggling so much. So Grace told her we were high. Then Petra thought we were funny and got out her phone and took our picture.

Grace wanted to make out, since Hanna kept saying how great it was. But there was no place to go, since Hanna and Claude were in the car. So we both squeezed into one of the cushy armchairs outside Nordstrom and put our coats over ourselves and played "where's my hand."

"Where's my hand?" whispered Grace, snuggling against me.

"In my pocket," I said.

"Where's my hand *now*?"

"Deeper in my pocket," I said. "Where's *my* hand?"

"Ga-vin!" she gasped, pushing my arm away. "We're in a public place!"

"Okay, now where's my hand?" I said.

"On my waist," she said.

"How about now?"

"Higher on my waist."

"How about now?"

"Oh, that tickles. No fair!"

"Does it tickle?"

"Yes, IT DOES. Don't, don't, AAAAHHHH!!!! NO! Stop it. GAVIN!!!"

I stopped. "Where's my hand now?" I said.

"No. It's my turn," she said. "Where's *my* hand?"

"In my armpit, where it's gonna get crushed."

"How come you're not ticklish?"

"Because I'm a boy and I have no emotions."

"Okay, now where's my hand?" said Grace. "No. Wait. Where's my *finger*?"

"On my chin."

"Now where?"

"My nose."

"Now where?"

"My muth."

"Does it taste good?"

"It taith all right."

"Where's my finger now?"

"In my ear. And it's wet. And that's gross." I twisted my head away. "Where are my fingers?"

"They're walking up my leg," she breathed into my ear. "Toward my special private personal area. Where they're not *allowed*."

"But they're still walking."

"They better not be walking."

"But they are."

"Then their little legs are going to get smashed!"

When Hanna and Claude reappeared, the four of us drove to Logan's house, where Petra and some other people had gone. For some reason Hanna decided to bury the hatchet with Petra and was super nice. Then we all smoked more weed and everyone got super giggly again. By the end of the night the group of us were lying on the living room carpet in the dark. That's when I began thinking about Antoinette again. I was still pissed about our conversation at the dance. I still felt the sting of her *minion* comment.

But I rarely saw her at school, and anyway, who cared what someone like her thought about my life? Her and her weird friends. As I lay beside Grace, breathing her silky hair, kissing her slender neck, running my fingertips over the soft skin of her shoulders, I reflected that my life was pretty damn good the way it was.

Naturally, since weed was cool now, Claude had to get some, since he was Claude and people expected him to have everything. I offered to help.

The first thing we figured out was that Bennett Schmidt was our school's main weed source. Claude and I both rolled our eyes when we heard this. Bennett was one of the biggest creeps in our class. He'd worn these dorky wire-rim glasses all through middle school and had terrible acne for years. He was best known for beheading live ants during a science class project in fifth grade. And then showing people—girls mostly—the twitching bodies through the microscope.

On Saturday we called Bennett and rode to his house on our bikes. His mother answered the door. She knew who Claude was—everyone did—so she was a bit surprised at the sight of us.

"Is Bennett here?" said Claude.

"Yes. Yes he is," she said. "He's downstairs in his room."

When she didn't move, Claude said: "Can you get him, please?"

"Oh," she said, flustered. She turned and called down the basement stairs. "Bennett! You have visitors!"

Bennett appeared from the darkness below. He told us to come down. Claude didn't want to go down there. Neither did I. But it didn't appear we had a choice.

We descended the stairs and entered Bennett's basement lair. It was pretty much what you'd imagine: a marijuana emporium. There were assorted posters: Snoop Dogg, *The Big Lebowski*, a big picture of Bob Marley with dope smoke coming out of his nose. There were different versions of the pot leaf stuck here and there. The ceiling was low. The lighting was dim. You had to respect the guy for dedicating himself so thoroughly to the drug-dealer thing. He used to be the gross-out king. Now he'd turned himself into Dr. Weed.

Bennett pointed at an old sofa that was along the wall opposite his unmade bed. Claude didn't want to sit. Neither did I. But this was part of the process.

I followed Claude as he maneuvered around a dirty coffee table. With great disdain, he lowered himself onto the old couch. I did the same.

"So you're interested in some cannibis," said Bennett.

"Why else would we be here?" said Claude.

Bennett was not affected by this insult. He went to his large metal desk and unlocked one of the drawers. He took out several small plastic bags and lined them up on a tray. Then he brought the tray over to the coffee table and placed it, with some formality, in front of Claude and me.

"This is what I have at the moment," he told us. He

proceeded to tell us what countries the different bags were from, what their different effects were.

"I don't care where it's from," said Claude. "As long as it gets you high."

"I like the Moroccan," said Bennett. "It has a more grounded feel. It's not so cerebral."

I glanced at Claude to see if he was going to laugh in Bennett's face. But he didn't. Bennett was showing a certain confidence throughout this interaction. He wasn't intimidated by Claude, not now. Claude had his status. And Bennett had his.

Claude unwrapped a couple of the plastic bags and studied the contents. I looked too. The clumps of marijuana at the bottom of each bag did look somewhat different from each other.

"Should we have a taste?" said Bennett. He pulled up a chair across from us and produced a small white pipe. He reached for the bag of Moroccan.

"I'm not going to smoke it here," said Claude, with growing annoyance. "How much is it?"

Bennett put his pipe away. "The Moroccan is forty," he said calmly. He took the plastic bag and rerolled it into a neat slender tube. He tossed it back onto the coffee table. Claude handed over two twenties.

"Can you believe that guy?" Claude said when we got outside. "What a moron."

"Do you remember that girl Antoinette?" Grace asked me one afternoon, while we were making out in her parents' bedroom.

I nodded that I did.

"Oh my God, I heard the weirdest thing about her." Grace sat up suddenly to tell me. "Supposedly, she went with Bennett Schmidt to a Southridge party? And everyone was really drunk? And they started making out? And then they started *switching off*."

"Switching off" was a term used for make-out parties that involved uncool people from redneck high schools like Southridge. When those people wanted to kiss different people, they didn't bother spinning a bottle. They *switched off*.

"And now she's supposedly *with him*. With Bennett! Can you believe that? He is so gross. Remember him in fifth grade? Chopping up those ants in science class?"

I nodded that I did. I scooted closer to Grace and tried to caress her back. But she was lost in thoughts of improper make-out games. She scooted away.

"Someone should tell her," said Grace. "She's never going to be accepted if she hangs out with people like that."

"She just moved here," I said. "She didn't know him in fifth grade."

"And *switching off*?" said Grace in disbelief. "With Bennett and some Southridge guys? That's disgusting!"

"Yeah, but what's the difference between that and spin the bottle?"

"Spin the bottle has rules!"

"Not when you play with Hanna," I said.

"And with spin the bottle you know who you're playing with. You know the people. It's not some random Southridge guys."

"She knows Bennett."

"It just sounds icky to me. And poor Antoinette! First her brother jumps off a bridge. And then those weird girls start following her around. And now she's with *Bennett* of all people."

"Yeah . . . ," I said.

Grace became reflective. "God, high school is so different than I thought it would be."

"How so?"

"People are just so . . . They can't control themselves. And they have so many problems! Why can't they just have fun? And do fun high school things?"

"I'm with you on that," I said, trying to kiss her neck.

But Grace was not interested. She slid off the bed and refastened her bra strap. The make-out session was over.

"Gavin?" she said, a new seriousness in her tone.

"Yeah?"

"Do you think Hanna and Claude are soul mates?"

"Uh . . ."

"Because you know Claude better than anyone," she said.

"Yeah, I probably do."

Grace finished buttoning her shirt. She went to her mother's full-length mirror and fluffed out her hair. "Hanna says that Claude doesn't think they're soul mates."

"What are they, then?"

"I don't know. Not soul mates."

"Did he say they weren't?"

"No. But they were talking about soul mates and he said he didn't know what it meant exactly. Meaning he didn't consider her to be his. Do you see what I mean?"

"I think so."

"If he's acting like he doesn't know what a soul mate is, that means he doesn't think Hanna is his."

"Yeah, but maybe what he's saying is he doesn't know what *other* people mean when they say 'soul mate.' Because different people probably have different ideas about that."

"But your soul mate is supposed to be your best friend," reasoned Grace. "And the person you love more than anything. That's what Hanna says."

"I'm sure Claude considers Hanna his best friend. And the person he loves more than anything."

"She's still mad, though. Why is he saying he doesn't know what a soul mate is? Why would you even say that?"

"Yeah, but you know Hanna. She looks for reasons to be mad."

"No she doesn't. She loves him. And so she wants to know if they're soul mates or not."

"If she loves him so much, she shouldn't start a fight about it."

Grace frowned into the mirror and began brushing her hair. She didn't look at me again. I also noticed that Grace didn't ask me if she and I were soul mates. Which was unlike her.

Complicating things further, it was now the middle of May. Summer vacation was three weeks away. I wasn't sure what Grace and I would do during that time. In the summer people went places with their families. We wouldn't have our friends to do things with and go on group dates.

That's when I realized something Grace probably already knew: We were going to break up. This thought hit me like a truck. But I knew instantly that it was true. Of course we were going to break up. We couldn't go out forever. We weren't going to get married. We'd been together five months, which was already longer than most high school couples. Besides which, we seemed to have completely run out of things to talk about. Which was why we spent nearly every second we were together making out.

We were going to break up. I sat pondering this. And it would probably happen soon. That's why Grace hadn't asked about us being soul mates.

I was shocked. I was sad. I stared at her face in the mirror as she brushed her hair. My first love was coming to an end.

For the time being, though, we kept going as before. That weekend we went to the Westgate Pavilion and saw a movie with Logan Hewitt and Olivia Goldstein. We sat in the food court afterward and ate Pinkberry frozen yogurt. Grace ate all her blueberries, like she does, so I went back to get her more. I was standing in line when I heard familiar voices. I turned to find Bennett Schmidt and Antoinette standing behind me. They had come out of a different movie.

"Oh hey," I said.

They nodded back.

I had never seen them together in public. They looked pretty well matched: Bennett with that flushed, drugged-out look on his face, and Antoinette, who had recently cut her bangs in a bizarre way. "What movie did you see?" I asked.

Bennett said the name of the movie.

I looked at Antoinette. "Was it good?"

"It was okay," said Bennett.

I nodded and turned away. Nobody talked. The line moved forward.

"How does Claude like the Moroccan?" asked Bennett from behind me.

I turned back toward them. "He likes it all right," I said,

though I hadn't heard anything about it. Claude didn't care about weed. It was probably still stashed in his desk somewhere.

"How are you doing?" I found myself asking Antoinette.

"I'm doing *great*," she said, with deep sarcasm. I didn't know what that was about. Maybe she was embarrassed to be seen with Bennett. Or maybe she disliked me even more than I realized.

And then Grace appeared. She came up behind me and slipped her hand around my elbow. I felt myself blush. The situation became even more awkward than it already was.

"I don't want any more blueberries, I decided," Grace told me, smiling at Antoinette.

"Okay," I said.

The four of us stood there for a second, Grace and Antoinette staring each other down, Bennett and me avoiding eye contact. It was painful. Grace finally pulled me away.

I did manage one last glance back at Antoinette, who gave me a broad, mocking smile. *Wow*, I thought. *She seriously hates me.* Which made me feel bad in a way.

But as soon as they were gone, I was relieved to be free of them. Angry Antoinette and creepy Bennett—who needed people like that around? For one fleeting moment, I loved Grace more than ever.

On the first day of June, my mother knocked on my door and told me my dad wanted to see me on the deck. That didn't sound promising. I went downstairs and found him sitting outside, in the late-afternoon sun, having a drink. I could tell he was going to lecture me about something, but I didn't know what. My brother had been accepted to Cornell University by then. Maybe he was going to gloat about that. Or maybe he wanted to discuss my 2.8 grade-point average and my nonexistent extracurriculars.

I paused at the sliding glass door, to watch him. My father was still wearing his suit and tie. The tie was loosened and pulled over to one side. He swirled the ice cubes around in his glass. It occurred to me he might be drunk.

I slowly pulled the door open. I wasn't looking forward to this.

"Come out here, Gavin!" boomed my father. "I want to talk to you."

I went outside and sat down across the table from him, in one of the deck chairs. We hadn't cleaned the outdoor furniture yet. It was still dirty from the winter. My dad didn't seem to notice. I could see some of the dirt from his chair had gotten on his suit.

"So your mother tells me you're not playing any tennis tournaments this summer."

This was true. I had dropped like a rock in the state tennis rankings over the school year, partly because I had skipped most of the big tournaments, but also because I was in the sixteen and unders now. Other guys had begun to emerge at this new level, guys I had been able to beat in previous years but who had suddenly grown four inches, or hired better coaches, or who knows what. There were also new people, superior athletes, who had for some reason picked up tennis racquets. I had been ranked as high as #2 in the state in the twelve and unders. I had dropped to #11 in the fourteen and unders. Now, in the sixteens, I was ranked #94 or something.

"I think I want to try other things," I told my father.

"And what other things do you want to try?" he said, slurring his words slightly. "What else exactly are you good at? Besides tennis?"

"I don't know," I said slowly, carefully. "That's what I want to find out."

My father took a sip of his drink. He stared out into the large yard of the large house he had bought for our family, which Russell and I had grown up in.

"Mom says you've dropped in the rankings."

"I have," I said calmly.

"And why is that?"

"The other guys have gotten better."

"And you have no problem with that?" he asked.

"There's nothing I can do about it."

"You could get better yourself."

"There's a certain factor of talent," I said coldly. "I'm good. But some people are really good. I can't beat those people. No matter what I do."

"So you say," grumbled my father.

"Those are the facts of it."

"Those are *your* facts of it."

I sat there. I stared into the yard.

"There's something about you," said my father. "Something I've been trying to figure out for a long time now. And I think I know what it is. I think I've finally put my finger on it." He paused dramatically, then turned to look me in the eye. "*You think you're better than other people.*"

I sighed and stared into the yard.

"And you know what?" continued my father. "That is about the worst quality a person can have. If you were a great tennis player, then maybe you could have an attitude like that and get away with it. But as you've just said yourself"—he sipped his drink—"you're not a great tennis player."

I said nothing.

"I wish I knew what to say to you," said my father. "I would tell you to look to Russell. To learn from your brother.

To see how a person can be confident and still not alienate the people around them. It's the difference between confidence and arrogance. A confident person, other people will rally around. But an arrogant person . . ."

He was right. I was arrogant. And difficult. And defiant. But it was only with him that I was like that. I wasn't like that around other people. Other people liked me just fine.

"The problem with you is . . . ," said my father. He stopped to consider the best way to describe the problem. "You don't think about the other guy. Now, maybe you can find a job working in some remote location. Or sitting in a cubicle. But those aren't good jobs. Trust me. Good jobs require dealing with people. And if you've got an attitude, who will want to deal with you?"

"Russell's the one who thinks he's better than everyone," I said quietly.

"*Russell* . . . ?" said my father, his nostrils flaring suddenly. "I'll tell you something. Russell is going to be *very* successful. He's going to do better than I've done. And I've done pretty damn well, as you can see from where you're sitting at this moment." My father waved his hand to indicate our large house and yard. "I don't have any idea where *you're* going to be sitting in twenty years," he said. "Not anywhere good, at the rate you're going. Which is what I'm trying to tell you."

He's drunk, I said to myself. I sat there. I bounced one of my knees up and down. A warm breeze blew across the yard. Bits of sunlight peeked through the maple trees that divided our property from the Winslows'.

"So what are you going to do with your summer?" said my father. "If you're not going to play tennis?"

I'd thought about this already. My mom had found me a job at the Garden Center, which was a local nursery owned by one of her friends. And the other thing was, my brother had a fancy camera he'd gotten for Christmas the year before and had never taken out of the box. During my landscape painting phase, I'd convinced him to let me look at it. It was complicated, but I'd figured out the basics. What I hadn't done was take it outside and actually try it.

"I'm going to take pictures," I told my dad.

"Take pictures," he snorted. "Like what? With your phone?"

"With Russell's camera."

"And why are you going to do that?"

"Because that's what I want to do," I said.

"Oh, good," said my father. "Only do what *you* want to do. That's a good strategy. The world always needs more people like that. I can see the ad now: 'Wanted: Person who only does what *he* wants to do.'"

My dad laughed at his own joke. He took a long swig of his drink.

On graduation day, my brother won numerous honors and awards. He also gave one of the commencement speeches for our high school. Standing at the podium, he talked about looking forward, staying true to your ideals, contributing something to society. I couldn't imagine what my brother would actually *contribute* to society. He'd *take* his fair share from society, that was for sure. But whatever. The speech sounded good. Everyone clapped.

My father had a big party in our backyard afterward. There were caterers and a tent. Since my brother's friends tended to be as boring as he was, it was a pretty dull affair. There was Russell's best friend, David Stiller, who was going to Stanford and was a cross-country runner. And his uptight friend Patricia, who was going to be a heart surgeon. And Hassad, who already wanted to be a banker.

As the party wound down, Claude stopped by. He came in the backyard, said hi to my parents, then we walked out to the driveway.

"What's going on with you and Grace?" he asked me. Obviously Hanna had told him to talk to me.

I shrugged. "Seems like she's not really into it anymore."

"Are you?"

I shrugged. "I don't know. I mean, she's great and everything."

"Hanna said you guys were probably going to break up," said Claude.

"Yeah. I think so."

Claude squinted in the sun. "You had a good run."

"Yeah. It's probably time."

"You should do it soon," said Claude. "Get it over with. So you're free for the summer. And her, too."

I nodded. I knew he was right.

"What about you and Hanna?" I asked. "What are you guys doing for the summer?"

"We're gonna be apart for most of it. She's teaching theater at a summer camp in July. And then she's going to Norway with her parents."

"And you're playing tennis," I said.

"Yeah, I've got this new coach. We're doing all the tournaments. Seattle, Boise, California."

"*California*," I said, shaking my head. California had all the best tennis players.

"Yeah, that won't be fun," said Claude. "But this coach is all about the quality competition."

I nodded.

Claude looked down the street. "And Hanna's still giving me shit about Petra. If you can believe that."

"What's her problem?"

"She's always gotta have something going on. Something to battle over."

"Huh."

"It's ridiculous," said Claude, kicking a rock into the street. "But you know what? I like Petra. I'm not going to shut her out of my life."

"Yeah."

"What are you doing this summer?" he asked me.

"My mom got me a job at the Garden Center. Watering the plants and stuff."

"That's cool."

"I'll make some money."

"Money's cool."

"Yeah," I said. "We'll see."

"All right," said Claude. "I gotta roll. Gotta go practice the backhand."

"Good luck in California."

"Good luck watering the plants."

Despite Claude's encouragement, I still couldn't figure out how to break up with Grace. Two weeks into the summer we were still together. When Logan had his first pool party, he invited the two of us as a couple. As I drove my mom's car to Grace's house, I wondered if this would be the night we would finally end it.

I picked up Grace and we drove to Logan's. It was nice out, warm. We had the car windows down. We made small talk. The vibe wasn't terrible between us. But it wasn't good, either.

Things were more comfortable once we got there. Petra handed Grace a Bud Light and dragged her off. I sat by the pool with Logan and some of the guys. Claude was in Seattle playing his first big tournament of the summer. We always missed him when he was gone. Nothing was quite as fun without him.

Later, when the sun went down, it got cold. Logan told me I could borrow a hoodie, so I went upstairs to his room. I was looking through his drawers when someone knocked on the open door.

"Hello?" said Hanna.

"Hey," I said, still digging through Logan's sweatshirt collection.

"What are you doing?" she asked.

"Getting a hoodie."

"Yeah, it's kinda cold out . . ."

I found a hoodie and unfolded it. It looked like it might fit.

"I'm sort of cold too," she said, coming into the room with her beer. "Is there anything that would fit me?"

I found a sweatshirt that was a medium and handed it to her.

She put it on over her T-shirt and bikini bottoms. I put on one too. It was a large.

"I couldn't help noticing something, Gavin," said Hanna, pulling her hair through the neck hole.

I felt a tingle of excitement when Hanna said my name.

"What's that?" I asked.

"You and Grace."

I went to Logan's mirror and pulled my hoodie on. "What about us?"

Hanna came over to the mirror too. She stood beside me, close enough that our arms touched.

"I don't think she's happy," said Hanna.

I looked at her once in the mirror.

"Do you think it might be time for you guys to move on?" she asked.

"Yeah," I said. "It probably is."

"I know she loves you. And I know you love her. . . ."

I nodded that this was true.

"Have you guys had sex?" asked Hanna.

She must have known we hadn't. Grace was one of her best friends. But I shook my head no.

"Hmmmm," she said. "Well, that's probably for the best. In terms of not breaking each other's hearts too bad."

"I know," I said. "We should break up. I'm just not sure how to do it."

Hanna smiled at that. "Of course you don't. Grace is your first girlfriend. You've never done it before!"

I nodded. I was embarrassed in a way, but I was also enjoying this private conversation with beautiful Hanna. It was rare that a person got Hanna's full attention. I certainly had never had it. Not like this.

She turned toward me and gripped the front of my hoodie. She gently tugged me from side to side in a teasing way. "It's hard to break up," she said. "I know. And even though you still love someone, even though you'll probably always love them, you still have to do it. If it's time. It's not good to drag things out."

Tears came into my eyes. Partly because I was about to lose Grace forever. But also because Hanna was so close to me. She was touching me. The brightness of her presence, the glow of her warmth: It melted you instantly. There was no defense against it.

"I know it's hard," murmured Hanna, gazing up into my face. "But when the time comes . . ."

I nodded. Hanna's forehead was about eight inches from my nose. I could smell her. She smelled of chlorine, of shampoo, of herself.

"You think I should do it tonight?" I said.

She nodded.

When I didn't say anything, she reached down and took my hand in both of hers. "What is it, Gavin? Are you worried you won't find someone else?"

"No," I said.

"Because I happen to know a lot of girls who like you."

"Yeah?"

"Of course," she said, grinning. "*Sooo* many girls think you're cute. They tell me . . ."

I knew then that something was going to happen. The

sensation was one of rolling down a hill, of gathering speed, slowly at first and then not so slowly.

"Oh, Gavin . . . ," purred Hanna. She nestled up closer. The tips of her breasts pressed into my chest. I could feel the softness of them. "Do you have any idea how cute you are?" She touched my chin with her forefinger. "Do you have any idea at all?"

This was not good. And I knew it. But Hanna, oh my God, to be near her, to be touched by her, to breathe her. To have those gorgeous green eyes on you, holding you, enticing you, inviting you to do things you knew you shouldn't but would be an idiot not to. I knew what I was about to do. And I knew what I would lose if I did it. But I still went ahead. I couldn't help myself. I kissed her.

She was shocked, of course. Or she pretended to be. But Hanna was not a person who shrank from a challenge. She kissed me right back. She was no priss. There was a single unforgettable moment of pure connection, of perfect equality, of love almost. Then it turned into something else: a test, a trial run, an experiment. Hanna was trying me on for size. She was checking me out. She was doing this because why not? She was young. Why shouldn't she sample what was available to her?

But oh, the taste of her. The velvety texture of her tongue and mouth. The perfect warmth and softness of her body as I pressed her closer to me. My brain swam in my skull. I felt like I was in a different world, a different universe.

And then, from behind me, I heard the faint whisper of another female voice: *"Oh no."*

That was Grace.

And then a louder gasp. And a different voice: "OH MY GOD! WHAT ARE YOU GUYS DOING!?"

That was Petra.

The two of them were standing in the doorway. They had come looking for us. And they had found us.

Needless to say, Grace and I broke up that night. Our last moments as a couple were spent in Logan's driveway, in the dark, both of us damp and cold in our bathing suits.

"I'm so sorry," I pleaded.

"Don't even say that!" she cried.

"I still love you."

"Don't say that, either!"

Hanna had hurried away to call Claude and confess to him what she'd done. Petra had slunk off to text everyone else what had happened.

In the driveway, Grace was trying to be pissed off. She was trying to do what Hanna would do in that situation. But mostly she was stunned. And sad. We both were. We both cried in the darkness of the driveway. Our first experience of completely sharing ourselves with another person had come to an end. All those doors, so newly opened, would now be shut again.

To her credit, Hanna never lied about what happened. It was her fault, she told people. She had flirted with me because she was sick of Claude talking to Petra on the phone at all hours of the night. The cause of the incident was Hanna's jealousy. "It's my worst trait," she told people.

Because of her honesty, Hanna and Claude would eventually survive the incident. After some deep, intense conversations, both of them vowed that they would provoke the other no further. Claude would stop talking to Petra. And Hanna would keep her hands (and lips) to herself. And so everything worked out in the end: Grace was free to enjoy her summer without me. Hanna and Claude continued together, their love even stronger for having been tested in this way.

As for me, I drove home alone that night, the smell of Hanna still lingering on my body. I thought about her when I went to bed. A lot of things had happened that night. I didn't know how to order them in my head.

I woke up the next morning and went to work at the Garden Center. I put on my apron and rubber boots and began my daily ritual of hosing down the asphalt and watering the plants. I hadn't talked to Claude yet. I would have to call him, of course. I was not looking forward to that.

During my lunch break, I called his cell. He was still in Seattle that day, playing the Washington State Regionals. He was either at his hotel, or playing a match. He didn't answer.

I tried not to worry about it. If anyone would understand, he would. Hanna was so alluring. Who could resist her? Not me. Not anyone. And it was really just a joke anyway, one of Hanna's ironic flirtations. Hanna didn't like me. So I'd leaned in and kissed her for a few seconds? It was like playing spin the bottle. We were drunk. It was stupid high school stuff.

Or was it?

I called Claude again at two. He was still not answering. It probably was a big deal. *Shit.* I began to seriously worry.

I called later that afternoon. It was now sinking in, the seriousness of the situation. I'd made out with my best friend's girlfriend. Jesus. What was I thinking? I was going to lose my best friend. And possibly more than that.

When I finished my shift, I sat in my car and called his number every two minutes. Finally it didn't go to voice mail. *"What?"* snapped Claude.

"Claude!" I said.

"What do you want?"

"Listen," I said, my voice shaking. "This thing with Hanna. I'm so sorry. It was a terrible mistake."

"Yeah, I would say so."

"It was a joke. Really. I was drunk. I don't even know what happened."

"You made out with my girlfriend. That's what happened."

"I know. And I'm so sorry. But it wasn't like it sounds. Claude, seriously, I'm sitting here, and I honestly can't believe it happened."

"Neither can I."

It went on like that. Me making excuses, trying to explain. Claude snapping back. Then he hung up.

I sat there, holding my phone in my lap, staring numbly out my car window. Claude was my *best friend*. And I had made out with his girlfriend. How could I have done that?

Days passed. I was afraid to call anyone. At work, I would look at my phone. Who could I talk to about this? Who could I explain myself to? Logan? One of the other guys? They wouldn't want to talk to me.

I went home after work. I watched TV with my mom. I would check my phone, thinking someone might call, someone might want to check in. But nobody called. Nobody wanted anything to do with me.

A week passed. Finally, I got up my courage and called Logan. When he didn't answer, I left a message. I did this several times. Then, finally, he called me back.

"Bro, you fucked up," he said.

"I know I fucked up."

"I mean, you *really* fucked up."

"I know I did," I said, my voice shaking. "You don't think I know?"

"I mean, I get it," he said. "I understand. Hanna's Hanna. But Claude's your *best friend*."

"I know. I know."

"And now it's like, you're so in the wrong, how can anyone forgive you?"

"It's true, I know. But what am I supposed to do? Who am I supposed to talk to?"

"It can't be me," said Logan. "Not for a while, anyway. Claude's my friend too. I can't act like nothing happened."

"So we can't hang out?" I asked.

"Sorry, bro."

"But for how long?"

"How long?" said Logan. "I don't know. A while."

"How long is that?"

"A month?"

"A *month*?" I said. "But that's half the summer!"

"Hey, you did this to yourself."

"A couple weeks. That's enough. Come on. I lost my girlfriend. I don't have tennis. I don't have anything."

Logan sighed. "Okay, a couple weeks."

"All right," I said with relief. "A couple weeks. Thanks. Thank you."

So that's what happened. Out of loyalty to Claude, Logan didn't talk to me for the rest of June and part of July. And nobody else did either. What could I do? This was my punishment.

So I worked. I volunteered for extra shifts. I read a paperback about a serial killer that someone left in the storage room at the Garden Center. At night I drove in the hills or down by the river. I went to the big bookstore downtown and looked at photography books of World War II or rock stars or old movie actors I'd never heard of. Which was fun in a way. But not as fun as hanging out with my friends.

And then one day Antoinette came to the Garden Center. She was with her mother, who bought some plants. Antoinette stayed in the car. She was reading something on her phone. She had an even weirder haircut now. It was short and round, almost bowl shaped. It made her look like a nun.

I was in my apron and rubber boots, hosing down the parking lot. She hadn't seen me yet. She probably didn't know I worked there. I came closer. I blasted the asphalt in front of her door just enough to bounce a few drops through her open window.

"What the—??!!" she said, reaching for the window button. But her mom had the car keys. She couldn't roll it up. That's when she looked out and saw it was me.

"I should have known," she said. "If you get my phone wet . . ."

"Sorry," I said.

I moved away and sprayed the asphalt in the opposite direction. She went back to her phone. Then she stopped and looked at me.

"Nice apron," she said.

"Nice haircut," I said back. "You look like a nun."

She stared at me for a moment. I kept spraying.

"I heard you and Grace broke up," she said.

"Yup."

"I hope you learned something," said Antoinette, looking back at her phone.

"What would I have learned?"

"I don't know. That boring people are boring?"

"She wasn't boring."

"Not to you she wasn't."

I blasted a gum wrapper with my hose and guided it into the gutter.

"What about you?" I asked. "How's Bennett?"

"He's okay," she said from the car.

"Me and Claude bought weed from him once."

"That's what he said," said Antoinette. "He said you were assholes."

"We were," I said.

She watched me spray a crate of flowers.

At that point the manager yelled at me from inside the nursery. I dropped my hose and hurried in. "Help Mrs. Renwick with these plants," he told me.

There were two big potted plants. I picked the first one up and lugged it to the parking lot. Antoinette got out of the SUV to watch. She didn't help. Her mother, who had no idea who I was, or that I knew Antoinette, opened the back door. "Careful with the top," she said. I struggled to get the heavy plant inside the car.

I went back and brought the other one out. I wrestled it

into the car as well. Mrs. Renwick began talking to someone on her phone, so it was just me and Antoinette standing there when I got the door closed.

"What are you doing this summer?" I said, wiping my hands on my apron.

"I'm going to Germany," she said.

"What's in Germany?"

"My dad. My real dad. He's in the army."

"What's he do in the army?"

"He sits behind a desk. He's a major."

"Is that high up?"

"It's pretty high up."

Mrs. Renwick, still on the phone, came back and pointed for Antoinette to get in the car.

"Give me your address," said Antoinette. "I'll send you a postcard."

I wasn't sure if she was serious, but I dug in my apron and found one of my little pencils. I wrote my address down on a scrap of paper.

"Have fun," I said, handing it to her.

"I will."

It was that night that I finally tried out my brother's camera. It had been sitting in its case in the back of my mom's car for a week.

There was no reason for Russell to own such a complicated camera, but my father had insisted. It probably cost a couple grand. It had a million special features, most of which prevented you from taking pictures.

In July, in Oregon, it was still light out at nine p.m. So after work I drove to the east side industrial district. There were some skateboard spots down there and train tracks and some homeless encampments. "The Wilds" was what the skater kids called this area. I parked in a gravel lot and slung the absurdly expensive camera around my neck. I started walking. Every time I saw another person, I worried I might get robbed. But I did manage to take some pictures. And with the fancy camera, they looked pretty good.

As I walked around, I thought about Antoinette. It had been nice seeing her. I thought back over our conversation at the Garden Center. Then I would see something interesting and stop and take a few pictures. It was a nice way to spend a summer evening. It was the only fun I'd had since the Hanna incident. But then, as I was taking a few last shots, the camera's autofocus froze. I tried everything I could think of to unfreeze it, but it remained stuck. Which is what happens when you buy the most complicated camera on earth.

The main focus of the Meeks family that summer was out-fitting my brother for his journey east to Cornell University. Deliveries showed up almost daily on the doorstep: sweaters, khakis, dress socks, boxer shorts . . . these arrived in boxes from Brooks Brothers, J.Crew, Banana Republic. Style-wise, my father seemed to think that to go back East to college was to travel back in time to the days of cardigans and penny loafers. Russell and I shared our last brotherly moments of rolling our eyes at our father. A few weeks after Russell left, I found a stash of all the more ridiculous clothes my dad made him buy, stuffed in a box in the back of an upstairs closet. At college, Russell would wear jeans and sweatshirts like everyone else.

Much to my surprise, about halfway through my first tennis-free summer, I began to miss it. And then Logan Hewitt called. He and Olivia wanted to play tennis and they wanted me to come. Olivia had a friend who would join us.

This was at the beginning of August. We were well past the two-week friend embargo by that point. But Logan was still maintaining a certain distance from me. So I was happy for any chance to normalize things between us. It helped that Claude was constantly on the road. Logan was as bored as I was.

I drove to the public courts and met Logan and Olivia in the parking lot. They didn't have real tennis clothes. The other girl—Rachel Lehman, from Hillside High School— was wearing cute cutoffs and a brightly striped T-shirt that said ASPEN COLORADO on it. Logan had on board shorts and Vans slip-ons. Olivia wore a tank top and a skirt.

We hit the ball back and forth. It felt good to hold a racquet again, to stroke the ball, to follow through. Logan was pretty good, and Rachel had played before, but Olivia could barely hit the ball back. That part was hard for me, hitting dink balls to no real purpose. We couldn't play an actual game. Every once in a while I'd whack one with some pace to Logan. That felt good.

Afterward, the four of us got sandwiches and juice drinks at the little market down the road. I tried to talk to Rachel a little. She was very cute. Even more so once you got close up. But I couldn't get her to say much. So we mostly listened to Olivia and Logan.

We walked back to our different cars in the parking lot. Rachel was driving her parents' Lexus, and I had my dad's new Mercedes Coupe, which my mom was letting me drive since he was out of town. Rachel smiled a certain way when I unlocked the Mercedes. She seemed to approve. I approved of her as well. I approved a lot.

• • •

It turned out the feeling was mutual. Logan called me the next day and said that Rachel told Olivia that she liked me and that I should ask her out.

So I did. I was much smoother this time, having learned my lesson with Grace. I called Rachel. I made a date. I made sure not to talk too much. The date was to go ice-skating at the Sherwood Town Center, since Olivia said Rachel was a big ice-skater.

We met on a Friday night. As promised, Rachel was very good at ice-skating. She was extremely cute in general. It was fun to watch her do anything, even just lace up her skates. So then I started to really like Rachel Lehman.

Unfortunately, when I called her a couple days later, she said she was leaving for the San Juan Islands on a sailboat with her parents. She hadn't mentioned this before. She would be gone the rest of the summer. That seemed like an odd thing to not tell someone. It pretty much put an end to our summer romance.

So back to the Garden Center I went. Hosing down the parking lot. Carrying the fertilizer. Hanging out at the pool with Logan and Olivia when they invited me, which was not very often. Eventually, I got a postcard from Antoinette. On the front was a painting of a guy from the 1800s, standing on a mountain peak, looking down at the clouds. "Wanderer in the Mist," it was called. It was a landscape painting.

On the back she'd written:

Frankfurt is hot and boring, but I went to Berlin
last weekend with a friend. Never made it to the
youth hostel. Met some wild Australians. Partied
for three days straight, had to hitchhike back
because we spent all our $$$. —Antoinette

I must have read that postcard ten times. Not in a romantic way, but because it was so interesting to imagine Antoinette running around some city in Germany. What a strange girl she was.

I put the postcard on my wall with a thumbtack. Every couple days I would turn it around so that some days it was the painting, "Wanderer in the Mist," and other days it was Antoinette's message of crazy adventures from across the ocean.

The day my brother left for college, we loaded up the Toyota RAV4. This was early evening, the end of August. The landscaping guy had cut our front lawn that day and trimmed the hedges. Our house, our yard, the entire neighborhood had a clean, wholesome, well-kept feel to it. Gentle Portland. Familiar Portland. It would be a hard place to leave. I thought it would be.

But not Russell. He was eager to go. He was sick of my dad, sick of being coached and lectured and advised. You could see it in his face. He was like: *Get me out of here.*

It was a long drive to the airport. My poor mother cried through most of it. My dad got mad at her when she couldn't compose herself long enough to get a picture of the three of them in the departures area. I took the picture: the two proud parents and their Ivy League son. That's what my dad wanted. What he got was my mom with her Kleenex and my brother looking vacant and scared and my dad pissed off at everyone.

Driving back from the airport, I thought about my own college situation. Where would I go with my 2.8 grade-point average and my lack of any other talents except tennis, which I had already been washed out of? I would end up somewhere. That was one good thing about my father. No matter how much he claimed he didn't care about me, that would change when college time rolled around. He wouldn't want to be telling his golfing buddies that his other son went to community college. He and my mom would figure out some way to make me look good.

As the beginning of the school year approached, I sent Antoinette a chatty Facebook message, thanking her for the postcard. She was back from Germany, according to Facebook. But she didn't message me back. I thought maybe she and Bennett were having an intense reunion, but then I noticed that she had changed her relationship status to single, and I quickly looked through the rest of her page to see what was up. Had she broken up with Bennett? Not that it was so important. But I was curious. I looked through her posts, but there were no clues. There was barely anything about being in Germany. Antoinette was not the type to put anything too revealing on Facebook.

A couple days later, I happened to tell Logan about the Antoinette situation. We were at Nordstrom, at the back-to-school sale. He was surprised by the way I was talking about her.

"Wait? So you *like* Antoinette?" he asked.

"Well, no . . ."

"Then why do you care if she broke up with Bennett Schmidt?"

"I don't . . . it's just . . . I'm curious about her."

Logan shrugged. "I don't know, bro. To me, a girl like that? What's the upside? She dresses like a freak. She's got the unibrow going. Her brother jumped off a bridge. Not that that means there's anything wrong with her. But, dude, there's probably something seriously wrong with her."

"Could be," I admitted.

"If I were you," said Logan, "I'd stick with the normal girls. They're cuter. They're *cleaner*. They're easier to deal with."

"Yeah, like Rachel," I said. "She sort of disappeared, though."

At that moment, Logan became suspiciously silent.

"What?" I said. "Do you know something about Rachel?"

"No," he lied, thumbing through some shirts.

"Dude, you know something. Come on, tell me. What happened?"

Logan sighed. "All I know is what Olivia said, and I don't know if it's true."

"What is it?"

Logan lowered his voice: "I guess Rachel thought you were still friends with Claude and Hanna."

"What?"

"She thought you were . . . you know . . . tight with those guys. She didn't know about the pool party. And the Hanna situation."

"Wait," I said. "So she only liked me because she thought she could hang out with Claude and Hanna?"

"I'm sure that's not the only reason."

"Jesus."

"What?" said Logan. "Girls do stuff like that all the time. Everybody does."

"I don't," I said.

"Yes you do," said Logan. "That's why you went out with Grace."

This was painful to hear. Doubly so because it was true.

"So we're all shallow assholes," I said.

"Don't beat yourself up," said Logan. "We're humans. We do what humans do."

So yeah, the last days of summer. It was a difficult time. The last thing I did before school started was take my brother's camera to a camera shop downtown. I didn't catch the official name of the shop, but the big sign in front said PASSPORT PHOTOS.

I went in and there was an old man and a younger guy there. The old man was doing something in the back. The young guy was sweeping behind the counter and whistling to himself. There were no customers. I wondered how much business they had, since everyone had cameras in their phones now. How many people used real cameras?

When he could see that I needed help, the younger guy stopped sweeping. He was in his midtwenties, I would guess.

He looked foreign, Italian or Middle Eastern, maybe. He seemed to have a lot of energy that wasn't getting used up.

I put my brother's camera on the counter. "I'm having trouble with this," I said. "The autofocus froze. I can't get it to do anything."

"Did you reset it?" said the guy.

"I tried."

"You got the manual?"

"No. I couldn't find it."

He took the camera from me. He looked it over. "This is a serious camera," he said.

"It's my brother's."

"He's got good taste."

I nodded.

"Yeah," he said, trying it himself. "Looks like you're froze up." He began to push things. He held one button down. He turned something else. When this didn't work, he took out the battery and rubbed it on his pants. When he put it back in, the autofocus whirred to life. "There we go," he said, as the various functions came back on.

"Cool, thanks," I said.

"Yeah, these cameras tend to freeze up," he said. He checked the view-screen and began to scroll back through the pictures I'd taken in the Wilds. "Great quality, though. Jeez. Look at these."

I stood there, waiting.

"What'd your brother do with this?" he asked.

"Nothing. He got it for Christmas."

The guy laughed. "He got *this* camera for *Christmas*?"

I nodded, trying to smile.

"Well, he's a good photographer anyway," said the guy. "Did he study photography?"

"No," I said. "He never used it. He never took it out of the box."

"So who took these pictures?"

"I did."

"You did?"

I nodded and blushed a bit.

"You got a good eye, kid," he said. He looked at more of the pictures. "What's your name?"

"Gavin."

"Okay, Gavin," he said, pushing some more buttons. "I think we got this figured out. Let me check the manual online."

I waited while he brought out a laptop and set it on the counter. He looked up my camera.

"What's your name?" I asked.

"Richie."

"Are you a photographer?"

"I am."

"What kind of pictures do you take?"

"I take passport photos," he said, pointing to the big sign outside that said PASSPORT PHOTOS.

"Oh, right," I said.

JUNIOR YEAR

You see something happening and you bang away at it.
Either you get what you saw or you get something else—
and whichever is better you print.
—*Garry Winogrand*

If your pictures aren't good enough,
you aren't close enough.
—*Robert Capa*

My summer vacation had turned out okay, I thought, considering how badly it started. I'd laid low, made a little money, hadn't aggravated the Claude and Hanna situation. Once school started, I assumed things would go back to normal. Claude would forgive me for kissing Hanna. He knew it wasn't my fault. Hanna said it wasn't. And Claude and I had been friends for so long. That had to count for something.

But when I got back to school I had a rude awakening. For one thing, Hanna, who I thought had been gone for the summer, had been home for the entire month of August. She'd had a big party at her parents' house. Not only was I not invited, but I hadn't even known about it. Also, two sophomore girls, Ashley and Krista, had suddenly emerged over the summer as the new party girls, and there had been several parties at Krista's parents' McMansion, where people had skinny-dipped and done beer bongs and jumped off the second-floor balcony into the pool. Supposedly, at one of these parties, Grace hooked up with a senior football player named Austin Wells and now they were in love. Which you'd think someone would have mentioned to me, out of common courtesy.

I slowly realized that Logan had been at most of these parties and hadn't told me about them, either to spare my feelings or because he had been instructed not to. I figured this was Hanna's doing, or Claude's. Maybe Grace was even behind it. She had been the most hurt by finding Hanna and me together. I guess finding your first boyfriend in the arms of your best friend would be pretty traumatic, though I noticed it hadn't stopped Grace from remaining friends with Hanna.

As the shock of this new reality set in, I found myself remembering other people who'd experienced devastating social downfalls. I remembered this guy Kyle, a basketball player who'd buddied around with Claude and me freshman year. He seemed destined for social success at Evergreen, but then his dad went to prison and suddenly his family had no money. He quickly faded from the scene. Or this girl Fiona Martin from eighth grade, who everyone liked. Even Hanna wanted to be her best friend, but something happened to her, too. She had health problems and gained a lot of weight, and by the time she hit high school she had become completely invisible.

Was that going to happen to me? I didn't know. It seemed like it might. I mean, I hadn't disappeared. I was still here. I still hung out with Logan and Olivia sometimes. I was still tall and blond and good at tennis. How far could I fall?

Quite a ways, it turned out.

• • •

There was a big party about two weeks into the school year, at Madison Decker's house. She was one of the editors of the school magazine and not an experienced party thrower. You could tell by the way people talked about it, the party was going to be huge. I asked Logan if he was going, but he and Olivia were doing something else that night. I wondered what that meant exactly. Probably there was a better party somewhere else and I wasn't invited. But I refused to worry about it. And on Friday I did something I'd never done before: I went to a party by myself.

I parked a few blocks away and walked up the street to Madison's house. The party was the same night as our first home football game, so a lot of kids from the game had shown up. Little packs of bewildered freshmen and sophomores were standing in the street and in the driveway. For some of them this was their first high school party ever. And it showed.

I slipped through the people, a little embarrassed to be there at all, but I kept up a good front. People brightened when they saw me. I was still—by reputation at least—one of the cool kids. Someone asked me about Grace. "We broke up," I said bluntly. Someone else—amazed to see me alone— asked if Hanna and Claude were coming. I didn't answer.

I went inside and found my way to the kitchen where the juniors and seniors were. None of my real friends were there. No Claude, Hanna, Petra, Olivia, Logan, or the rest of them. They were obviously somewhere else, doing something much more fun.

I made the best of it. I got a beer. Someone spilled orange juice on my Nikes. Madison was there, freaking out because so many people had shown up. She had no idea what was coming. But I knew. In about an hour every drunk kid on the West Side was going to appear. Madison would be lucky if her house was still standing by the end of the night. Even now people were telling her to call the police. Someone else was reporting that a freshman had passed out in her bathtub. And then two sophomores, wrestling in the living room, broke the coffee table in half. Poor Madison. "This wasn't supposed to be that kind of party!" she cried, which is what people like her always say.

I stayed for forty-five minutes. To stay any longer would make me look bad. As I walked back to my car, I heard someone yelling down the street. I looked and saw Antoinette and another girl running hand in hand up the hill toward the party. They ran by me, breathless and laughing. The other girl I knew vaguely. Her name was Kai. She had an even weirder haircut than Antoinette. The two of them were absurdly overdressed. Antoinette wore a fur coat and Kai had sparkly stuff all over her face. Both had bright red lipstick on, which no normal Evergreen girl would ever wear.

They didn't see me, so I called out, "Antoinette!" She

slowed down and stared at me blankly. She was very drunk. They both were. Kai immediately pulled on her arm, dragging her forward.

"The party sucks," I called after them.

"We don't care!" yelled Kai into the air.

They continued up the hill. I got in my car.

So yeah, junior year, a lot of stuff was different. And not just for me. There were new friendships, new cliques, new couples. One day I was at my locker when I heard a shriek behind me. I turned and here came six-foot-three-inch Austin Wells carrying tiny, slender Grace Anderson slung over his shoulder. "Coming through! Coming through!" he shouted. "Emergency girl removal!" Everyone jumped out of the way, laughing and pointing at Grace, who was also laughing and making faces as she beat her little fists against Austin's huge back.

Of course, there were rules against carrying people in the hallways. But that didn't stop Austin. He turned out to be this big, goofy, teddy-bear-type guy. And with Grace being so small and skinny, a lot of carrying went on. But people liked them, you could tell. They became a very popular couple. This gave Grace a new confidence. She'd been so timid and reserved with me, but now she'd run up behind Austin and jump on his back. It became their thing. Everyone loved how much they were in love.

Meanwhile, the rift between Claude and me remained. There wasn't actual hostility between us, but there wasn't any communication, either. I would see him in the halls and sometimes we'd exchange a head nod. But that was it. I could follow what was happening in his life through other people. It hadn't been a great summer for him tennis-wise. He had made it to the finals of the Idaho Junior Championships but had not done well in California or in Washington State, either. He looked different too. Something in his face had changed slightly. He was still very good-looking, but he seemed to have lost some of his Claude swagger. I assumed this was because of the tennis. Getting your ass kicked all up and down the West Coast, that was no fun. It made me glad I had bailed on that.

And then there was Hanna. I didn't talk to her, either. And yet I didn't hate her. It was hard to hate Hanna even if you had a good reason, which I did. For the new school year, she'd changed her hair. She had new highlights and her hair was a different shape, curving inward around her neck. She had obviously asked her stylist for a fresh look for junior year. But it looked sort of cheesy, and the next week she had it changed again, more like her old hairstyle but still with the highlights.

Despite hating Petra for talking to Claude, Hanna and Petra had somehow become friends over the summer, while Grace, who mostly hung out with Austin Wells's friends, had moved away from them both. This made sense in a way. Hanna had really hurt Grace by making out with me at Logan's party, though that wasn't how other people saw it. That mess was generally considered *my* fault, which was true in a way. Though to be honest, it wasn't a huge topic of conversation. That was summer stuff—ancient history. Nobody cared once school started.

The main thing was how popular Grace and Austin became. People were always talking about them, even more than Hanna and Claude. They were more real in a way. Though Hanna and Claude were pretty real too. That was their dirty little secret: They really were in love. I'm sure from the outside it didn't look that way. Most people considered them shallow and spoiled (they were often referred to as "Ken and Barbie"). But they really did share everything with each other. That part was never an act.

As for me, I had no girlfriend and barely any guy friends left. I didn't even have my older brother to make fun of anymore. That actually became a problem, going home to that big empty house every night. I missed Russell. I'd go shoot baskets in the driveway and think about the epic games we used to play with the neighborhood kids. I was always a better athlete than he was and was the same size as him for many years, though he would still win somehow, often by talking us out of something or changing the rules. At those moments it became obvious he was genuinely smarter than me. But in other ways, he was a total dork. He always liked the worst music. He'd get super into Porsche cars or Rolex watches and he'd rattle off specifications to you, or tell you how incredibly expensive something was, as if that proved beyond a doubt how great it was. I wasn't like that. Sometimes the plainest thing was the best thing.

Russell had the better room of the two of us. Now that he was gone, I would go in there sometimes, to look at things or to steal a pair of socks. As a senior, he'd arranged the room like an office, like my dad's. He had a big desk and a fancy chair. He would be a good lawyer, that was pretty obvious, though he never expressed that as his objective. That was because Dad told him not to. Dad told him to keep his options open, to go into law only if that's what he really wanted. But Russell didn't know what he wanted. Except for money. He knew he wanted that. How else was he going to get all those Porsches and Rolex watches?

One night I was in my room, messing around with my brother's camera, and my phone rang. It was Antoinette.

"Do you wanna go driving?" she said. I could tell she was outside somewhere.

"Driving where?" I asked.

"Just driving, with Kai and me."

I thought about it a second. I wasn't doing anything else. "Okay," I said.

"Where do you live?"

I told her my address. "Can I bring my camera?" I asked.

"Bring anything you want."

They arrived outside my house ten minutes later. They honked their horn.

I mumbled some explanation to my mother and headed out the front door. I strode down the driveway and crawled into the backseat of Kai's beige Subaru. Kai was driving. Antoinette was in the front passenger seat. When I closed the door, Kai hit the gas and we screeched away down the street. I said nothing as I tried to protect my camera from Kai's bouncy driving style.

"Is that new?" said Antoinette, looking back at the camera.

"No. It's my brother's."

"Can you take pictures in the dark?"

"With a flash."

"Can you buy cigarettes?" said Kai.

"Cigarettes?" I said. "I don't know. I never tried."

"We need cigarettes," said Antoinette.

"What do you need cigarettes for?"

"Uh, like, to smoke?" said Kai.

"We thought, since you're tall . . . ," said Antoinette.

"I'm not *that* tall."

"People card us because we look weird," said Kai. "Which is so, like, sexist or lookist or whatever."

"You have to be eighteen," said Antoinette.

"Will you do it?" said Kai.

I looked out the window of the car. "I can try," I said.

We pulled into a Safeway. Kai and Antoinette thought this was the best place. I left my camera and went inside. I bought a liter bottle of Cherry Coke, a bag of Sun Chips, a pack of gum, and then asked for two packs of Marlboro Lights. The checkout lady, to my amazement, sold them to me. I thanked her and went out. Back in the car, I tossed the two packs of cigarettes into the front seat. Kai hit the gas and we screeched out of the parking lot.

So then they smoked. And I ate Sun Chips. Nobody really talked. Kai put on the radio and bopped around in her seat as she drove. Antoinette didn't bop around. She was looking at something on her phone. I watched the two of them. I wondered if they did this every night.

They wanted to go to a place called Command Control. This was an arcade downtown, on a scuzzy block near the bus station. Command Control had pinball machines, *Pac-Man*, *Space Invaders*, and other games from the past. It was also full of skeevy, downtown, bus-station-type people. Kai and Antoinette showed no fear and walked straight in. I had my camera around my neck and gripped it a little extra tightly as I squeezed in among the leather jackets and home-made tattoos. One guy had two tiny metal studs sticking out of his forehead. I tried to maintain a neutral expression on my face.

Kai wanted to play a game called *Street Fight in the Bronx*, but it was currently occupied by a huge woman with dyed black hair and pockmarks. So then Kai was freaking out and she sent Antoinette over to the woman to ask how long she was going to be. Antoinette came back and said she was almost done.

So then Kai got to play *Street Fight in the Bronx*. Antoinette and I walked around and looked at the different games. It was very dark and noisy in there. It smelled like mold and cleaning chemicals. Then Antoinette wanted to go outside and smoke. I followed her out. We sat on the curb of the street, her smoking and me trying to act casual with my four-thousand-dollar camera while bums and criminals and drug dealers hovered around.

"So I heard what happened to you last summer," said Antoinette.

"Oh yeah?"

"You got seduced by Hanna. Which is how you lost your girlfriend."

"Oh that," I said, lifting my camera and focusing on the parking lot sign across the street.

"Why didn't you tell me that?" said Antoinette. "When I saw you at the Garden Center?"

"It was private."

"So private the whole school knows about it," said Antoinette.

"It wasn't that big of a deal."

"How can you say that? You lost your best friend! And your girlfriend. Who now goes out with that lunkhead football player."

"They're a good couple, though, don't you think?"

"I don't care about people like that," said Antoinette, smoking.

"Well, neither do I."

"Really? So you're not a jock anymore? What are you, then? A photographer?"

I was still looking around through my viewfinder. There were a bunch of people standing outside the Starlight Theater on the next block. I picked out two girls and zoomed in on them. The camera electronically adjusted itself, bringing their faces into focus.

"What are you?" I asked Antoinette.

"Me?" said Antoinette. "I'm just the same. I never change."

"You've got a new friend. Kai."

"Yes, I do."

"That's something different. You had different friends last year."

"Oh, my 'suicide friends,' as you guys called them."

"I didn't call them that."

"Your friends did."

"What happened to Bennett?" I asked.

"We broke up."

"What happened?"

"Nothing. It ran its course. It was mostly a sex thing anyway."

I stared through my viewfinder. The two girls outside the Starlight were also smoking cigarettes.

"Have *you* had sex yet, Gavin?" asked Antoinette.

"No," I said.

"You better get on that," she said. "You don't want to be the last virgin at Evergreen High School."

"I won't be."

"Oh yeah? You got someone lined up?"

I ignored this. "How old were you when you lost your virginity?" I asked.

"Ha-ha," she said, putting her cigarette out on the curb. "Wouldn't you like to know."

Back in the Subaru, Kai hit the car in front of us as she tried to leave her parking spot. She hit it pretty hard. There was a crunch.

"Shit," she said.

"Kai!" said Antoinette.

Kai quickly shifted into reverse. "It's their own fault they parked too close!"

She pulled back and hit the car behind her. *"Shit!"* she said again.

"Stop hitting the other cars!" said Antoinette.

"I'm not trying to hit them!"

"Hurry. Someone might come."

Kai pulled forward and hit the car in front of us again.

"I can't believe this," said Antoinette.

"What!?" said Kai. Finally she maneuvered out of the parking spot. She hit the gas and the Subaru screeched into the street.

"Can you drive by the front of that theater?" I asked Kai when we stopped at the light.

"Why?" said Kai.

"I wanna take a picture of those two girls."

"Gavin's a photographer now," explained Antoinette.

Kai looked at the theater. "You want to take a picture of *those* girls?" said Kai. "They're not even cute."

But when the light turned green, she did it, swerving into the closer lane and pulling up in front of the theater.

When I saw that she was cooperating, I lowered my window. I moved back away from it so I wouldn't be too obvious.

Kai pulled the car right up against the curb and stopped. The girls were perfectly framed beneath the marquee of the theater. It was a great shot: the two of them, in their hipster clothes, looking bored, looking cool. It was perfect. I clicked off a half-dozen shots.

"Hey, girls," called Kai out her window. The two girls stopped their conversation and looked at us. I clicked off several more shots.

"What's up?" said Kai.

The girls sneered at her once and went back to their conversation.

"Oh, another thing," Kai said to them. "You're ugly."

One of the girls flipped us off. Kai hit the gas. The car screeched into the street. For a moment nobody said anything. Then we all burst out laughing.

The next day, in the cafeteria at lunch, I had my usual problem of where to sit. At the beginning of the year I had avoided Claude and Hanna's table completely. But then sometimes if there were a lot of people sitting with them I'd sit there too, off to one side. If Logan was there, I could always sit next to him. But if Claude and Hanna were sitting alone, or with one or two other people, I usually went elsewhere. Not that I would be shunned or anything. Nobody was antagonistic toward me. It was just awkward.

That day, though, before I looked to see where Claude and Hanna were, I looked for Antoinette and Kai. I'd never eaten with them, but maybe I should. We could talk about our crazy night. Of course they probably didn't think it was that crazy. They probably did stuff like that all the time.

But then, as I stood scanning the tables, I remembered that Antoinette never came to the cafeteria. That was one of her things back in her "suicide friends" days. She had gotten an actual note from her mother to be excused from ever eating lunch there. Some of her other suicide friends had done the same. They had claimed that the cafeteria was "shaming" and made you feel bad about yourself if you didn't have the right clothes or friends or whatever.

I'd assumed that was bullshit at the time. But it was kind of true in a way. That huge, noisy room was not a fun place when your social position was in question. Lunch had always been one of my favorite parts of school. But not so much now.

That night, at home before bed, my dad called me into his office upstairs. He was sitting at his desk, doing something on his computer. He still had on his shirt and tie from work.

I came in and sat in the armchair. He continued to do whatever he was doing. It took a while. Finally he sent off an e-mail and sat back and considered me for several seconds.

"Your mother said your clothes smelled of cigarette smoke last night."

I was caught off guard by this.

"Oh, uh . . . yeah," I said. "I was in a car with some people . . . who were smoking."

"Which people?"

"These girls from school. I don't know them very well."

"Why were you in a car with them?"

I shrugged. "I just was."

My father stared at me. He sat forward. "Since she smelled the cigarette smoke, your mother looked through the pockets of your coat. She found a receipt for two packs of Marlboro Lights."

"Oh yeah," I said. "Those weren't for me. Those were for the girls."

My dad pursed his lips. "A year ago you were a state-ranked tennis player. And now you're smoking cigarettes?"

"Dad, I don't smoke. It was these two girls from school. I'm not even friends with them."

My father watched me without listening. "It's not necessary to explain," he said.

"But it is. Because I didn't smoke those—"

"I don't *care*," he said with that quiet power he can muster in his voice. My lawyer dad was very good at talking, arguing, making you feel inferior, making you feel like an idiot. "Your life is your own now," he said. "Do you understand that?"

I sank into silence.

"These years," he said. "Sixteen to eighteen, these are the years when we, your parents, we let you go. We release you into the world. It's the time when you start taking responsibility for your own life."

I nodded vaguely.

"What can I do?" he continued. "Ground you? Lecture you? You know how unhealthy smoking is. And how socially unacceptable."

"—but I didn't—"

"It doesn't matter if you did or not. That's what I'm trying to tell you. This is your life. You can do whatever you want. If you want to wander off into the smoking sections of the world, then okay. Since you don't appear to have any other plans or goals."

There was no point arguing with him. He continued on about choices, lifestyles, the decisions that affect one's life over the long term.

As he talked I felt that sinking sensation in my chest that I often got during moments when my father and I completely misunderstood each other. We weren't on the same planet at such moments. We weren't even in the same universe. In that way, he was right. It was my life now. He sure didn't know anything about it.

When he was done talking, I went back to my room. I ate some of the Sun Chips from that same bag I bought with the cigarettes. I picked up my phone and found Antoinette's number. I called and let it ring a couple times. Then I hung up.

Eventually I went back to looking at my photos from the night before. I'd moved them onto my big computer and was manipulating them in various ways. There were about thirty pictures in all. The best one was of the girl flipping us off. I'd zoomed in at the last minute and got this slightly blurry, slightly shadowy perspective on her face. She had this hard, dull look in her eyes. She didn't even look American. She looked like a girl from another time, another country, on the streets of some war-torn city. . . .

"Huh . . . this chick flipping you off . . . I kinda like that one," said Richie. "Where'd you take these?"

"Downtown," I said. "Outside the Starlight Theater."

We were standing at the counter of Passport Photos. Richie had transferred my photos onto his laptop. "Hmmmm," he said.

"The light's messed up," I said.

"But the blurriness kinda works," said Richie.

"Yeah, but I don't know how I did it."

"That's okay. You'll learn."

"And it's too dark."

"It is too dark," Richie agreed. He spent a few minutes talking to me about light. He even tried to sell me one of those handheld light meters.

"I'll tell you, though," he said, going into the back. "You want to take pictures of people on the street? This is your baby." He returned with an older camera, a Canon. I could tell from the casing that it was rock solid. It was still digital, but much simpler to operate. You could figure it out in a few seconds.

"And then you gotta look at this," said Richie. He dug

around under the counter and pulled out an old paperback art book. It was called *The Americans* by Robert Frank.

He plopped it down in front of me. "This guy invented street photography."

The book itself was old and curled up at the corners. I put down the camera and opened it. It was all photographs. One per page. They were black and white, from the fifties and sixties, it looked like. They were mostly people, all different kinds. A cowboy. A nurse. People on a bus. Rich people in tuxedos. Teenagers around a jukebox. They were in big cities, small towns. The people in the pictures seemed to have no sense of a photographer being present. The guy who took them must have hung around for a long time. He'd waited so long that everyone forgot he was there. And then he got the shot.

"What do you think?" said Richie. He was smiling. He could tell what I thought.

"These are great."

"Hell yes, they're great. Take it home. Study it. That's pretty much all you gotta know right there."

So that's what I did. I went home, ate dinner, did my usual bare minimum of homework. Then I got out *The Americans*. I looked through each picture in the book. Obviously a person could study these pictures in a technical way, the angles and the light. But I didn't notice that stuff. Not at first. I liked how they made you feel. Most of them were sad or revealing in some way. A bored waitress. An angry factory worker. A tired old person, thinking about the past. It was kind of astonishing how much they affected you. The pictures had been taken half a century ago, and yet they felt so new, so alive.

After looking at that, I went back to my own photos of the girls at the Starlight. They didn't look so good now. They looked obvious and amateurish, like something a high school kid would take.

Later, though, on a whim, I sent one to Antoinette, the one where the girl was flipping us off. My phone rang five seconds later. "Oh my God," she said. "That picture is hilarious!"

"I know!" I said.

"They look like they're from another century. How did you do that?"

"I have no idea."

"The one girl's cute. With the skirt."

"I don't know if I'd use the word 'cute,'" I said, blowing up that same picture on my computer again.

"Well, she's no Grace Anderson."

"Hey, leave Grace alone," I said.

"At least these girls have some style. Grace doesn't have anything."

"Grace has plenty of style. It's just more . . ."

"What?" said Antoinette. "Mall based? More suburban? Grace is an idiot."

"Just because someone is from the suburbs doesn't mean they're an idiot."

"Oh yeah? You sure about that?"

"People have to grow up somewhere," I said. "It's probably better to grow up in a safe environment—"

"The suburbs aren't *safe*. Who told you that? The suburbs destroy people. They rot your brain."

"They're not rotting my brain."

"How do you know? Do you think people know when their brain is rotting?"

There was a click on the line. "That's Kai," said Antoinette. "I sent her your picture. Gotta go."

I didn't talk to Antoinette again for almost a week. That was the thing with her. It was like you were friends for a day or two and then she would totally disappear. Then she would reappear a week later and you were friends again. I didn't know where she disappeared *to*. You didn't really see her around school.

And then one day she came to her fifth-period geometry class totally high. Apparently she had done this before. She got called on by the teacher and had to go up to the board. She was supposed to do a proof—which she couldn't do—and then she couldn't find her way back to her desk. The whole class was snickering behind the teacher's back. Then, when Antoinette did find her desk and tried to sit, she missed the chair. She landed so hard on the floor she knocked herself out. So then Principal Brown had to come, with the school nurse. When they couldn't wake her up right away, they called the paramedics.

I heard about this between classes. Everyone was talking about it, and the ambulance was still in the parking lot with its lights flashing. Antoinette had been brought to the main office by then. I hurried to see what was happening, but several teachers were blocking the door. Also, all the adults were talking about Kai. She and Antoinette had both taken a Xanax, it turned out. Kai had run off. She'd left campus. Nobody knew where she was. Which was why the police were called.

The police showed up a few minutes later. Not only did they have their flashing lights on, but they blasted their siren a couple times as they pulled into the faculty parking lot. The whole school was buzzing with excitement. When the bell rang, nobody went back to class. A general chaos had taken over, especially when the policemen came marching down the hall with their radios and their guns.

The teachers kept telling us to go to our classes. But nobody did. I stayed by the office as long as I possibly could, trying to see inside, or at least hear what happened. The expressions on the teachers' faces were so grim and serious, I wished I had my camera. Meanwhile, the students were loving it. Antoinette had knocked herself out! And Kai was being chased by the cops! It was the most exciting day ever at Evergreen High, and now we were missing a whole class because of it!

Eventually Principal Brown announced that any students not in class would be suspended. So finally we went. We took our time, though. People were still running around, yelling back and forth. Back in our classes nobody could focus. The entire day was disrupted. Even the teachers gave up.

After school, in the parking lot, people told and retold the story of Antoinette falling on her ass. They discussed which direction she fell. They described the sound of her body hitting the floor. They told how Principal Brown got down on his hands and knees and whispered to her as she lay unconscious on the floor. This was also the first time I heard the nickname "Antoinette Trainwreck." This phrase became very popular for a while. For months afterward, anytime Antoinette showed her face—in a class, in the hallways—people would giggle and whisper to each other: "There she is, *Antoinette Trainwreck*!"

The next day Antoinette's and Kai's punishments were announced. They were both suspended for three days. Kai was lucky that was all that happened, since she almost got hit by a car, stumbling down the West Beaverton Highway. That's what the police told Principal Brown when they brought her back to school.

At lunch, I texted Antoinette. We had the following text conversation:

Me: *You okay?*
Antoinette: *They think I have a concussion*
Me: *What did your parents say?*
Antoinette: *Very mad*

That was all I could get out of her. So then I texted Kai.

Me: *You all right?*
Kai: *Ya*

Me: *They said the cops found you*

Kai: *Ya*

Me: *What did the cops say?*

Kai: *"Get in the car"*

Me: *And you did?*

Kai: *Ya*

Me: *Your parents freaking out?*

Kai: *Uh, ya.*

I didn't hear any more from them, and then they came back to school on Friday. Everyone was looking forward to that. I thought they might show up all embarrassed and apologetic, but they did not. They walked in more defiant than ever: Kai with dark eyeliner and a very short skirt, and Antoinette wearing her fake fur coat and a scarf like she was a rock star. Everyone wondered what would happen. Would Principal Brown send them home? Would he suspend them again? Would Mrs. Parsons get out her ruler and measure Kai's skirt to see if it met the dress code?

It was a pretty entertaining day. Not that people were on their side. Most people disapproved or felt sorry for them. *Antoinette Trainwreck*. Sure, she was having fun now, but a drug suspension on your high school record? And then showing up dressed like that? Good luck getting into a good college.

Other people complained they got off easy, that it wasn't fair, that if a normal person did the same thing, they'd be punished much worse. But since they were such freaks to start with—and with Antoinette's tragic past—nothing that bad happened to them.

Hanna and Petra had their own take on it. They understood the power of reputation, so they had to respect any girls who could pull off such extreme attitude. "I love it," Hanna told a bunch of us at lunch. "The way they do whatever they want. I mean, look at Antoinette. She's not afraid if people think she's a slut. She could care less."

"She's not a slut," I said.

Everyone laughed.

"What?" I said. "Who has she had sex with besides Bennett?"

"*Kai*," said Petra.

Everyone laughed again.

"That's what I heard," said Petra. "They're lesbos."

"They're not *lesbos*," scoffed Logan. "Antoinette went out with Bennett. All they did was have sex."

"Sex with Bennett?" said Petra. "Oh my God. That's *disgusting*."

"I respect them," said Hanna loftily. "They decided they wanted to be the bad girls. And they've done it. Everyone knows who they are. And everyone knows what their deal is."

"Maybe she hasn't gotten over her brother's death," said Olivia. "Maybe she's acting out because of that."

"Oh, come on," said Hanna. "That was a year ago."

"And she was weird anyway," said Petra. "She was like that when she got here."

"It's almost too perfect, though, isn't it?" said Hanna.

"If you wanna be the crazy messed-up chick? To have your brother jump off a bridge?"

"Her dad is a major in the army," I said.

"Exactly," said Hanna. "The whole thing is like out of a book. She wants to be a tragic figure? Good for her. Maybe she'll get her wish."

And then one day I came back to my locker before lunch and found Grace Anderson standing there. That was a surprise. She appeared to be looking for me.

"Hey, Grace," I said.

"Hey, Gavin," she answered, smiling bashfully.

"What's up?"

"Not much," she said. "I was wondering if I could talk to you for a minute?"

I couldn't imagine what she wanted. But I said okay. I put my books away and followed her down the hallway and out to the breezeway.

"How's it going?" I said as we walked.

"Good."

"How's Austin?"

"Good. Really good."

That was all the small talk I could manage. But it was nice to see Grace again close up, to be talking to her and having her actually acknowledge me instead of looking through me like I didn't exist, which was what she usually did.

Outside, Grace stopped and faced me. "The thing I need to ask you . . . ," she said.

"Yeah?"

"It's about Claude."

"Claude?" I said.

"Hanna's worried about him."

"What's she worried about?"

"There's something going on with him," said Grace. "He's acting strange. His parents want him to take medication for social anxiety."

"Claude has *social anxiety*? I find that hard to believe."

"They don't know what it is. Maybe it's depression."

"That doesn't sound like Claude," I said.

"Have you seen him though? Have you talked to him? It's true. He's different."

I looked away. "So what do you want me to do about it?"

"Hanna says he doesn't have any friends."

I laughed. "What are you talking about? He has a million friends. He can be friends with anyone he wants."

Grace shook her head. The expression on her face reminded me that Grace was not an idiot, despite what Kai and Antoinette said. Grace understood certain things. She had been cute and popular her entire life, and when other cute, popular people were in trouble, she could feel their pain.

"Hanna thinks you should talk to him. That he misses you."

I shifted my stance. "Hanna? Who completely fucked

up our friendship to start with now wants me to fix it?"

Grace nodded. "Hanna didn't mean to do that. It was just her jealousy. She's working on that."

"She's *working* on it?" I said. "Oh great. Good for her."

"But don't you want to be friends with Claude again? He was your best friend."

"Yeah, well, maybe things have changed."

Now Grace did a little pout, her version of one of Hanna's classic moves. "Well, if you don't want to . . ."

"It's not that. I mean, yes. Of course I do."

Grace brightened. She hit me with her killer smile. "Hanna would *soo* appreciate it."

"*Hanna,*" I grumbled. I stared at the ground for a second. Then I looked up into Grace's face. "What about you? Why are you tangled up in this?"

"They're my friends," she said. She paused a moment. "And you're my friend too. I hope. If you want to be."

I blushed when she said that. "Of course I want to be."

We both stood there for a moment.

Finally, I said: "I have to tell you. It's hard seeing you and Austin Wells having so much fun. It makes me feel like I wasn't much of a boyfriend."

"You weren't that bad. You tried. You were nice." She shrugged in her cute way. "And anyway, we were younger then. We were sophomores. We didn't know what real love was."

• • •

So then I had a new mission: Figure out how to talk to Claude. Not that he avoided me. But we had developed the habit of not talking to each other. So now we had to break the habit.

I came up with a plan. I parked my car—my brother's RAV4—next to Claude's BMW in the parking lot and then waited in it after school so I'd catch him. I was stalking a dude, basically.

When I saw him walking toward our two cars, I got out and pretended to do something on my phone. When he got closer to me, I looked up. We gave each other the usual head nod. He unlocked his car with his remote.

"Hey," I said to him.

"Hey," he said back, tossing his book bag into the rear seat.

Then he hesitated a moment. We both looked at each other over the roof of the BMW.

"I never got to hear how the tournaments went last summer," I said.

Claude grunted. "Not too good."

"I heard you made the finals in Idaho."

"Yeah," he said. "But I got killed in California." He shook his head. "I wanted to strangle my coach."

"Huh."

"I did finally beat Jake Jorgenson in Seattle," he said. "That felt good."

"Wow. Jake Jorgensen."

"But he's done," said Claude. "He doesn't care anymore. He was playing out the summer for his parents' sake. Same as me."

"So that's it? You're done?"

"Well, if you can't get out of the second round of half your tournaments, yeah, I'd say you're done."

I nodded.

"You did it right," said Claude. "You got out at the right time."

"I just peaked earlier than you."

"My dad finally fired the coach," said Claude. "We had to pay him all this extra money for breaking the contract. My dad was pissed. But whatever."

"*Dads,*" I said, shaking my head. "What's their problem?"

"They put their shit on you," said Claude. "Whatever they couldn't do, you gotta do."

"I guess so."

We lapsed into an easy silence. It was nice talking to Claude.

"How's Hanna?" I said.

"She's okay."

"Just okay?"

"I dunno . . . She gets bored. She always needs something new. New dramas."

"Sounds like Hanna," I said.

"It's not a great mystery she's like that. But what can I do?"

"*Chicks*," I said, shaking my head.

"Exactly. *Chicks*."

"You guys will be all right," I said.

Claude nodded that this was probably true. He looked at his watch. "I gotta roll," he said.

"All right," I said.

"Good talking to ya," he said.

"Likewise," I said back.

It was in October that I was out raking leaves with my mom and my phone rang. It was a number I didn't recognize. I answered anyway; it was Richie from Passport Photos.

"Hey, kid," he said.

He'd never called me before. It was strange to hear his voice on the phone.

"What are you doing this weekend?" he said.

"Uh . . ."

"I got a photography gig," he said. "In Seattle."

"Yeah?"

"From a magazine. *Travel and Leisure*. Ever heard of it?"

"Sure," I said, though I hadn't really.

"Paid gig. Gonna drive up there Saturday. You wanna go?"

"Me . . . ?"

"You can be my assistant. Ask your parents."

I put the phone to my chest and turned to my mother. "Can I go to Seattle this weekend?"

"What for?"

"The guy from the camera store has a gig up there."

"What sort of gig?"

"Taking pictures," I told my mother. "For a magazine."

"Ask your father."

I lifted the phone to my face again. "What sort of gig exactly?"

"A pro gig. A travel piece. Some guy wrote an article and we'll take the pictures. The Space Needle. Pike's Market. All that. We'll spend the night. I'll pay you."

"Really? How much?"

"Fifty bucks."

I turned to my mom. "He said he's going to pay me."

"Who is he?"

"The guy from the camera store."

My mother frowned. "Ask your father."

There was a big case going on at my dad's law firm. He'd been coming home late and going straight to his upstairs office, where he worked even later.

I knocked on his door. He told me to come in. He was eating microwaved lasagna from a plate. He had two computers going at once.

"Hey, Dad," I said.

He stared up at me. He looked very tired. Very stressed out.

I didn't want to take up too much of his time. "I have to ask you something."

"What?"

"You know how I was trying out Russell's camera?"

"Yes?"

"Well, I've been hanging out at this camera store. And talking to the guy there. He has a paid job taking pictures of Seattle. For a travel magazine. And he wants me to go with him. And be his assistant."

"Who is he?"

"His name is Richie."

"What kind of person is he?"

"His uncle owns the Passport Photos store downtown. He wants to be a photographer."

"And what will you do?"

"I'll be his assistant. I'll carry stuff."

"And why did he pick you?"

"He likes my stuff."

"What stuff?"

"My photographs."

My father frowned. The idea of me as a photographer was so ridiculous to him, he couldn't talk about it. "Well, I don't care. Ask your mother."

I didn't ask her. I went into my own room and called Richie and told him I'd do it.

That was on a Wednesday. So I had a couple days before we went. At first I didn't think about it much. I was like, okay, I'm going to Seattle on Saturday. I'd been to Seattle before. I'd played in tennis tournaments there. But then Thursday at school, it hit me what I was doing. I got more excited and a little bit scared. I had no idea what it was like, being on a real photography job.

On Friday there was a big party at Krista Hoffman's McMansion. Krista and Ashley had become the new party girls over the summer. Krista was a pretty visible person in general, for a sophomore. She was always running around, being adorable with her wavy blond hair. Her whole face squeezed together when she got excited, which was a lot.

So then, since Claude and I were becoming friends again, he called me and we rode over together in his BMW. Hanna, who still ignored me for the most part, came up to me when we arrived and gave me a hug. So everything was basically cool with the three of us again. Which was a great relief.

The party was awesome. Krista was running around in this white dress, with a red ski hat with a big puffball on top that everyone was swatting at. She was being the party girl, I guess. She literally bounced up and down when she talked.

I was excited about going to Seattle the next day, so I was in a good mood. We started dancing, Hanna and Logan and some other people. Olivia showed up too, with Rachel Lehman, of all people, who I hadn't talked to since she left for the San Juans halfway through the summer. She did her usual thing of looking super hot and then not talking. So you had no idea what she was thinking. I tried to act casual and just smile at her.

Hanna and Claude left pretty early, so I wandered around and got a beer and went into the backyard. Bennett and some of his drug buddies were out there. They had started showing up at such places—the better parties—that year. They had taken over the big patio table, so I sat with them. They were smoking a joint and grinning like people do when they're high.

Then Antoinette and Kai showed up. So now they were coming to the cool parties too. They looked suspicious of the whole thing and a little out of place. They walked into the backyard and sat on a bench against the wall and lit cigarettes. I watched Bennett watch Antoinette. The word was that Antoinette had broken his heart pretty badly. Judging from his facial expressions, that was an accurate description. I had never thought—or cared—about the two of them as a couple. But I thought about it now. She must have recognized that he wasn't the total loser everyone thought he was. In some ways she had helped him evolve out of his loser-ness. But what did he see in her? The same thing I saw. Her confidence. And that quality she had where she seemed to be thinking all the time. She wasn't just some pissed-off teenager. She had a plan. It was like she knew the future and was already preparing for it. She was going to learn the things she needed to learn. She was going to do the things she needed to do. And the rest of it: high school, social life, teachers, parents . . . it was just noise to her. It didn't matter in the slightest.

• • •

Later that night I ended up smoking a joint with Logan and Olivia and Rachel Lehman, in Krista's sister's bedroom. Logan and Olivia were giggling and goofing around. Rachel and I smiled at each other a lot but didn't really talk.

Logan got up to piss. And when he didn't come back, Olivia went to look for him. So then Rachel and I were sitting there together in the dim light, both of us stoned and sipping on our Amstel Lights.

"How's school?" I asked her.

"It's okay," she said.

"That was fun playing tennis last summer."

"Yeah," she said.

We sat there.

"You look really high," I said, grinning.

"So do you."

"Your eyes are like little slits," I said.

"Your eyes are all shiny."

Now she was grinning too. And doing flirty things with her hair.

"I wanted to hang out with you more last summer," I said. "But you went on vacation for, like, five weeks!"

"I did."

I laughed. "You broke my heart," I said.

"Did I?"

"A little bit."

"Well, I'm here now," she said.

114

We looked at each other for a moment. Then I leaned in to kiss her. With great smoothness and grace, she met my lips with hers. Wow. She was a great kisser. I mean, unbelievable. I scooted closer.

We made out. The door opened at one point, but neither of us looked up. It closed again.

Later, when we returned to the party, she ran off with Olivia. I didn't see her again that night. But that was okay. We had seriously made out, which meant I could call her again.

The next morning my alarm went off at six a.m. I gathered up my stuff for Seattle and went downstairs and ate some cereal. I let the thought *I made out with Rachel Lehman* go through my mind once. Then I got back to business.

I drove in the dark to the address Richie had given me. It was on the east side, in an odd neighborhood I had never been to before. The houses were older and small and they had old-style concrete driveways that were so narrow they could barely fit a modern car. This was Richie's uncle's house, it turned out. Richie lived in his spare room.

I tapped lightly on the front door as I had been instructed. Richie came to the door and opened it and shushed me to stay quiet. There was a lot of crap on the floor. Lights, umbrellas, tripods, rolls of cable and cords, several different camera cases.

I quietly grabbed some of it and followed him out the

door. When he got outside and saw the RAV4, he stopped.

"This yours?" he whispered.

"Yeah," I whispered back.

"Let's take your car."

"I can't."

"Why not?"

"My parents."

"What about them?"

"They didn't give me permission to drive to Seattle."

"How are they going to know? C'mon. Open the door. Hurry up."

"But what if they find out?"

"How will they find out?"

So we took my car.

We were on the interstate when the sun came up. Richie drank coffee and rocked his head to the radio. He had his foot up on the dash. He wore black jeans and motorcycle boots.

"This is a sweet ride," he said to me.

"It's not mine. It's my brother's."

"Where's he at?"

"He's at college. Back East."

"Nice. I like the sound of that. *College. Back East.* That's what I should have done. Instead of hanging around my uncle's shop."

I drove. "Well, you got a good gig at least," I said.

"*Travel and Leisure*. How much do you get paid for this?"

"Not enough," he said.

"That's okay," I said. "It'll be good experience. You're getting your foot in the door."

"Yeah, yeah. *Good experience. Foot in the door.*" He sipped his coffee. "You got a lot to learn, kid."

In Seattle, Richie wanted to drive, so we traded places. From his shirt pocket, he pulled out a list of the places that were featured in the travel article. This list was titled: SHIT WE HAVE TO HAVE.

The first on the list was a restaurant called Maud's Kitchen. I punched the address into the GPS and it showed us where to go. We arrived at ten thirty, as brunch was beginning. A long line of people were standing outside. Richie pulled over in a NO STOPPING zone and hopped out. I watched from the car while he walked briskly toward the restaurant entrance and disappeared inside. I looked up at the NO STOPPING sign and checked around for cops or meter maids or tow trucks.

A minute later he came hurrying back out. "This is perfect. Place is packed. Let's go." He opened the back door and grabbed some of the stuff. He motioned for me to grab the cords and two of the lights. He started back into the restaurant.

"Richie!" I called to him. "We can't park here."

He'd been too distracted to think about that. He looked up at the sign. "Pull it around. Park in the lot. And hurry!" He headed back into the restaurant.

• • •

I didn't know what lot he was talking about. We hadn't seen any lot. Nor did I know what "around" meant. I shut the doors that Richie had left open and hopped into the driver's seat. I pulled forward and took a right. That seemed like "around." But in fact that was a pretty steep drop down a hill. And there wasn't another right to take for three blocks. I passed a parking garage, but I didn't see an entrance. I turned right again and found myself under the freeway, on a dead-end street. I started cursing. I turned around and headed right again, thinking I'd at least be heading back in the direction of Maud's Kitchen. I went straight ahead for a while, assuming the restaurant would reappear on my right, but it didn't. So I turned left and then left again and found myself going up a ramp. This turned into a freeway entrance, and a few seconds later I was merging into traffic. I was back on the interstate. I was on my way to Canada.

Things were a little tense when I finally got back.

"*Where have you been?*" Richie snarled at me under his breath as he simultaneously smiled at the manager of Maud's. The manager was not thrilled to have his packed restaurant disrupted by a disorganized camera crew.

"You said there was a parking lot," I hissed back. "But there wasn't one."

It all worked out in the end. We got some good stuff at Maud's. Richie became obsessed with getting an aisle shot, so you could see several booths in a row, at an angle, with the best-looking diners most visible. Richie even made one booth rearrange itself to get a woman with big sunglasses on the end. We had to readjust the lights several times. It took a few minutes, but we got it.

Next up was Pike's Market, where the fish guys threw the salmon back and forth. It was one of Seattle's most famous tourist attractions.

Richie surveyed the situation. He didn't like it. "What am I supposed to do with this?" he said. "Everyone's already seen this a million times."

"Yeah, but it's what they want," I said. "Flying fish" was second on the list of SHIT WE HAVE TO HAVE.

"Yeah, well, you take it, then," he said, handing me his fancy Pentax.

So I took a bunch of shots from different angles, until I was pretty sure we had something good.

After that we walked through the market and took pictures of whatever else looked interesting. Richie did the shooting. I carried the gear. Richie was good at catching odd things: an old Chinese lady with her plastic bags, a stray cat eating fish guts off the floor. It was a lesson in population density. That many people crammed into a small space created a lot of photographic possibilities. Richie was all over it.

• • •

That night we checked into the Holiday Inn, which *Travel and Leisure* was paying for. I walked down the street to McDonald's and got us two Big Mac meals. I felt pretty important standing in line, with my light meter still hanging from my neck. My first pro gig. I liked the feel of it.

Back at the hotel we watched SportsCenter and ate our Big Macs. Richie promptly fell asleep in his clothes on top of his bed. I brushed my teeth and actually got under the blankets. I was pretty tired. And pretty excited. And not only that: *I had made out with Rachel Lehman the night before.* I was like a jet-setting journalist, traveling to distant cities, fighting my way through crowded markets, all the while knowing that my beautiful girlfriend was waiting for me at home.

Not that Rachel was my girlfriend yet. But it was fun to think about.

The next day, after we had all the SHIT WE HAVE TO HAVE places crossed off, we drove down to the waterfront. Richie took shots of different things. The boats. The skyline. Wood chips floating in the water. He explained that you wanted to have a bunch of extra random stuff on a gig like this. It gave the photo editors options.

That night we got back on the interstate and headed home. While Richie slept, I drove and daydreamed about Rachel Lehman. I thought about kissing her at the party. How soft her lips were. How shockingly cute she was. But then I remembered how she didn't talk. And there was her strange disappearance last summer. And the fact that she didn't want to hang out if I wasn't friends with Hanna and Claude.

Well, I *was* friends with Hanna and Claude again. So maybe she would like me now.

Back in Portland, I drove us to Richie's, where we unloaded the gear. We were so tired we didn't say a word to each other.

It was two in the morning when I got to my own house. As I turned into our driveway, I saw a person standing out by our big spruce tree. He was on the opposite side of it from the house. I looked closer. It was my dad. He had his parka over his shoulders. He appeared to be talking on his phone.

I eased the RAV4 into its usual parking spot. Since it was so late, I got my stuff and headed straight into the house. Whatever my dad was doing, I didn't want to bother him. He was probably standing out there so he wouldn't wake my mom while he talked over his big case.

I took my bag upstairs and down the hall to my room. I left it there and then, without turning on any lights, crept back to the hallway that looked out toward the spruce tree. I peeked out one of the windows. Because the tree blocked the view, I couldn't tell if my dad was still out there. And I couldn't hear anything. I watched. I listened. He must have seen my car come in and gone back inside.

What was he doing? Maybe he'd gone out there to piss. I did that sometimes late at night. If I had to piss and nobody was awake, I'd walk out into the yard. Just to be outside for a second, to look at the stars. But my dad wasn't really a *look at the stars* kind of person.

On Friday I had my second date with Rachel Lehman. We went downtown, to this new gourmet pizza place Hanna kept raving about.

I could tell from the beginning something was not right with Rachel. For starters, she had sounded surprised when I called her. Had she forgotten about the party? Then she wanted to meet me at the restaurant for some reason. She didn't want to be picked up.

I tried to stay positive. We met and got our table and ordered. When the waiter left, I asked her what else she had done over the weekend, but she wouldn't really answer. So I told her about my weekend, driving to Seattle and assisting on the photo shoot. I made a funny story out of getting lost on the freeway.

Rachel smiled.

I asked her how she and Olivia had become friends.

She couldn't answer because she was drinking her Diet Coke.

The pizza came. I carefully pulled a piece off the special silver tray and slid it onto her plate.

"So what's going on with Claude these days?" she said

suddenly. It was the first complete sentence she had spoken.

"What do you mean?" I asked.

"He's still with Hanna, right?"

"Yeah," I said. "Didn't you see them at the party?"

"She seems very difficult, if you ask me," said Rachel. "I don't see how he puts up with it."

I stared at her across the table.

"He deserves better," she said, picking at her pizza with her fork. "He deserves a dignified girlfriend. Not a loud-mouth drama queen. And the way she assumes everyone is just going to do whatever she wants . . ."

I said nothing. "I didn't know you knew Hanna."

"I don't. Thank God. But I know Claude. We went to summer camp together. Did you know that?"

"No," I said.

"He was the first boy I ever kissed," she said, smiling dreamily at the memory. "He was kind of my first love."

"Well, that explains a lot," I said.

"Do you think he and Hanna will ever break up?"

"I'm sure they will someday," I said. "Or they'll get married. Or they'll die." I was trying to be funny, but Rachel wasn't listening.

"It's just such a waste is all," she said, putting a tiny bit of pizza in her mouth.

After that Rachel retreated back into her silence. It was amazing how she didn't talk. You could say things, ask her questions, it didn't matter. She just didn't speak.

Afterward I walked her back to her car. I'd planned on kissing her again. I'd been looking forward to it for a week. But it was pretty clear that wasn't happening. She got out her keys and opened her door.

"Should I call you again?" I said.

"If you want," she said.

When I got home, I threw my coat down, flopped on the bed, and stared at the ceiling. The good thing about Rachel Lehman was she shut you down so fast, you didn't have time to get your hopes up.

Eventually, I dug my camera out. Not my brother's camera, but the Canon that Richie had lent me. I had brought it to Seattle and taken some random shots with it. I'd gotten a couple good things. And I liked the camera. I thought I should buy it from Richie. He could deduct the fifty dollars he owed me for assisting from the price. I might never see that fifty dollars otherwise.

Later, I went downstairs and ate a bowl of Cheerios. I could hear the rain dripping from the gutters outside while I ate. I had forgotten about Rachel Lehman while I had been fiddling with the Canon. I resolved to continue to forget about her.

Then I heard my dad's footsteps upstairs. I could tell when it was him and not my mother. He was heavier and he thudded more. He went to the bathroom, did something there, flushed the toilet, and then moved down the hall to his office. I could hear the big office door close.

At that moment, I had a rare feeling. I felt sorry for my dad. I didn't have any reason to. Just his life. And now without Russell here, and working all the time, and whatever else went on in his life.

I wondered if he was actually happy. He acted so smug and self-satisfied. He definitely considered himself "a winner." People listened to him. People did what he told them to do.

At least my brother would be back from college soon. At least he had that to look forward to.

Back upstairs I had a friend request on Facebook from someone I didn't know. Britney Vaughn was her name. I clicked on her profile and looked at her picture. She was the girl from the Starlight Theater, whose picture I'd taken, the girl who flipped us off.

There was also a message from her. It said: *Excuse me, why are you posting pictures of me on Facebook? I did not give my permission to be photographed and I did not give permission to have it posted.*

I *had* posted it but only that one and not with Britney's name on it. I didn't even know her name then.

Now I did. Britney Vaughn. I looked at her profile some more. She was a street-fashion type, like Antoinette. Weird clothes, weird haircut. She had a more definite style than Antoinette, though. She was more punk, with black stockings and black Vans and way too much eye makeup.

Not knowing what else to do, I confirmed our friendship and wrote her back. *Sorry. I didn't know your name. I'll take it down if you want.*

I sent this and waited. A minute later she wrote back: *You should pay people if you're using their image for personal gain.*

It's not for personal gain, I wrote back. *I just liked it.*

Okay, she wrote. And then a moment later: *Do you know Antoinette and Kai?*

Yes, I wrote.

That changes things, she wrote.

Why does it change things?

It just does.

In what way? I wrote.

But she never answered.

"Oh, those girls hate us," Antoinette told me at school the next day. "Thanks to Kai insulting them. And flirting with their boyfriends."

"Wait, Kai was flirting with someone's boyfriend?"

"She didn't *really* flirt with them," said Antoinette. "It was just this stupid thing. At this stupid party. And they made a big deal about it. They wanted to fight us."

"Like fight you, like a real fight?"

"I guess so."

This was another thing that happened with Kai and Antoinette. You wouldn't see them for one weekend and then you'd hear about these crazy adventures they'd had.

"And what happened?" I asked.

"The one girl was too drunk. She could barely stand up. And then Britney claimed she couldn't find her shoes."

"And what party was this?"

Antoinette shrugged. "Some Agenda party."

"What's Agenda?"

"It's a dance club. Downtown. For people under twenty-one."

I had not known there were dance clubs for people under twenty-one. "Who goes to it?"

"Teenagers mostly."

"Do you go to it?"

"Sometimes."

"What's it like?"

"It's a dance thing. They play music. People dance. You know what dancing is, don't you?"

Russell came home from college the week before Christmas. The three of us drove to the airport to get him: my mom, me, my dad. My brother's flight had been delayed by a snowstorm in Minneapolis. He'd been traveling sixteen hours by the time he landed at PDX at midnight.

He looked pretty different. He wasn't all Brooks Brothers, that's for sure. He had a plain blue hoodie on and jeans and Nikes. His hair was messy and he had a neck beard going. His eyes looked like he hadn't slept in days.

My dad took his shoulder bag. I rolled his suitcase. You knew right away Russell would make a huge deal about how difficult finals had been, how tough Cornell was in general. This first semester had been a great ordeal: the stress, the pressure, the competition. His first semester, he confessed to us at the baggage claim, was the hardest thing he'd ever done in his life.

My dad loved this. He wanted to hear every detail. So Russell spent the car ride home telling us about the demanding professors and the three-hour exams. He told us about finishing essays on political ideology as the sun came up. He described the "brain food" and the Red Bull and the all-night cramming sessions at the library, which stayed open twenty-four hours during finals. Last of all was the big party Russell and his hallmates tried to have after finals: making margaritas and then falling asleep before they could drink them because they were so exhausted from so much work.

My father beamed with pride. My mother looked worried for Russell's health. I said nothing and watched out the window at the passing cars.

Two nights later, a bunch of other recent Evergreen graduates showed up at our house. These were Russell's close friends: David Stiller, Hassad, and some others who had gone to elite colleges. They too had stories of insane workloads and impossible reading lists. How had they done it? How had they survived? Listening to them, it was like they'd climbed Mount Everest or won a war.

My dad was smack in the middle of this too. He ordered gourmet pizzas delivered and a case of expensive beer. Russell and his friends were not of legal age, but that was okay. Since they had proven themselves in the academic big leagues, they were entitled to a few adult beverages.

I hung around in the background of all this. Skeptical as I was, I could tell Russell and his friends really had been through something. They had pale, sallow faces. People had lost weight, or gained it. They had bags under their eyes. One of the girls described having to study for finals while her roommate had an anorexic meltdown. The roommate had stopped eating at Thanksgiving. They had to call an ambulance and fly her home to Denver.

In bed that night, I thought about everything I'd heard. I envied Russell and his friends the intensity of their experience. Was there something similar that I could do? With my grades and my test scores, I'd assumed I was destined for University of Oregon. If I could even get in there. If I couldn't, possibly Portland State. But maybe I could go somewhere else. Like art school. I didn't know anything about art schools. I wasn't even sure I was interested in "art." But maybe I needed to think about it.

"Art school?" said Richie, when I asked him about it at Passport Photos. He made the hand gesture of a guy masturbating. "It's bullshit. Are you kidding me? What will you do in art school? Pay somebody thousands of dollars to tell you what looks good? You either know or you don't."

I was there with the Canon, trying to talk Richie into selling it to me. He wanted a lot for it. And now there was the small issue of the gas up to Seattle, which I had paid for, plus the fifty dollars he'd promised me for assisting, both of which I wanted him to take off the price of the Canon.

Eventually we worked it out. I could have sold Russell's camera and bought ten Canons, but I had a feeling he would want it back at some point, which he did. When he asked for it, I brought it to him and he complained that I'd changed the settings, which I had. Then I had to sit down and explain how it worked, which wasn't easy with such a complicated camera.

Eventually, he took a few pictures of Mom and Dad and himself and vowed to take the camera back to college. I tried to explain that it was too complicated for casual use, but he didn't think so. My dad agreed. That camera cost a fortune and had all the newest technological advancements. Obviously that was the one you wanted.

After all that, Russell took the camera upstairs and locked it in his desk and forgot about it.

As Christmas approached things got pretty hectic around the house. My father had his annual office party to organize. Plus his big case was still pending. He was up late almost every night, working in his office.

My mother had her own obligations. She did volunteer work at several places, including the middle school where Russell and I had gone. There was a big Christmas play and a bake sale, which she was in charge of.

Russell, who claimed he wanted to "do nothing but sleep and watch TV," was constantly meeting up with friends. He surprised everyone by going on several dates with a woman we'd never heard of, Carmen, who went to Dartmouth and was a friend of a friend.

We also had the Oswalds over for dinner. They were my parents' best friends. Henry Oswald was a lawyer too, like my dad. He and my dad were their usual self-important selves.

The fact that Russell had just completed his first semester at Cornell should have overshadowed any stories the Oswalds had about their own kids, but that didn't stop Henry Oswald from telling them anyway. Little Abby Oswald was taking special music classes because she had a previously undiscovered talent for the cello. We got to hear all about this. My father was visibly pained, but put up with it, just like Mr. Oswald had to put up with him when the conversation went back to Russell's unbelievable workload at Cornell.

Another night a different carload of Russell's high school buddies showed up at the house. These were the friends who had not gone to elite colleges but had stayed closer to home to attend Oregon, Oregon State, or worse. They had to be dealt with diplomatically. Russell pretended to sympathize with their difficult exams and nodded along with their stories about keg parties and fraternity pranks. But Russell didn't take these people seriously. My dad ordered only one pizza. And no beer.

In the midst of these holiday activities I got the urge to hang out with Antoinette. I'd barely seen her in recent weeks. But surrounded by the endless college talk, I felt a need to hear her snarky, sarcastic voice. What I really needed was to get out of that frickin' house. So I called Antoinette. I asked her if she would take me to Agenda, which had been festering in my mind as something I needed to see.

Antoinette picked me up in her mom's car, a silver Toyota Camry. I'd brought the Canon, which I'd stashed in my backpack.

"How was your Christmas?" I asked her.

"The usual."

"What's the usual?" I asked.

Antoinette sighed. "My mom trying to be cheerful. Then completely losing her shit. Then trying to be cheerful again. And then losing her shit."

"She's still thinking about your brother?"

"She's always thinking about my brother. She'll be thinking about my brother until the day she dies."

I nodded respectfully. "What about you?"

"What about me?"

"Is it always on your mind?"

"Sometimes it is," she said. She thought for a second. "And then I forget about it. And when I realize I forgot about it, I feel guilty."

I nodded. I watched the passing houses along the road. "What happened to him exactly?"

"He impacted a hard surface at a high rate of speed."

"You know what I mean."

She drove for a while, thinking about it. "I don't know what happened to him."

"What did the doctors think?"

"The doctors? There weren't any doctors."

"He didn't go to therapy or anything?"

She shook her head.

"What about the police?" I asked. "Or your family?"

"Nobody knew he was going to do that. I mean, we knew he was depressed. He was always depressed." She changed lanes, checking her rearview mirror. "I did learn one interesting thing though."

"What's that?"

"My dad tried to kill himself when he was nineteen."

"But he didn't succeed," I said.

"He didn't try as hard. He took pills. And then puked them back up."

"Well, that's good."

"I think my dad might be gay," said Antoinette. "That's the feeling I've got from my mom over the years."

"Yeah?"

"Marcus might have been too. But who knows. It's not like anyone's going to discuss it. Being a military family and all."

Agenda was right downtown. We parked across the street. I got out the Canon. Antoinette watched while I slung it around my neck.

"Actually," said Antoinette, "I don't think they allow cameras inside."

"It's small," I said. "They won't notice."

"I think they'll notice."

"No they won't," I said. I tucked the strap under my shirt and hid the camera beneath my coat. With my hands in my front pockets, you couldn't tell it was there.

"They're pretty strict," said Antoinette.

"They won't see it," I said. "I've been working with this pro photographer guy. We just did a gig in Seattle. He knows all the tricks."

"If you say so," said Antoinette.

The Agenda security guy found my camera. It took him about two seconds.

We went back to Antoinette's car.

"So who is this guy you work with?" asked Antoinette, while I untangled the Canon from around my neck.

"His name is Richie," I said. "He works at the Passport Photos place downtown."

"And you get paid?"

"He gets paid. And then he pays me."

"And you call it *a gig*?"

"That's what Richie calls it," I said, returning the camera to my backpack.

"I gotta say, Gavin, ex-boyfriend of idiot Grace Anderson, that's sorta cool."

We went back to Agenda. They let us in this time, after another thorough search.

I don't know what I was expecting of Agenda. I guess I thought it would be like a high school dance, awkward kids smiling bashfully at each other from across the room. It wasn't like that. People were dressed very cool, for starters. The guys looked intense. The girls looked like they'd snap your head off if you looked at them wrong. It wasn't what you'd call a welcoming vibe.

We sat on a bench along one wall. Eventually the music started. It was pretty hard-core electronic dance music, which I like. The beat was crisp and powerful through the large speakers. It sounded fantastic. As the music got going, people appeared from various nooks and crannies. The dance floor filled up. Then the lights went out and a ball started to turn above the dance floor. It sent laser lines, bending and twisting through the room. I turned to Antoinette to say something, but it was too loud. Instead, she grabbed my arm and pulled me onto the dance floor. And so we did that. Antoinette and I danced.

The dance floor got pretty wild. It was way cooler than any high school dance. Two girls appeared beside us who were dressed up like . . . I don't know what . . . sixties girls? They had thick fake eyelashes and short dresses and different-colored tights. And they were great dancers! Super casual and not moving too much, but totally sexy.

They never looked at anyone and kept the same unreadable half smiles on their faces. Then I looked over at Antoinette and realized she was like them, super chill and relaxed and moving just enough and in just the right way to be totally *hot*. Since when was Antoinette *sexy*? But she was. She totally was.

We danced for a long time. People would come and go off the dance floor. You'd get to know the different people by their look, their style, the way they moved. One girl bobbed her head from side to side. One guy in white jeans did slow-motion reptile moves, like a snake. And since we were all stuck inside—you couldn't leave Agenda once you came in—we settled in with each other.

After an hour, it got pretty hot and sweaty. We took a break and bought cans of Coke, which cost four dollars each and weren't even cold. More people came in. The night was just getting started, it seemed. And with everyone dressed to the teeth, with their own carefully honed styles, it was really a spectacle. I would have killed to have my camera.

We left around midnight. Outside, I couldn't quite believe what I had seen.

"So what do you think?" asked Antoinette.

"It was great," I had to admit. "I didn't know there were such places."

"Yes, dear Gavin. There are."

"I want to take pictures in there."

"Well, you can't."

"Maybe there's some way."

Antoinette dug a cigarette out of her bag. "Why do you always bring your camera when you do stuff with me?"

"Because there's interesting people."

"They're not *that* interesting."

"To me they are."

Antoinette leaned against her car and lit her cigarette. "Maybe instead of taking pictures of interesting people, you should try to be one."

"How would I do that?"

"Are you serious?"

"Yes."

"Well, you could start by going out with someone interesting for once."

"Like who?"

Antoinette smiled in a funny way. At first I didn't know what she was smiling about. But then I saw that she was looking past me, down the street.

"How about Britney Vaughn?" she said.

Britney Vaughn was coming up behind me, her and another girl. The two of them stopped a few feet away.

"Hello, Britney," said Antoinette.

"Hello, Antoinette," said Britney. But her attention soon shifted to me. She looked me up and down. "You're the guy who took my picture."

"I am," I said.

She was going to say something mean but then thought better of it. I knew why. It was because she had posted my picture of her on Facebook, the one where she was giving us the finger. It had 280 likes. It was so popular she was now using it as her profile picture.

"My name's Gavin," I said.

Britney didn't answer.

"You're welcome for the picture," I said. "People seem to like it."

"I'm going to delete you," said Britney. "Now that I see what you look like."

I didn't respond, but I understood what she meant. By Agenda standards, I looked like the most boring suburban prep imaginable.

"Everyone is still pissed at you," she said to Antoinette.

"What for?"

"Flirting with Ryan," said Britney.

"Kai flirted with Ryan. Not me."

"Bad things happen when you flirt with other people's boyfriends," threatened Britney.

"Oh yeah?" said Antoinette, taking a long, bored drag of her cigarette. "Like what?"

Britney Vaughn had to think about that for a while. Then, watching Antoinette, she said, "You got another cigarette?"

Without answering, Antoinette felt in her pocket. She found her cigarettes and threw the pack to Britney.

I watched all this. My camera was right behind me in the car, but I didn't dare reach for it. Britney, who had a plain, lumpy face, opened the pack. She flicked it a certain way and a couple of the cigarettes stuck out of it.

"Can I have two?" she asked Antoinette.

"No, Britney, you can have one."

Britney then gestured to her friend. "Can she have one?"

"Yes," said Antoinette, looking away. Britney handed the other girl a cigarette, then stuck the one she was holding behind her ear, then took a third cigarette out of the pack. She lit it. The other girl lit hers.

Antoinette said: "You guys do know that Ryan was hitting on every girl he saw that night, right?"

"He was drunk," said Britney.

"So whose fault is that?"

Britney didn't answer. She stared at Antoinette's car. "This your car?"

"Yes," said Antoinette.

"I always knew you were rich."

"I'm not rich, Britney. It's a Toyota."

Britney, with her lumpy face, took a while to digest this information. She did not give the impression of great intelligence. Then she stared at me again. "Why are you hanging out with this guy?" she asked Antoinette. "Is he your personal photographer?"

"He goes to my school," said Antoinette.

"Oh," said Britney, looking at me again.

"As a matter of fact," said Antoinette, "Gavin was just telling me he likes you. He wants to ask you out."

I turned and gave Antoinette a glare I didn't know I possessed.

"Him?" said Britney, looking me up and down. "But he's so white bread. He is sorta cute though. Hey, could you guys lend me twenty bucks?"

"No, we can't lend you twenty bucks," said Antoinette.

"Ten?"

"Britney, you came over here to threaten me. You were going to beat me up last week. You can't ask me for money."

Britney smoked her cigarette. Antoinette smoked hers. Britney became bored and turned to her friend. They made some sort of nonverbal decision.

"We have to go," Britney said to Antoinette.

"You sure you don't want to go out with Gavin here?" Antoinette said.

Britney turned and looked at me one last time. "No thanks," she said.

We left Agenda and drove around for a while. I got my Canon out. It felt good to hold it in my hands again. I tried to take a close-up picture of the dashboard in the dark car interior. Then I took some pictures of Antoinette while she drove. She didn't do the usual things people do, like act shy or put up her hand. She just drove. After a while I started pointing the camera at things outside: signs, buildings, people walking on the sidewalk.

When she dropped me back at my parents', I wanted to say something, thank her for taking me around. But I thought that might sound stupid. Better to say nothing.

Upstairs, in my room, I downloaded my pictures onto my big computer. I knew they were going to be too dark and they were. Still, the ones of Antoinette driving her car were interesting. I'd caught something, some hidden part of her. It was there in the murky image. I could feel it, even if I couldn't actually make it out.

Unfortunately, in photography, if you can't see it, you failed. *Seeing it* is kind of the whole point.

JUNIOR YEAR
(PART TWO)

A thing you see in my pictures is that I was not afraid
to fall in love with these people.
—*Annie Leibovitz*

The best fashion show is definitely on the street.
Always has been, and always will be.
—*Bill Cunningham*

At Evergreen everyone was in a good mood after the holidays. People had gotten phones, cars, video games for Christmas; they'd gone on vacation. Some people had suntans, most noticeably Claude and Hanna, who had gone to Hawaii together with Claude's parents. Going on vacation as a couple was an impressive step in a high school relationship. No other couple had done that, not that I had heard of. But I guess Claude and Hanna were so beautiful and mature and perfectly matched that nobody minded that they slept together, not even their parents.

Something was off between Claude and Hanna though. I sensed it immediately when they got back. Hanna, instead of luxuriating in the attention she would inevitably receive, being tanned and even more gorgeous than usual, was suddenly uninterested in it. She seemed bored with people and annoyed with school life in general. She didn't tell funny stories about Hawaii at lunch, like she normally would have. Nor did she make fun of Claude in some sexual way, which she loved to do: how he fell off the bed during sex, or had a condom stuck to his jeans during dinner. And then a week later she and Claude had an actual fight in the cafeteria, right in front of everyone. I couldn't tell what it was about, but Hanna became so angry, I thought she might throw something. And this wasn't Hanna's usual dramatic play acting. This was actual anger. I'd never seen her like that. I'd never seen either of them like that.

That moment was also significant because Krista Hoffman was sitting next to me at the time. As the group of us sat there, stunned and embarrassed, it was she and I who exchanged looks of *did that just happen?* It was also at that moment that I realized that whenever Krista sat with us, she always took that same spot at the table, right next to me.

Krista had also returned from winter vacation with a tan. It looked especially good on her, with her freckles and her bouncy blond hair. She was having a great year. She always looked fantastic and she seemed to be everywhere, at all the parties, always with the cutest sophomore girls or the best-looking guys. She had begun to hang around us, too, sitting with us at lunch sometimes, saying hi at parties. Not that she talked much. She tended to shut up when Hanna or Petra were around. She understood they were her social superiors. But she still liked to be around them. And apparently she liked to be around me, too.

I realized this one day when I came back to my locker and Krista was hovering a few feet away. She didn't see me at first. I came up behind her and surprised her and she immediately turned red and started waving air at herself. I made a dumb joke about sophomores not being allowed in the junior/senior wing. She blushed, which was extremely cute.

Nothing happened that day at my locker, but within a week, Logan, Olivia, and I ended up at Krista's McMansion. It wasn't a party; it was more just Krista and some of her friends hanging out.

People were mostly downstairs or outside in the hot tub, which was extra steamy on a cold night in January. At one point Krista and I were in the hot tub with some other people. Krista kept smiling at me like she does. Eventually, some of the other people left the tub and went inside. Krista stayed. I did too. It seemed like something was going to happen, but I wasn't sure what. More people left. And then the last person left. And then it was just us, alone in the green glowing water.

"Kind of a quiet night," I said to her.

"Yeah," she said. "People always want me to have big parties. But sometimes I'd rather just have my friends."

"Less damage to the house," I said.

"It gives you a chance to talk to people."

"Yeah, that's nice."

Krista moved into the middle of the tub and hovered in the deeper water in front of me. She lowered her head into the water, until just her face was in the air. Then she popped back up and gave me her biggest, brightest, most scrunched-faced grin.

"You have the best smile," I said to her.

"Really? What does it look like?"

"Like pure happiness and fun."

"That's me," she said. "Pure happiness. And lots of fun."

"What do you think is the funnest thing to do?" I asked her.

She thought about it. "I like kissing," she said.

"Yeah, kissing's pretty good," I agreed.

"And other things."

"Yeah," I said. "Other things are good too."

We both went silent then. But it was a good silence. The best kind. The very best kind.

We ended up in her room. It was not like with Rachel Lehman, where it was all about a single kiss. With Krista—since we were in our bathing suits and practically naked already—it moved from kissing to "other things" pretty quickly. It was like both of us were waiting for the other to slow things down. But neither of us did.

Finally, sensing my hesitation, Krista pulled away. "Are we going too fast?" she said.

"No, no," I said. But we were. To me we were.

"I'm sorry," she said, wrapping a towel around herself. "I get carried away sometimes."

"No, no," I said. "It was me. It was my fault."

"I'm only a sophomore," she said.

"No. Really. It's okay."

"Is this too weird?" she said seriously. "Do you want to say this never happened?"

"What? No. Of course not. Do you?"

"No?" she said.

She still looked worried though. So I moved toward her. I put my arms around her. I hugged her and rocked her and kissed the top of her head.

Eventually she turned her face up and kissed me on the lips. And then it started all over again.

So then Krista and I were together. We were a couple. Maybe it was good that it happened so fast. I didn't have a chance to screw it up.

It was odd timing too, because two days later the news swept through school that Hanna and Claude had broken up. This was huge news. By this time, Hanna and Claude were the most respected, envied, and admired couple not just in our class, but in our whole school. And at other schools too.

Nobody knew what happened. I couldn't find Claude at lunch, and his car was gone from the parking lot after sixth period. Hanna supposedly ran out of her history class in tears. And then the next day neither of them came to school.

So then the rumors started, rumors about Claude and Petra. Claude had been seen walking with Petra. Petra and Claude were talking after school. Petra's car was parked at Claude's house. People speculated: Petra had never stopped loving Claude. She had been pining away for him since freshman year. Things had possibly happened, physical things, sexual things. And of course with Hanna and Claude having their mysterious problems, this was her chance. All this time she had been waiting and biding her time and now Petra had returned, to claim what was hers.

Meanwhile, I was with Krista Hoffman. I wasn't sure how exactly that was going to work. It wasn't like with Grace, where we could just follow our friends around and always be together. Most of Krista's high school life took place in the freshman/sophomore wing at school. It was possible to not see her at all during the day. And though she was accepted by the older kids, most of her close friends were in her own grade. Unlike Grace, she wasn't the kind of person who dropped her old friends because she got a new boy-friend. From our first couple conversations, I learned that Krista had pretty much *always* had a boyfriend. Needless to say, she wasn't a virgin.

On Saturday we played tennis. Krista knew I was a ten-nis player and she wanted to try out for the girls varsity that spring, so it made sense. She'd never played competitive tennis before, so when we met up at her parents' athletic club, I was surprised how good she was. She had a small, compact body and was fast on the court. She had a reputa-tion as this party girl, but she could clearly focus when she wanted to. She was competitive and a natural athlete.

It was a good first date, playing tennis. It gave me a

chance to be confident and good at something in front of her. It gave her a chance to run around and get out her aggressions. Also she was super hot in her tennis outfit. A lot of the guys at the club were totally watching her, I noticed.

After tennis I drove Krista home. She invited me in to take a hot tub, which would be good for our muscles, she said. Her mom seemed fine with this, so we went up to her room and changed into bathing suits, during which Krista seemed even more gushy and smiley than usual.

I followed her out to the hot tub with my towel. She got in first, and I followed. The green foam and bubbles gurgled around us. Krista did her thing where she went in the middle, into the deepest part, and lowered her head all the way down into the water until only her face was still in the air.

"Remember the other night when we were in the hot tub together?" she said.

I nodded that I did.

"You said I was super fun," said Krista, grinning.

"And you are," I said, grinning myself. *We are totally going to have sex*, I suddenly realized. *Like soon. Like when we get back up to her room.*

"I like it when you say nice things to me," said Krista.

"You're an easy person to say nice things to."

She lay back again. I moved into the center too and put my head back and looked up. There was a light drizzle falling. The light of the hot tub illuminated the tiny drops of moisture as they fell, so they looked like a million tiny beings flying down at you, attacking you, but then swerving away, just at the last minute.

Upstairs, I could see that Krista had things planned out a certain way. First, she wanted to take a shower. Together.

I hesitated for a moment. "But what about your mom?" I said.

"She won't know."

So we did that, taking off our wet bathing suits and sneaking down the hall, holding our towels around ourselves. The McMansion bathroom was quite luxurious, with lots of white tile and silver faucets and everything super shiny and new.

She turned on the shower and held her hand under the water until it got hot. I stood waiting, holding my towel around my waist. I had never gotten totally naked with a girl before. Not with all the lights on. There were a lot of lights in that bathroom.

"Do you want me to go in first?" she asked.

I nodded.

She grinned at me. "You're shy, aren't you?"

"I guess so," I said, laughing a little.

She dropped her towel and went in the shower. She sort of hopped around a little, while she adjusted the water temperature.

"Okay," she said. "It's warm now. You can come in!"

I dropped my own towel and got in with her. It was

a little weird to be two people in one shower. It was also very weird to be naked with a girl like that. I mean, I knew people took showers together. Hanna and Claude did it. But it seemed strange to me. I felt very exposed.

"Oh my God," she said. "You're trembling!"

"Just a little," I said.

"Here, get under the hot water."

She switched positions, so I was in the water stream.

"Let me wash your back," said Krista. "Turn around."

So we did that. She had a fancy sea sponge, which she moved up and down my back. It did make me feel better. Then she soaped me up with some organic lavender soap from England, which she claimed had special calming qualities.

"Now you wash me," she said, smiling up at me like she did. It was weird to wash a person. But I did it. And then I liked it. And then we kissed a little and then a little more. And then it was time to get out of the shower.

We got in her bed. She had condoms in a little drawer right beside her bed, which seemed odd to me, since wouldn't her mother see them? But I didn't stop to think about it.

It was very easy, very comfortable, the actual doing it part. I guess I was relieved to not be standing in that shower. Krista didn't hesitate to guide me and move me around. She was very sweet about it, which seemed like a good sign. And also that was just her personality: taking charge, teaching you, helping you do things a little out of your comfort zone. I could tell I was going to learn a lot from Krista Hoffman.

It was almost midnight when she let me out her front door. She was wearing a bathrobe then, her hair all over the place, since she'd never dried it properly. Her mother was gone to some other wing of the McMansion. We had never even seen her dad.

"Thanks for the tennis game," she said, giving me a last squeeze.

I had totally forgotten that we'd played tennis.

I gave her a last kiss and began the walk down her driveway to my car. I was a little shaky on my legs. And then, in my car, I had to sit for a minute and gather my thoughts. My brain was as messed up as my legs. The only clear sentence that came into my head was: *Well, that was fun*.

Then I started the car and drove away.

So then I was super into Krista. It was an odd relationship though. We fooled around so much. Sometimes that was the only thing we did. We'd make a plan to go somewhere and I'd drive to her house to pick her up and we'd never leave her bedroom. Her mother didn't seem to have any problem with this. We were free to hang out, take showers, take hot tubs, whatever we wanted.

Eventually—while we were lying in her bed—I asked Krista: "So your mom's cool with us hanging out all the time?"

Krista nodded that she was. "We discussed it."

"What did she say?"

"We both agreed that it was better if I was home and not in the back of some car somewhere. . . ."

"What about your dad?"

"He knows to mind his own business."

So that was that. It still seemed odd to me though. I was used to the idea that you had to earn certain things from your girlfriend. You'd take her places and do stuff and have long conversations *and then* you'd do the other stuff. But Krista wasn't like that. She was into physical things. She

loved sports. She loved riding her bike fast. She loved anything that felt good to her body. "If I like someone, I want to
feel them," she told me. "What am I supposed to do, pretend
that I don't?"

During this same time, Antoinette and Kai were having
adventures of their own.

In February, Kai got caught smoking pot in the parking
lot with some senior boys. One of them had already been
accepted to a prestigious college so there was a big contro-
versy about whether our principal should tell the college or
not. The senior and another boy blamed it on Kai, saying
it was her idea, and her pot, and that they didn't actually
smoke any. I guess Kai went along with this. I didn't know
the details. It was quickly hushed up.

Not long after that, Antoinette was at a party where a
Hillsdale drug dealer accidentally shot himself in the foot.
This guy was Hillsdale's version of Bennett. He was showing off and waving a pistol around and it went off. The
police came and an ambulance. And then the police wanted
to search everyone at the party. Antoinette refused to be
searched. So they arrested her and took her to the police
station and called her mother.

The thing about that was: Nothing happened to her.
Antoinette didn't get in trouble or suspended because it
was off school grounds on a weekend. And anyway, people
were used to Antoinette by now, so it wasn't a big deal. Of

much more interest to our students was that this Hillsdale guy was stupid enough to shoot himself in the foot. This became a running joke. When we played Hillsdale in basketball, the Evergreen students chanted: "Shoot! Shoot! Shoot your foot!" which was considered very funny and a major burn on Hillsdale.

Naturally, I avoided telling Kai and Antoinette about Krista for as long as I could. I knew what they were going to say, and as soon as they heard, they said it.

"Krista?" said Antoinette. "Krista Hoffman? *She's* your new girlfriend? You go from Grace Anderson to Krista Hoffman? What are you, in the Dumb Girl Olympics?"

That got Kai going too. They hit me with the McMansion jokes. And the blond jokes. And then even worse, the sex jokes. I would eventually get these from everybody. The sex jokes started because I stupidly asked Logan if it was bad in some way to have too much sex. I thought this was just between us, but since we were kinda drunk at the time, apparently not. So then I got a lot of "Poor Gavin's little Gavin" comments. Krista probably wasn't thrilled about that, but she didn't care. She was like Antoinette in that way. She didn't care what people thought. And anyway, we were going out. We were a couple. You couldn't criticize us for doing what couples were supposed to do. Though you could definitely make fun of me for worrying about it.

• • •

I was still in touch with Richie from Passport Photos that winter. Richie was getting fairly regular assignments from *Portland Weekly* to take pictures of new restaurants or bands or local events. Richie would ask me to come along. Sometimes he would pay me; most times he wouldn't. The main thing was, he wanted people to see that he had an assistant. "It makes me look pro," he said. "And it's good experience for you."

Then Richie got another overnight gig. This was in Vancouver, BC, for the same magazine, *Travel and Leisure*. We drove up in the RAV4, through Seattle and then into Canada. The border guards made us open up our equipment cases, and Richie had to show them the e-mails from his photo editor in New York to prove we had a real job, though we obviously did. Richie had gotten better in that way. He was more confident, more pro. He was still his funny, fast-talking self, but now when he told people he was a photographer, they believed him. I felt like that too, as an assistant.

The gig in Vancouver was to cover a big international art show. Most of the stuff on the SHIT WE HAVE TO HAVE list involved the art museum downtown. The first morning, we took shots outside, of a big sculpture and of some of the foreign tourists in their weird eyeglasses and pointy shoes.

The rest of the day we were inside, shooting the artwork. My favorite was this one room that had three huge car wash cylinders, standing in a row, the ones that spin and have the cloth strips that wipe down your car. Not moving, they looked like three enormous Christmas trees. But then, while you were standing there, one of them would start spinning, going faster and faster, so that the cloth strips would stretch out from the centrifugal force. Then it would slow down and a different one would start to spin. Then another. Then they'd all spin at the same time. I know it sounds sort of pointless, but when you were watching it, and hearing it, and feeling the vibrations in the floor . . . well . . . it was pretty mesmerizing.

Lots of the art pieces were like that. You'd stand there and try to figure out what the point of it was, or if there even was a point. And then you'd be like, *Who could have thought of that?* And all you could think was: a very strange person.

Richie wasn't into the art. He thought most of it was bullshit. He liked the people more. He was always taking pictures of the best-looking women and then trying to chat them up. I kept telling him about the car wash cylinders, but they were in a special room, in the basement, and he couldn't be bothered to go down there. Finally he checked it out, and then he liked it. He took a bunch of pictures of it. He said, "I should have brought my car."

That night, Richie went out for drinks with some of the
people from the museum. I stayed in our hotel room and
watched Canadian TV. There was a McDonald's a couple
blocks away, and I thought about walking down there later
for some food. But then I thought, what am I doing? I'm in
Vancouver, BC, on a Saturday night with a bunch of great
cameras sitting all around me!

So I got off the bed and dug out this old Nikon that
Richie always brought but we never used. It shot actual
film, which we had a couple rolls of, buried in the bags.
Film was kind of the ultimate test of a photographer, Richie
always said. You had limited shots and you had to figure
out the light and focus yourself. And you couldn't see it
immediately. You had to trust yourself, and hope you got
something, without knowing if you actually did.

Richie had shown me how to load the Nikon. You pulled
out one end of the film coil and ran it through the spools
and then attached it on the other side. When it was ready to
go, I put it around my neck. It felt clunky, having no battery
and no electronic parts of any kind. It was like a spear or an
ax, a primitive tool from prehistoric days.

I rode the elevator down to the lobby. From there I went out into the street, into the darkness of Vancouver, the first foreign city I had ever been to.

I had thirty-six shots in the Nikon. That made things interesting. You couldn't just blast away at something randomly like you do with modern cameras.

Outside, it was cold and there was a slightly salty ocean smell in the air. I pulled my collar up around my neck. I walked down the street and then turned down an alley. They had great alleys in Vancouver, full of junk and Dumpsters and metal doorways. Electric wires ran along the top of them. I walked the length of this one, taking a few pictures when there was enough light.

Back on a major street, I got a couple shots of a streetcar, which was brightly lit inside and full of dressed-up people. They were holding on to the poles above their heads and talking excitedly to each other, since it was Saturday night. I walked along the streetcar route and eventually found a kind of square, where the car traffic was blocked off and there were several cafés packed together. This was the hangout spot, it appeared. There were lots of young people: inside the cafés and outside, on the street, and around a couple food trucks. These were the most stylish people I'd seen, so I began to walk around, taking a shot here, a shot there, checking out people's clothes and the general vibe of the place. And that's when I met the two art-school girls.

I'd noticed them when I'd first started walking around. In that entire square of cool people, they were the coolest of all. And when they saw me taking pictures, they came right up to me and started asking me questions. I told them about Richie and our gig at the art museum. They told me they studied at the art college there in Vancouver. They were originally from smaller towns in central Canada, but where they came from, if you were interested in anything artistic, you had to move to Vancouver. They told me about their classes. Art history and design and one called Concepts of Visual Fluency. They both had cool raincoats and eye makeup that went out to the side. They liked my old camera and that I was shooting real film. That was big with the students at their school. Film cameras and vinyl records.

I told them I wanted to go to art school but I didn't know anything about art. They said, "You know enough." They said I should definitely go, that I would love it, that I would regret it forever if I didn't. They gave me their phone numbers in case I wanted to ask them questions, or if I was ever back in Vancouver and wanted to hang out. When they left they gave me European kisses, one on each side of my face. It felt so strange and warm, feeling a person's cheek touching your cheek.

After that I felt energized. I hadn't caught a streetcar before because I didn't know how to pay. But now I jumped on the first one I saw. And then at the next stop a big gang of drunk college students got on. I snuck up behind some of them and took close-up shots of their faces. I think they noticed but they didn't seem to care. Since I was shooting film, I'd have to stop and wind the camera by hand after each shot. It helped create a rhythm. Aim, shoot, wind. Aim, shoot, wind. At one point I got a great shot of these four guys crammed together in the back of the streetcar, laughing and arguing and shouting over each other. You could feel the energy of Saturday night coming off them. I thought, I should do a series of different social groups out partying and call it "Saturday Night." Of course, the photographs would need to be good, and in focus, which I wasn't sure these would be.

I jumped off the streetcar downtown and walked around the big hotels. There were a lot of people there, too, but these were more tourist types and older people in nice clothes who'd been to the symphony or opera or whatever. I got pretty bold and went right in on people. I shot this rich lady in a fur coat. Another woman said, "That's awfully rude!" when I stepped in front of her and got a close-up of her face. But I turned and walked away and nothing happened.

In the end, none of these pictures came out very well. The light was bad; the focus was off. But there was a definite *excitement* in all of them. It was like whatever energy I felt when I took a picture, that same energy would be there in the final image. Like a swooping shot felt like it was swooping and a brash, in-your-face shot had a reckless, stealing-something quality.

• • •

We drove back the next day. I dropped Richie off, and when I pulled the RAV4 into my own driveway, it was one thirty in the morning.

I had school the next day, so I grabbed my bags and hurried inside. I was surprised to find the lights on in the kitchen. That was odd. And the coffeepot was on. I turned it off. I couldn't imagine who would be awake. My dad wouldn't be drinking coffee, not at this hour. And my mom was usually the first to bed in our house, since she got up the earliest.

No, something was up. I found myself creeping forward, through the kitchen. Several of the cabinets were open. There were random things on the counter. A pair of my dad's shoes. A tube of toothpaste.

I continued farther into the house. There was stuff in the hall. One of my dad's suits, still in its dry-cleaning bag, was lying on the floor of the entryway. I looked in the closet. It was usually packed with coats and parkas; now there were gaps and spaces.

I heard a noise upstairs. Then footsteps. "Gavin, is that you?" said the voice of my mother.

She appeared at the top of the stairs. She was wearing a bathrobe. Her face was red and blotchy and she was holding a ratty Kleenex in her hand.

She came partway down the stairs and stopped and sat.

"Something's happened," she said.

"What?" I said.

She unrolled the thick knot of Kleenex in her hand. "It's about your father," she said. She touched the Kleenex to her nose.

"What about him?"

"He left."

"Where did he go?"

She opened her mouth. She couldn't speak.

I stood there, holding my bag, watching her.

"Where did he go?" I said again.

"He has a girlfriend now," she said. "He's staying with her."

I barely slept that night. It was a new feeling to have Mom and me be the only people home. That house just got bigger and bigger.

I drove to school the next day. Nobody knew about my father yet, and I kept it that way. I tried to imagine what kind of person would fall in love with my dad. My mother had said she worked at his office, as if that explained it. And now he was living with her somewhere? Where? In a house? In a hotel? It was mind-boggling. The whole thing seemed utterly impossible.

I got through first and second periods. During third period I went to the restroom and sat in one of the stalls. A text had already come from my father. I deleted it unread. I took several deep breaths. I tried to steady myself.

Logan came by my locker after fourth period and we walked to lunch. Claude sat with us. Petra was there too. Krista was not there, which was good. I would have to tell her what had happened. As my girlfriend, she would be the person who would help me through this. But I wasn't sure how that would work. She was younger than me, and she wasn't a very emotional person.

Most of the lunch conversation that day was about Mr. Knutson, the gym teacher. Claude and Petra were making fun of him. They told the old story about how he appeared to have a gym sock stuffed in the front of his sweatpants freshman year. Hanna, who wasn't at the table, had loved to make fun of Mr. Knutson. She could talk like him and imitate his gestures. Anyway, it felt good to laugh and not think about my father for a few minutes.

When last period was over, I hurried out to the parking lot. I had this idea that I needed to be home for Mom. I'm not sure why I thought that. As I was walking to my car, I saw Krista talking to some of her friends. I went over to her.

"Hey," I said.

Krista reached out and grabbed me by the arm and pulled me close to her. Her friend Sophie was telling a story about a drunk guy at a party.

"Actually," I whispered to Krista, "I have to go."

"What's up?" she said, looking up into my face.

I turned her around and walked her away from the others. "It's my dad."

"What? Did he die?"

"No, he didn't die. . . . He just . . . He moved out."

"Oh."

"I should probably go home."

"Where did he move to?"

"I'm not sure."

"Okay," she said. "Well, I have to go listen to Sophie. We're going shopping. She has to be home by six."

"Okay."

"Will you text me later?"

"Yeah, sure."

She squeezed my arm. "Maybe you can come over," she purred.

"Yeah, maybe," I said.

When I got home, my mom was upstairs. I could hear her talking on the phone. I wasn't sure what to do, so I made myself some cereal and ate it. Then I sat there, waiting for my mom to come down, or for something to happen. But nothing did. I texted Krista that I probably couldn't come over. She was a little annoyed, it sounded like.

So then I went to my own room and lay on my bed. Coming home probably wasn't the best idea. I went to my mom's room and asked her if I should make some dinner, but she said no, she wasn't hungry.

So then I texted Kai. She and Antoinette were watching a movie at Kai's house. I told them I was stuck at home, with my mom, and that something was going on with my parents, they were splitting up, it looked like. Kai texted back: *?????!!!!!*. She and Antoinette immediately offered to come pick me up. I wasn't sure I wanted to be around them in the state I was in. I didn't want to start crying or do something embarrassing. But the minute I hesitated, Kai texted: *We're coming over.*

So they picked me up. The second I got in the back of Kai's Subaru, I felt a huge weight go off me.

At first they didn't say anything. We just drove. Antoinette gave me some gum. I chewed it and looked out the window. Finally Kai looked at me in the rearview mirror. "So when did this thing with your dad happen?"

"Last night," I said.

"He just left?" asked Kai.

"I guess so. My mom said he has a new girlfriend."

"Uh-oh," said Antoinette. It was the first time she spoke.

"That sucks," said Kai.

"I'm just like . . . I don't know what to do," I said.

"There's nothing you can do," said Antoinette, quietly chewing her gum.

I chewed my own gum. I could feel tears coming. I didn't know why I was so sad. Who was I sad for?

Kai drove. Nobody really talked. Eventually Kai asked Antoinette where we should go. Antoinette suggested McDonald's since they had McRibs, which they only had a couple times of year. So we went there.

At first we were going to do drive-through, but then we went inside. I started to feel better once we were standing in line in the bright and colorful McDonald's. I thought, *Thank God they came and got me.*

• • •

A week later, Krista called.

"Hey, Gavin," she said.

"Hey," I said. I was at the supermarket, buying cat food and paper towels and some other stuff my mother had forgotten when she went shopping.

"What's up?" she said cheerily. I could imagine her face scrunching up like it did.

"Not much," I said. "I'm at the supermarket."

"Do you have to do the shopping now, because of your dad?"

"I hope not. But yeah. For the moment."

"I'm so sorry that happened."

"Thanks," I said.

"And I hope your mom's okay and you're okay."

"Thanks," I said again.

"The thing is, I sort of need to talk to you about something. . . ."

That didn't sound good. Not that I was surprised. I had told Krista more of the details about my dad leaving. She had not responded well. She seemed to think she would be expected to act morose and gloomy all the time. And to stop having fun.

"What do you need to talk to me about?" I said.

"See. The thing is, Tyler Young really likes me."

"Tyler Young?"

"He said he's been waiting for me to be single for so

long. He's been watching me. Since the beginning of freshman year."

I realized then who Tyler Young was. He was this dumb senior who did a lot of coke and had parties on his parents' boat. He was—I realized in that instant—the perfect guy for Krista.

"And the thing is," she said, "since you're kind of . . . well . . . you have a lot going on right now and I want to help you and be a good girlfriend and all that, but I'm not that good at things like parents breaking up. My parents are still together and I can't imagine . . . I mean . . . well . . . it doesn't seem like you even want me around, the way you're acting all depressed and everything. I mean, I still like you. And you're super nice. But Tyler. He *adores* me. You should hear what he says about me. And he's a senior, so he won't be here that much longer. So I feel like he's the one I should be with right now. So I'm sorry. But I think it's for the best. Don't you?"

"No," I said.

"Well, I'm sorry," she said. "And I hope you're okay. I can't talk any more because Tyler is coming over. And the other thing is, Tyler said he always thought you were a really cool guy. He wanted me to tell you that."

"Thanks," I said, standing in the frozen-pizza aisle of the grocery store. I stared into the frosty glass.

"You guys are going to have sex, aren't you?" I said. "Like right now, when he gets there."

"I don't . . ."

"You've probably already had sex."

"Since Tyler's my boyfriend now and you're not, I don't think I should answer that. Good-bye."

She hung up the phone.

32

I avoided my dad completely during this time. He called, texted, sent e-mails. I ignored or deleted everything. My mom thought this was a bad idea and told me I needed to talk to him. So then I texted him back. He suggested we meet and have dinner at one of his favorite restaurants.

I drove downtown and parked. By then I hadn't seen him in two weeks. Despite his questionable parenting style, my father had always been physically present in my life. To not see him for that long had been a shock.

Entering the restaurant, I saw I was early. The beautiful hostess offered to seat me, but I ignored her. I sat by myself on the little couch in front. I looked at my phone and chewed on a toothpick.

My dad finally arrived. He was coming directly from work. He had his navy blue suit on. His hair was freshly cut and his face had more color in it than usual. Possibly he'd been to a tanning salon.

I found it easy to be in his presence again. I greeted him and then didn't say anything. I did what I always did: I let him take control.

He was a regular at that restaurant. The beautiful

hostess greeted him, "Good evening, Mr. Meeks." She smiled at us both. We were led to a large booth in the back of the room.

"How's your mother?" was the first thing he said. He took a sip of his Scotch, which had arrived within seconds of us sitting down.

I shrugged, nodded, did my usual noncommunicative-teenager act.

My father frowned. He seemed to consider his options on how best to deal with me. At that moment I was reminded of how smart he was. He was so good at getting what he wanted. Me and my mom, we had no chance against him. Whatever he wanted to happen, that was what would happen.

We ordered, and when the food came we ate. He started to talk: "The key, for now, is to minimize the disruption of your mother's life. And of yours. The two of you will stay in the house. You will continue to be provided for. You and I will see each other on a regular basis. I will of course be having discussions with your mother about the details of our separation."

I said nothing.

"I've talked to Russell. He's very concerned, of course, but his life shouldn't be affected. I want him to remain focused on his studies."

I pushed my food around with my fork.

"How are you feeling about everything?" said my father.

I shrugged.

"I'm very sorry this happened. I'm sorry for you and your mother. Despite what you might think, I do get great satisfaction out of being part of this family, of providing for you and making you and your brother and your mother as happy as I can. That will not change, though of course the details of our lives will be altered somewhat."

"Somewhat," I repeated, a tiny zing of anger flashing in my chest.

"Like I said, I will do my best to maintain things as they are."

I slipped into silence again. I had questions. I had things I wanted to say. But I had reached my limit of new information about the breakup of my family.

"If you're wondering what happened on my end . . . ," my father said, clearing his throat. "I met someone. A coworker. I tried to be careful. I tried to not let it develop into something that would affect my family. But sometimes these things are beyond our control. Sometimes we can't choose who we love and who we need to be with. At a certain point it becomes counterproductive to live a lie, or to pretend you feel one way when you actually feel another."

I nodded along with this. Not that I agreed. I just didn't want to hear any more. I didn't want to know my father's opinions on love or *being with someone* or whatever the hell he was talking about.

He talked more. It got pretty bad. I wanted to put my hands over my ears and start humming, but I couldn't do that in the fancy restaurant. So I tried to think of other things. School. Photography. Anything. Then I found that if I focused on one spot on my plate, I could sort of disconnect in a way. I could put myself in a trance for a few seconds.

". . . I've contacted Clark Jennings," my father was saying when I came back. "He's an excellent divorce attorney. He's an old friend. Your mother knows him. I know him. That's another area where I hope we can reach a quick and mutually satisfactory . . ."

I focused on a pea in my pasta and again tuned him out. It wasn't that hard. It was like going dancing that night at Agenda. Turn your brain off and let the music take over. Become one with the parts of your environment that weren't trying to destroy you.

I didn't want dessert. My father signed the check. Walking out, he stopped to chat with the beautiful hostess. I didn't stop. I just kept walking, no good-bye, no hug. I could not stand to be inside that place one more second.

Outside it was dark, but it was downtown, so there were lights and people and cars on the street. I felt like I'd been holding my breath and now I could breathe. My father was still inside, and I started walking faster. Then I started running. I turned around the first corner I came to, so he wouldn't see where I went.

After another week of this, my mom went to visit her sister in San Francisco for a couple days. "A vacation from my nervous breakdown," she said as I drove her to the airport.

When I got home, it was just me in that big house. I went inside, into the kitchen, and made myself a sandwich.

I wasn't used to being home alone. It was late, and there seemed to be a lot of spooky noises from whatever part of the house I was not in. So I locked all the doors and turned on the TV and left ESPN on, really loud, most of the night.

The next night I felt more comfortable. I turned off the TV and put on music and turned it up loud so I could hear it throughout the house. I did a little homework upstairs and then got out the Canon and took some still shots in the kitchen, stuff that hadn't moved since my dad left: an apple, a bottle of wine, my dad's shoes, still sitting on the counter. I got pretty involved in this, and when I looked up it was two in the morning.

On the third night of being home alone I called Antoinette. I'd been updating her every couple days. She was a good person to talk to. Her parents had split up when she was eight. She'd had a stepdad for the last four years, who she referred to as "Bald Mike."

I invited her and Kai over. They came in Kai's Subaru. Kai said, "Look at you and your fancy house!" as she walked in the door. That made me a little nervous. I wondered if she might steal something.

Antoinette was more casual. She made herself at home. In the kitchen, she opened a bottle of wine, one of the nice bottles from the special rack of my dad's. I hesitated when she first pulled it out, but when I told her it was probably very expensive, she was like, "You don't understand, Gavin. You're in payback territory now. If this is your dad's most expensive bottle, then this is the one we're drinking."

So we drank it. And then lay around in the living room and listened to music. I even let them smoke cigarettes in the house.

"So Krista broke up with you?" Kai said to me. She was lying on the couch, her head on a pillow, blowing smoke toward the ceiling.

"Yeah," I said. "She dumped me for Tyler Young."

"And because your dad left," said Antoinette. "Which was cramping her style."

"Really?" said Kai. "She broke up with you because your dad left?"

"Krista doesn't *do* family problems," said Antoinette.

"Oh my God," said Kai. "Poor Gavin. And now she's

with Tyler Young? You know about him, don't you? He's seriously one of the dumbest people at our school."

"So I've heard," I said.

Kai smoked. She stared up at the ceiling. "I did shots with Tyler Young once. I literally thought he was pretending to be stupid. Like he was practicing for a play or something . . ."

"Why were you doing shots with him?" asked Antoinette.

"I don't know," said Kai, putting out her cigarette. She looked at me. "So what girl are you going to like now?"

I shrugged.

"Gavin doesn't decide who he goes out with," said Antoinette. "He lets other people pick his girlfriends."

"Really?" Kai said to me. "You let other people pick your girlfriends?"

"*No*," I said.

"*Yes*," said Antoinette.

"Maybe with Krista," I said. "She did make the first move."

"And Grace," said Antoinette. "You didn't pick Grace, and don't pretend like you did!"

"Who picked Grace?" asked Kai.

"Hanna did," said Antoinette. "And Claude. And the rest of them."

"The *beautiful people*," said Kai, sighing.

"Every school has them," said Antoinette.

"But you're one of them," Kai said to me. "So can't you have any girl you want?"

"I don't think that's how it works," I said.

"How does it work, then?" said Kai.

"The problem with Gavin is," said Antoinette. "He knows better."

"What do you know?" Kai asked me.

"He knows how dumb those people are," said Antoinette.

"They're not dumb," I said firmly. "Trust me. Claude is not dumb. Hanna is not dumb."

"No," said Antoinette. "But the ones who aren't dumb are mean. And cruel."

"That might be true," I said.

"So that's Gavin's dilemma," Antoinette said to Kai. "He knows the truth about his popular friends. But he's afraid to give them up. Because he doesn't know what lies beyond."

"What does lie beyond?" Kai asked.

"Weird people," said Antoinette. "People like us."

We drank more wine and they smoked more cigarettes. Eventually they had to go. I walked them outside. It was raining, so we ducked our heads as we walked out to Kai's car.

"Thanks for having us over to your palatial mansion," said Kai.

"Thanks for your dad's best bottle of wine," said Antoinette.

Kai gave me a hug, which I wasn't expecting. I immediately wondered if I might get a hug from Antoinette, too, but she turned away and headed around the car to the passenger side.

This left Kai and me standing together in the rain while Kai dug in her backpack for her keys. She couldn't find them.

"Kai?" said Antoinette, standing in the rain. "Can you hurry up please?"

"Just a second!" said Kai. She finally found her keys and pushed the unlock button on her key chain. Antoinette got in on the passenger side.

Kai looked back at me. In a low voice she said: "I know one girl you could like."

"Who?" I said.

"Antoinette," she whispered, watching my face.

"No," I said. "That would never work."

"Why wouldn't it work?"

"Antoinette and I are like matter and antimatter," I said quietly. "If we got together the universe would implode."

"And that would be a bad thing?"

"The universe imploding? Yes, that would be a bad thing."

"Are you sure?"

I looked at Kai. I had never really spoken to her in confidence like this. "I'm pretty sure."

"Good," she said. "So there's some wiggle room."

Antoinette, still sitting inside the rain-blurred car, yelled at the two of us. "Kai! Can we go please! It's cold!"

Kai got in the car, started it up, and drove backward down the driveway, nearly hitting our mailbox. Finally, the car disappeared into the rainy night.

I went back into my palatial mansion.

The next day I drove to the airport and picked up my mom.
She was quiet on the ride home. I helped her carry her bags
in and went up to my room.

A moment later she yelled up the stairs, "Gavin! Can
you come back down here please!"

I came back down the stairs.

"What is this?" she said. She was standing in the middle
of the living room with her arms crossed.

"What is what?"

"*This*," she said, waving one hand in the air. "It reeks
like cigarette smoke in here," she said.

"Oh . . ."

She beckoned me further into the room and pointed out
a tiny Mexican salsa bowl that had been pushed under the
sofa. It had several of Kai's cigarette butts in it.

"Oh, sorry about that," I said.

"I can't have you smoking, Gavin," my mother said,
suddenly on the verge of tears. "Do you understand that?
Not now. Not with everything else that is happening."

"I don't smoke, Mom. Some friends came over. Kai and
Antoinette."

She shook her head. I couldn't tell if she believed me or not. It didn't seem to matter. She snatched up the salsa dish, marched into the kitchen, and threw it into the garbage.

I went back upstairs.

My mother worked for a small advertising agency before she met my dad. This was in San Francisco, during her first years out of college. One of our photo albums was dedicated to this period, my mother's life in the early nineties. As a little kid I loved these pictures. Mom sitting on the fire escape of her apartment. Mom in black dresses and Doc Martens. Mom on a scooter or drinking cocktails after work at the trendy offices of the Echo Advertising Agency.

At one time she was engaged to one of the founders of Echo, Peter Frohnmeyer. He was very good-looking and fashionable. Apparently he was from a wealthy San Francisco family. There were lots of pictures of the two of them: at the beach, at a big New Year's party, on a boat. It was quite a life, judging from the pictures. It always looked like my mother was having a great time.

But then my dad had appeared on the scene. My tough-guy, no-bullshit dad. I never learned the exact story of how he stole her away from Peter Frohnmeyer. The most Russell and I were ever told was what a great victory it was for our dad. One of his many successes.

In another photo album there were three or four pictures of my dad at around the same time. He had moved to

San Francisco too. He was supposedly very poor when he was in law school and yet a year later he was somehow driving a convertible. He looked pretty good in these pictures, with all his hair and less flab in his face. But it's obvious from the most casual photos that he was the more serious person. A certain grim determination was visible in his face, even in the old Kodak pictures. Whatever he did to get my mother away from Frohnmeyer, I'm sure that was part of it. Frohnmeyer looked like a pampered rich kid in his pictures. My dad looked like a bulldog.

So that's what happened. My mother married the poor lawyer, had two kids, and soon found herself in Oregon. Which makes you wonder what would have happened if she'd stayed with Frohnmeyer in San Francisco. She would have gone to a lot more cocktail parties, that's for sure. And probably had more fun. She would have had a totally different life.

Back at school, Krista remained with Tyler Young through the spring. Fortunately, she was in the freshman/sophomore wing, so I didn't see her very often. The couple times I did, she was bouncing around like she does. I heard she'd made the girls tennis team. So that was good for her.

Claude and Petra were together now too. The rumors had been true. How exactly it went down was still a mystery. Claude wouldn't say much, even to me.

"She just got more and more impossible," was all he

really said about Hanna. When asked about Petra, he would be vague. "We're hanging out," he would say. If people pressed him on it, he would admit that it was now more than friends. And then he'd shrug. And people would be satisfied. He was Claude, after all. People assumed he knew what he was doing.

There was still something he wasn't saying. That was my impression. Something else had happened. I was sure of it. But I had my own problems: getting dumped by Krista, my dad walking out, the weirdness of my new home life. Besides that, I had to figure out college or art school or whatever I was going to do after high school. And it wasn't like when Russell was in this position. There wasn't the four of us sitting around the kitchen table, thinking through all his options. It was just me sitting at the kitchen table now. I was an army of one.

Then one night I came home and there was a Mercedes in our driveway. It was the Coupe, like my dad's, but instead of navy blue it was dark red. I parked in the street so it could pull out. As I walked up the driveway, I stopped to look inside. It had leather seats, a wood dash, all the extras.

But whose was it? I went inside and found out. It was Henry Oswald's, my dad's best friend. He was sitting at our kitchen table drinking coffee. My mother sat diagonally across from him. She also held a coffee mug. She averted her eyes when I walked in.

"Hello, Gavin," said Henry Oswald. He stood up and shook my hand. It was the first time I'd seen him since my father left.

"Hello," I said back.

He pulled on the front of his pants and sat down again. "Thought I'd swing by and check on you two."

"Oh," I said. "Thanks."

"How's it going?" he asked.

"It's going okay," I said.

"How's school?"

I shrugged. "Okay."

Henry smiled. "You're a junior, right? Are you thinking about colleges yet?"

"Not that much."

My mother glared at me. "Gavin, can you at least make a *little* effort?"

"What?" I said. "It's the truth."

My mother went back to staring into her coffee cup.

"I'm thinking of going to art school," I told Mr. Oswald.

He gave me a quizzical look. My mother also looked up with surprise. "Art school?" he said.

"For photography."

Henry Oswald considered this and began to nod. "Okay," he said.

My mother said nothing.

"I haven't looked into it yet," I said.

"That's funny," said Henry. "My brother went to art school. My brother, William. He lives in Seattle." He turned to my mother. "He studied painting and graphic design. At Cal Arts."

My mother seemed encouraged by this news. I also perked up. "Did he like it?" I asked.

"Art school? Are you kidding?" Henry Oswald chuckled. "He loved it. What's not to love? You sit around talking about art. He said they used to run around naked in the desert. Some of his classmates became famous artists."

This was interesting news.

"How are your grades?" asked Henry Oswald.

"Not that great," I admitted.

"Well, it's art school," he said. "You don't have to be smart. You have to be . . . you know . . . *wacky*."

I nodded. My mother nodded.

"What sort of photography are you interested in?" asked Henry.

"All kinds. The classic stuff."

"Do you have anything you can show people?"

"Yeah," I said. "I have some stuff."

"Well, send me something. And I'll send it to my brother. We can see what he thinks."

"Okay," I said.

Later, when he was gone, my mother rinsed out the coffee mugs.

"Art school, Gavin?" she said to me over her shoulder. "When did you get this idea?"

"I've been thinking about it for a while."

She put the mugs in the dish rack to dry. "Why didn't you tell someone?"

"Who was I going to tell?"

The next day I drove downtown and took my laptop into Passport Photos. I told Richie what had happened.

"Cal Arts?" he said. "No shit. And this guy can help you?"

"His brother went there. But I gotta pick out my best stuff to send him."

I opened my laptop, and Richie went over my photos with me. Despite his dislike for art schools, he understood the difference between what a place like Cal Arts would want versus a professional portfolio like he had. We went through my best photos one by one. They were mostly imitations of Robert Frank and the other photographers of the past. But as Richie said, at least I was copying the right people.

When we'd picked out my best ten pictures, Richie said his usual piece about art school. "Listen. I got nothing against it. All I'm saying is, you don't *have* to do it. The great photographers, they saw life a certain way. And they knew how to capture that through the lens. You can't teach that."

"Still, though," I said. "Would you go to Cal Arts? If you could?"

"If I was you? In your situation?" He thought about it. "I might go. I'd go for the chicks, to be perfectly honest, and the parties and all that. I mean, I'm sure it's fun. But I've found my own way. That's what happens. Everyone finds their own way."

Later, after we'd closed the shop, I walked through the rain to my car. I was planning on driving home, but I felt inspired by all the photography talk. So I got out the Canon. There wouldn't be much to shoot on a night like this. But I put on my rain poncho and tucked my camera under it. And I went for a walk.

• • •

I spent several more days thinking about the pictures we'd picked out to send to Henry Oswald's brother. They were okay, but I felt like I needed something else. My pictures were all style. And not even original style. I needed a subject. I needed something to shoot that I had some connection to, something that affected me in some way. Something I was afraid of, or thrilled by, or had a real opinion about.

So I called Antoinette. I asked her if I could come over and take her picture. She seemed surprised by this request. At first she hesitated. She said she was having her period and she looked like shit. I said it didn't matter.

I drove over in the RAV4. I knocked on the door. Her mother opened it and invited me in. I remembered her from the day Marcus committed suicide. She looked older, I thought. Not that you can tell with adults. But I could sort of tell.

Antoinette came down the stairs. And then her step-father appeared from the kitchen. This was "Bald Mike." So then the four of us stood in their living room, talking. I was shown a picture of Marcus, the brother who killed himself. There were also pictures of Antoinette's father, in his uniform, and her other brother, Paul. He was older than Marcus and had been in the military when Marcus died. He was still in the military. In South Korea.

Mrs. Renwick was tall and had a tight, narrow face. She watched me very closely. She couldn't figure out what exactly to say to me. Bald Mike said nothing. He wore glasses and had white tufts of hair on the side of his head. After about ten minutes of this, Antoinette brought me upstairs.

We went in her room. It was pretty small. Their house in general was smaller and more modest than my other friends'.

She closed the door. There was an open book, facedown on the bed.

"So what sort of pictures did you want to take?" said Antoinette.

I blushed slightly. "I need pictures of a person."

"What do you need it for?"

"To maybe go to art school."

"Art school?" she said, her expression turning serious. "Okay. Do I need to be, like, naked?"

"No," I said. "I was just thinking your face."

"Okay," she said. "Can I wash it at least?"

"Sure."

She went into the hall, to the bathroom. I heard the water turn on. I took a seat on her bed. I looked around her room. There was a lot of stuff on the walls: pictures, postcards, posters. It was too much to absorb all at once. So I took pictures of it.

Beside her desk was a bookcase. Probably every book in it was something I needed to know about but didn't. *The Tibetan Book of the Dead* was one of the titles I noticed. That sounded important. I lifted my camera and took a picture of the bookcase. Maybe someday I could use that photo as a reading list.

Antoinette came back in the room. "Okay," she said. "What do you want me to do?"

I didn't know. I looked around. "Maybe sit on the bed?" I told her.

She sat on the bed. I pulled a chair over, turned it backward, and sat on it, using the back of it to prop up my elbows. The Canon felt good to me by now. It was like an old friend. But something was wrong as I framed her in the viewfinder. She didn't look right. She looked nervous and confused and like she didn't trust me. Not me as a person, me as a photographer.

I checked the light, then focused and squeezed off about twenty shots. They weren't good. I stopped shooting. I wasn't doing this right. I was too nervous.

I tried some different things. I moved back a few feet. I tried standing on the chair and shooting down. I tried looking up from the floor.

She could tell it wasn't working. "Is there something you want me to do?" she asked.

"Uh . . . ," I said, checking my settings. "Maybe move around a little?"

Antoinette took a deep breath. She relaxed herself in some way. She started to focus herself on the camera, not by looking at it, but by inviting it to her in some way.

She looked to the side, and then further to the side. She pulled some of her hair into her face. It still wasn't great. But I stayed with it. I started moving closer, getting in tight on her face. I got so close I could see her pores, the wisps of pale mustache above her lip, a large mole hidden inside her thick eyebrow. I went for a straight-ahead view: her eyes in the center. Her oily forehead above. Her lips below. Antoinette was not what you'd call pretty. But her face was so full. It had everything in it. It was a thing you could look at, and study, and think about for a long time, if you wanted to.

I was in love with her, I guess, is what I'm trying to say. I was in love with her.

Thock . . . Claude's backhand sizzled across the net.

Thock . . . I smacked it back.

Thock . . . He hit an arcing topspin to my backhand.

Thock . . . I chopped it low and crosscourt and came to the net.

Thock . . . He blasted the ball right at my chest.

Thock . . . I jumped aside and managed to block it. The ball hit the top of the net, skittered along the tape for a moment, and then rolled over onto Claude's side.

"Oh, *come on!*" shouted Claude, running for it, and then giving up.

After the set, we sat side by side on the bench. He toweled off his face. "You know you could still get on the team," Claude said to me. "Coach Kemp would love to have you."

"I don't think so," I said.

"I wish you would," said Claude. "We got nobody this year. I'll have to carry the team."

"You've always carried the team," I said.

Claude didn't respond. He reversed the towel and wiped down the grip of his racquet. He'd been doing that since we were doubles partners in the twelve and unders.

"Krista made girls varsity," he said.

"Yeah, I heard."

"She good?"

"For someone who hasn't played much," I said. "She's a natural athlete."

"So I hear," said Claude, smiling for a moment.

We gathered our stuff. "How's Petra?" I asked.

"She's okay."

"What's it like? Getting back together with an old girlfriend?"

"It's all right. I mean, we've known each other so long."

"Is that good or bad?"

He shrugged. "Both."

We got our tennis bags and headed off the court.

"The thing about ex-girlfriends," he said as we walked toward our cars, "you miss them. You have all these great memories. But it's the good parts you're remembering. When you get back together, those parts are already over. You're starting in the middle."

I nodded. I always listened closely to Claude about girl stuff. He generally knew what he was talking about.

"What about Hanna?" I finally said. "Would you get back with her?"

Claude made a noncommittal sound under his breath.

"Why did you guys even break up?" I said.

Claude had not talked to me about this. He hadn't

talked to anyone about this. "That I cannot tell you," he said in a low voice.

"You *can't* tell me or you *won't* tell me?" I said.

"I can't tell you," he said. "Because I don't know."

"Wait. So you guys didn't talk? When you broke up?" I couldn't imagine this. Hanna breaking up with someone without long discussions and drama? It was unthinkable. "Is she okay?" I asked. "Hanna, I mean?"

Claude became deathly silent.

"Jesus," I said.

He opened the trunk of his car and threw his stuff inside.

"Like I said, we could use you on the tennis team," he said. He slammed the trunk down. He was trying to be casual and smooth, the old Claude, but I could see the tension in his face.

"Seriously, Claude, is Hanna okay?" I asked.

He stared across the parking lot for a moment, then shook his head. "I honestly don't know."

It was my mother who told me to go see Mrs. Fogarty, the college counselor at my school. She must have talked more to Henry Oswald about me going to art school. Whatever it was, if my mother was taking the idea seriously, that meant I could too.

"I think I want to go to art school," I told Mrs. Fogarty, sitting in her small office. She was older, about fifty. She looked like a librarian. I had met with her a couple of times over the years. She knew me as a tennis player and a B-minus student with a rich lawyer dad. I'm sure in her mind I was University of Oregon material all the way.

"Art school?" she said with surprise. "That's not something we've discussed before. When did you become interested in art?"

"Recently," I said.

"What sort of art are you interested in?"

"Photography."

"Oh," she said. "Did you join the photography club?"

Our school had this lame photography club. Three girls had started it the year before to beef up their college applications.

"No," I said. "I started helping a guy who's a professional photographer."

"Oh," said Mrs. Fogarty. "Well, that's good. He can write you a recommendation."

"Well, actually, he thinks that art school is sort of . . ."

When I didn't finish my sentence, she looked at me over her glasses.

". . . *masturbatory*," I said.

"Oh."

"He's more about being super professional. And not getting all intellectual about things."

"I see."

"Sorry if I'm not allowed to say that word. The other word."

"That's all right," said Mrs. Fogarty, turning to her computer. "If that's what he said . . ."

"Yeah, but he would probably do it though. Write me a recommendation. He just likes to complain about things."

"Let's hope he chooses his words wisely."

She typed my name into her computer and pulled up my file.

"Do you think I could do it?" I asked. "Go to art school? Is it hard to get into them?"

"It's hard to get into the good ones."

"How do they judge you?"

"Well, I'm sure your grades and your test scores count somewhat. But I would imagine your art would be the most important."

She looked at my grades and my test scores. "Hmmmm," she said. "Do you know where you want to go?"

"Cal Arts."

"Okay. We can look at that. Is there anywhere else you were thinking?"

"I was wondering if you knew some places."

"I know the Rhode Island School of Design. That's a very famous art school."

"Okay. That sounds good. And that's back East?"

"Yes, Rhode Island is back East."

I could imagine my father's smug smile if I asked to go to such a place. But the truth was I didn't care what he thought. I wasn't going to screw myself over to avoid his approval.

"Okay," I said. I wrote it down on the front of my notebook: RHODE ISLAND SCHOOL OF DESIGN. "Yeah, I'll do some research."

"As will I," said Mrs. Fogarty, who actually smiled at me for once.

37

The windshield wipers of the RAV4 flopped back and forth. I was with Richie, trying to get to a photo assignment. While we waited in traffic, I imagined Cal Arts, and Los Angeles, and people running around naked in the desert. I pictured palm trees, blue skies, kids sitting in drum circles in the sand, their sunglasses gleaming in the sun. How would I do in a world like that? What would those people be like?

Richie played with the radio, then shut it off. We were doing a shoot for *Portland Weekly*, taking pictures of some of the new artisanal cupcake spots that were popping up around town.

"Fucking cupcakes," said Richie, staring at the back of a stopped bus. "I did not get into this business to shoot fucking cupcakes."

I tapped my fingers on the steering wheel.

"Passport photos are more interesting," grumbled Richie.

"Passport photos are pretty interesting," I said. I had taken home an entire box of rejected passport photos from Richie's store recently. I'd scanned a bunch of them into my computer and was messing around with them. Since I was applying to art school, I was starting to have "art school ideas."

We finally arrived at the first cupcake shop. The woman who owned it was freaking out because we were late. She got a little controlling with Richie, about how to arrange the picture. He finally told her: "Listen, lady, we got it. This is what we do."

The next cupcake shop was run by an old hippie couple. Their cupcakes were made with special grains. They tried to explain this to Richie, but he didn't care. Their cupcakes were lumpy and had a greenish hue. Richie asked them if they had any better-looking cupcakes. "You know, *photogenic* cupcakes?" Richie told the man with the gray ponytail. "Like something you'd want to eat?"

The last place we went to, Hawthorne Bakery, was owned by two women who were quite young. They looked about Richie's age, midtwenties. They had an elaborate baking area built inside this old wood building. Everything was super clean and shiny and well lit.

One of the two owners wore an actual baker's outfit: the white apron, the white hat, she even had a smear of white flour on her cheek. The other was more the business person. She followed us around, telling us things about the bakery. When Richie asked her where she got the money to start the business, she talked about her investors and about demographic research and business models.

"Translation: she got the money from her parents,"

Richie said to me when we were outside switching lenses. We stayed at Hawthorne Bakery a long time, though. We took a lot of pictures. I realized Richie liked the other of the two owners, the one with the baker's hat. He must have taken a hundred pictures just of her.

Later, when we got back into the RAV4, he told me not to start the car. "That bakery chick, the one with the hat," he said. "What did you think of her?"

I shrugged.

"I wanna ask her out. What do you think?"

"With the flour on her face?" I said. "Yeah, she was cool."

"This bakery thing. I'm into it. It smells good."

"It looks like fun."

"I liked her," said Richie. "The one with the flour on her face."

"Ask her out," I said.

"I think I'm gonna ask her out."

"You should."

"Do you think she liked me?"

"Yeah," I said. "She smiled at you."

"Did she?" asked Richie. "Did she smile at me?"

"Well, you told her to smile. You were taking her picture."

"Fuck it," said Richie. "I'm gonna ask her out." He got out of the RAV4 and slammed the door. He went inside. I sat and waited. I could see him through the big front window. He went up to her, started talking, waved his hands around, like he did when he got excited.

A minute later, Richie came striding out. He opened the car door, sat down, slammed the door shut behind him.

He slapped a piece of paper on the dashboard. "Check this out," he said. On the top it said: HAWTHORNE BAKERY. Below that was a phone number and in female handwriting, NICOLE.

"You got balls," I said.

"Damn right I got balls," said Richie, rocking in his seat. "And now I'm shaking with nerves. Let's go get a beer."

We went to a restaurant down the street. We sat at the bar. Richie had brought the piece of paper with him. He kept looking at Nicole's name and number. "I think I like this girl," he said.

Richie had his beer and I had a sandwich. Meanwhile, there was something happening on the TV above the bar. Breaking news. A reporter was talking about a police shooting in Seattle. A fifteen-year-old African American girl had been shot by the police for shoplifting the day before. Now there was a protest, which judging from what we were seeing on TV, had turned into a riot.

Commentators were trying to explain what had happened, but they kept cutting away to show live footage from Elliot Square in Seattle. They showed a large angry crowd, arm in arm, shouting something at the police. They showed the police lined up in riot gear, preparing to hold them back.

"What the hell is this?" Richie said, watching the TV.

They showed a bunch of tear-gas canisters flying through the air. And people running through the smoke.

"Holy shit," murmured Richie.

They showed a guy with a TV camera running across the street. And then a journalist with a big Pentax camera getting knocked down by the cops.

"Did they just hit that guy?" said Richie. "Did the cops just tackle the guy with the Pentax?"

We both watched the fracas. It was crazy and fascinating.

"We should be up there," said Richie. "We should be shooting this." He turned and yelled for the waitress. "Hey! Hey, lady! We need our check!"

We paid our check and hurried to the parking lot. Though we were only shooting cupcakes that day, we'd put all the gear in the RAV4. That was one of Richie's rules: "Always bring everything."

I got in the driver's seat and started the engine. Richie was checking the traffic on his phone. It was 4:45 p.m. He thought we could be in Seattle in four or five hours.

"What about you?" he asked me. "Will your parents be cool with this?"

"It's just my mom. I'll call her later."

I drove fast. We caught a couple lights. In a few minutes we were on the freeway, headed north on Interstate 5. We drove for about ten minutes, and then Richie suddenly looked up from his phone. "Hey, what about your mom?"

"What about her?" I said.

"You gotta call her, right? You can't just take off."

I had thought of that too but had put it out of my mind. "It won't be a problem," I said.

"You gotta tell her. You gotta call her. Like now."

He was right. I dug my phone out of my pocket as I drove. I called.

"Hi, Mom," I said, over the car noise.

"Hi, Gavin."

"I wanted to let you know, I'm not gonna be home until late."

"Why? Where are you?"

"Uh, we were doing a shoot, Richie and I, and we . . . uh . . . we got a last-minute assignment."

"Doing what?"

"Shooting some stuff."

"No," said Richie loudly beside me. "You gotta tell her the truth."

"What's going on, Gavin?" said my mother. "Where are you?"

"We're going up to Seattle to take some pictures."

"Where in Seattle?"

"By the protests. For that girl that got shot."

"At that *riot*? No, you are not doing that. You're coming home. You're not going anywhere near that mess. People are being gassed. People are being arrested."

"Well, yeah, Mom. That's kind of why we're going. . . ."

"Gavin, you are not going up there. That's final."

I thought for a moment. I was steering with one hand, holding the phone with the other. "Well, that's great, Mom," I said. "I'll be home pretty late. Don't wait up."

"Gavin, you listen to me," said my mother's voice. "This is not the time to pull some stunt."

I swallowed. I felt so sorry for my mother sometimes.

Being married to my dad had drained her of all authority. Everyone was so scared of him, she was an afterthought. Nobody listened to her. Nobody did what she said.

But she had chosen her path. And now I had to choose mine.

"I know, Mom. I'll be careful," I said loudly into the phone.

"Gavin! Don't you do this. And you tell that Richie, if he doesn't bring you back right now, I'll have him arrested for kidnapping!"

"Okay, Mom. See you soon. Love you," I said. I turned off my phone.

"Is she cool?" said Richie.

"She's cool," I said.

I drove as fast as I could, and we arrived in Seattle a little after nine thirty. The main protest was in Elliot Square, near downtown. We drove in that direction, but were waved off at a police barricade. The official protests were over, but according to the radio, there was still a large crowd in the square. The entire area was closed to traffic. A curfew was in force.

We got as close as we could and parked. Elliot Square was ahead of us about fifteen blocks. We hopped out. We quickly got our gear together. I had the Canon. Richie had the big Pentax with the super-zoom lens.

Richie talked as we loaded our carry bags. "We'll walk

down there. We'll see what's up. We won't do anything too risky," he said. Then he stopped for a moment to emphasize his words: "And listen, if there's trouble, or you don't want to keep going, you bail. Okay? No shame in that. This was my idea. You're just a kid. . . ."

I nodded.

"I'm serious," he said. "They're gonna have mace. They're gonna have tear gas. You got anything to put over your face?"

I hadn't thought of that. But I did have something. I had a tennis towel, a little one, that was still in the back of the RAV4. I found it and rolled it into a triangular shape. I tied it around my nose and mouth and went to one of the side mirrors to see how it looked.

"I kinda have my own issues with cops," said Richie behind me. "I don't like them. So if I do something stupid and you don't want to be part of it, you get away. Okay? I'm serious."

I nodded. The towel fit so well over my face, it was like it had been designed for that purpose. Tennis towel/gas mask, it was two things in one.

"You got another key for the car?" Richie asked. I found one and gave it to him. We locked the RAV4. We double-checked that we had everything. Then we started to walk.

As the skyline of downtown Seattle loomed in front of us, the reality of what we were doing hit me all at once.

"If we get separated and we can't call, we meet back at the car," advised Richie. "So remember where it is."

I looked up at the street signs. But I was so adrenalized I couldn't focus enough to read them. I was swimming in adrenaline. I actually felt like I was floating, like I might lose touch with the ground.

"If you gotta run, just run. Don't worry about me," said Richie. "We'll be harder to catch if we separate. And if they get one of us, then we'll still have the other guy's shots."

I looked over at Richie. "Have you been in riots before?" I asked.

Richie frowned. "I've done all sorts of stupid shit."

We were both breathing hard now. We were walking as fast as our legs could go.

"What do the cops do if they catch you?" I said.

"They beat the crap out of you. And they take your stuff."

I swallowed at that.

"I'm not kidding," said Richie. "They will. So watch yourself."

I nodded earnestly to all these instructions. I even told myself: *Do what he says. Run if you have to.*

But I knew from tennis that you can't half-ass certain things. If you want to win, you go all out. You don't play it safe. I had a feeling the world we were about to enter would be like that. This was "all or nothing" territory.

•　•　•

We were about six blocks from Elliot Square when we began hearing the echoes of a voice coming through a loudspeaker. The sound bounced off the building walls. I heard the word "unlawful." I heard the words "disperse" and "arrested." My heart began to beat so fast, I thought I might have a heart attack.

Suddenly, a man came tearing around a corner, sprinting away from the square. Richie spun in place and got the shot: the running man, the black cityscape behind him. It hadn't even occurred to me to lift my camera. That's how nervous I was. I gripped the Canon. I had to calm down. My whole body was shaking.

We came to the next corner and now we could see Elliot Square itself. It was lit up by huge spotlights, like the ones they use when they're fixing the highway at night. You could see people moving around. Then the loudspeaker blared out again, this time much clearer: "THE PROTEST IS OVER. YOU ARE NOW TRESPASSING. YOU ARE NOW IN VIOLATION OF THE LAW."

Richie started to run. I ran after him. We were moving parallel to the square, trying to get closer to the center of the action. I could see in Richie's face, he was as excited as I was.

We slowed to catch our breath. We peeked around the next corner. We could see the police. They looked like an army. They were on horses. They were in cars. The ones on foot were crammed together in tight formation, with shields and helmets and black clubs.

At that moment someone yelled behind us. I looked back. About six cops in riot gear were telling us to stop. They could see Richie's big Pentax. "Run," said Richie quietly to me. We both broke into a full sprint. The cops, with their heavy equipment, had no chance. They didn't even bother to chase us.

We went three more blocks and then ran toward the light of the open square. When we got there, we were on the civilian side, about fifty yards behind the main crowd of protesters.

The minute you stepped into that open space, you could feel the electricity in the air. Every sensation was supercharged and dreamlike: the acid smell in the air, the brutal floodlights, the ominous rustle of all those cops waiting for something to happen.

I followed Richie as he moved up closer behind the protesters. They were mostly ordinary people, standing, talking, occasionally shouting something at the cops. A younger man picked up something off the street and heaved it forward, over everyone else's head, in the direction of the police. Several people yelled angrily at him to stop throwing things.

Richie and I moved cautiously forward until we reached the front of the crowd. There, across a wide concrete no-man's land, was the police force. The enormous floodlights behind them were aimed directly at us, so you couldn't look at them or see them very well. There was a line of cops in riot gear, and in the middle of it, a big military-style vehicle with a machine gun on top. If you squinted, you could see a guy up there sitting behind the machine gun. He wasn't exactly aiming it at us. But he sort of was.

The floodlights were so bright you could see every detail of everything. I started looking at the people around me. A lot of those near the front didn't look like protesters at all. They were anarchists: young guys, white guys, dressed all in black, with hoods and scarves over their faces. They threw rocks and taunted the police. They were there for the fight.

But other people were regular citizens, with normal clothes and gray hair and glasses. There were lots of African Americans. Mothers, it looked like, and older black men in suits, some of whom were probably church people or ministers or maybe politicians. There were little kids, too, running loose. One black kid kept running up to the front and back again. He couldn't have been more than six years old. He was so fast he was a blur down at knee level.

The voice on the loudspeaker came on again: "THIS IS YOUR FINAL WARNING. YOU ARE NOW GUILTY OF CRIMINAL TRESPASS. IF YOU DO NOT WANT TO BE ARRESTED, LEAVE THE AREA NOW."

Nobody was leaving, I noticed. A tall white man, who looked like a college professor, lifted up a little girl and yelled something toward the police. Other people started to yell. A dozen older black women came forward from the back. They had a banner from their church, which they held stretched out in front of them. Someone started to sing. Other people picked it up. Within a few seconds the whole square was vibrating with the beautiful hum of human voices.

Richie was shooting constantly. He was moving through the crowd, searching out the best angles, the most interesting faces. I was just standing there, in awe of the situation.

And then everything stopped. The singing, the yelling, the loudspeaker. The entire street went so quiet you could hear the police horse's shoes clacking on the pavement.

And then someone screamed.

And then another sound, a kind of low rumble. It sounded like the patter of rain, but bigger, heavier. It was the police in their boots and their horses. They were coming at us. They were charging the crowd.

39

I got knocked down immediately. That's how bewildered I was. But that was good because the minute I hit the ground I woke up. I scrambled to my feet. People were sprinting past me. I could hear things flying through the air, metallic pops. A very bright flash exploded to my right, scattering the crowd and adding to the chaos. People fell down. Other people helped them up. I managed to stop running and lift my camera to my face. But someone crashed into me, banging the Canon into the bridge of my nose. The flow of fleeing people drove me back. Someone grabbed the strap of my carry bag and actually jerked me backward. And then I got my first whiff of the tear gas, which scalded my throat and chest like burning gasoline.

It was too late for the tennis towel. The gas was already on my face. It felt like a swarm of hornets had landed in my eyes. I ran wildly, blindly toward the back of the square. I fell over someone and then collided with another photojournalist, who unlike me, had set his feet and was carefully shooting the scene behind us. I tripped and found myself on the ground again, rolling, stumbling, crawling on all fours.

I got to my feet and ran, despite the burning in my eyes

and lungs. When I got to the edge of the square, I cut down a side street. But the way was blocked. I turned and followed some other people, running down a different street, which led to an empty parking lot. There, a kind of emergency sanctuary had been established. There were tables and chairs and stacks of water bottles. People were pouring water on each other's faces. They were getting first aid.

I found myself waving at a middle-aged woman, begging her to squirt my face, which she did. I dug out my tennis towel and began dabbing at my hot skin. My cheeks and eyelids felt like they had been singed. My face stung so badly, I couldn't touch it, except with the wet towel.

As my vision cleared, I could see the aid givers better. They were volunteers, it looked like. They had white handkerchiefs tied around their upper arms. Suddenly, everyone began yelling that we had to move on. People hurried away, running farther from the square. I started to run too, but then something possessed me and I stopped and slipped into a doorway. *Don't run*, a voice said in my head. *Stop running.*

I moved as far back into the doorway as I could. A dozen cops came into the parking lot area, but only the volunteers remained, and a few of the protesters who were still recovering from the tear gas. The cops left them alone and went back toward the square. When they were gone, I crept back into the street and carefully moved forward until I stood at the edge of the square again. In the floodlights, you could see the tear gas drifting through the air. The main group of protesters were gone, but I could still see dark figures running among the trees. I saw someone pick up a tear-gas canister and throw it back toward the police. I looked farther to my right and spotted a serious skirmish going on between several cops and one of the anarchist kids. The kid wore a scarf and ski goggles. The cops hit him so hard on the side of the head the ski goggles flew off. When he crumpled to the ground, they swarmed over him, beating him with their clubs.

Also, there were photographers, lots of them. They were advancing, retreating, hovering around the action like referees at a UFC fight. These were not local people. You could tell by their clothes, their equipment, their total fearlessness. One guy, screaming in a foreign language, got into a shoving match with one of the cops. The cop tried to wrestle him to the ground. The guy fought him off. Then two more cops jumped in and rode him to the ground, slamming his camera into the concrete and shattering his lenses in a crush of glass and plastic.

I had to get out there. *Take one good picture*, said that same voice in my head. Apparently, this was some new part of me, which was *way* braver than I was.

But maybe I could get something. I looked out over the square. What was happening? I remembered the church ladies with the banner. What had happened to them? I scanned the area and eventually spotted their banner on the ground in the central part of the square. Looking closer, I saw the ladies themselves, partially obscured behind a statue. They were sitting in a row, their hands bound behind their backs. A couple cops were standing there too. I checked my Canon. Despite being bounced off the concrete several times, it was still fully juiced, still functional, still ready to go.

Take one good picture, said the voice again.

I ran into the square. It was surreal out there now. There were no sides, no boundaries. Cops ran one way and then another. Other people walked through the chaos as if nothing were happening. There were pops and flashes and smoke and yelling. The anarchist kids were the ones still fighting. They threw bottles at the police, then sprinted away. They were good at it. You suspected they did this all the time. For them, this was another day at the office.

But they weren't the story. The church ladies were the story. I made my way in their direction. I tried to keep my camera as inconspicuous as possible. Since I didn't have a big zoom lens, I didn't look like one of the pro guys. And also, my general demeanor separated me from the real photojournalists. They didn't hesitate. They went for every shot. I was kind of . . . well . . . I was a kid. And I was scared half out of my mind.

I worked my way across the square until I got close to

the statue. Then I made a dash and got behind it, out of sight of the church women and the cops on the other side. Once there, I sat with my back to the base of the statue, in the dark, and caught my breath. I pulled my strap around. I checked the Canon. I put the flash on. Then, gripping it with one hand and my finger on the button, I crawled on my hands and knees toward one end of the statue, easing my way silently around the marble base, until I could see the church women and the police. Nothing was really happening. The policemen were talking on their radios. They looked a little embarrassed, like they weren't sure what to do with a bunch of middle-aged church ladies.

The women were sitting on the ground, in a row, their hands secured by plastic ties behind their backs. Another woman lay on her stomach with her face on the ground, her hands and her feet bound behind her, like an animal. In the middle of this was a little girl, about five years old. She was holding on to the arm of one of the seated women, her mother possibly. The girl was sucking her thumb. She was sitting there, huddled against her mother, staring up at the cops and sucking her thumb. That was the shot.

I didn't move another inch. I eased the Canon around and lifted it to my still-burning face. I found the girl in my viewfinder. The leg of one of the cops would be in the picture. But that was okay. I activated the flash, which made a slight whirring sound. I had the shot. I lined it up. I gave it that one extra beat, to "let the picture become itself," as Richie often said. Then I slowly pressed down on the button.

There was a bright red flash. And that was the last thing I remembered.

When I opened my eyes, I was in an ambulance. But the light was too bright. And everything hurt so much. So I closed them again. . . .

When I opened my eyes a second time, I was lying on a gurney in a hallway somewhere with a big bag of ice on my face. I closed them again. . . .

When I opened my eyes a third time, I was in a darkened room with a bright light shining in my face. A man was leaning over me, tugging on the skin beside my nose. He wore bifocals and a surgical mask. He was deeply absorbed in doing something to my face.

"Hello," he said.

I didn't know if I could talk, so I looked up at him.

"I'm sewing up your face," he said. "Don't move."

He continued with his work. It was an odd sensation to be "sewn." He stuck the needle in, pulled it through, pulled it tight, and stuck it in again.

"Usually we staple these," he told me, "but yours is in a tricky spot."

I blinked my eyes once.

A nurse was beside him. The doctor wore light green

gloves. Most of what he was doing involved my nose, which didn't feel like it was in its usual spot on my face. I tried to move my mouth. Though my head was completely numb, my mouth seemed to work. I tried to talk: "Ith my nothe broken?"

"Your nose? I don't think so. We're waiting for the X-rays."

"What happenth?" I said.

"You seem to have received a blow of some kind," said the doctor.

"Wherth my camera?"

"We have it," said the nurse. "It's here."

"Don't talk," said the doctor. "Stay still."

So I did.

Richie found me. It was light out by then, seven thirty in the morning. I was in a waiting area, in a chair, my head back, an ice pack across my nose, my entire upper body tingling with Novocaine and painkillers.

Because I was a minor, the hospital needed my parents' permission to release me. Plus, there were forms and insurance papers I needed to fill out. There was also a bill for $1,276. Someone from the Seattle Police Department was on their way, to take my statement. Richie was the one they explained this to, since I was so drugged up I could barely think.

We sat there for a while, waiting for all this to happen.

Then Richie told the nurse I had to use the restroom. She pointed down the hallway. Richie helped me up and walked me slowly in that direction. When we got to the restroom, Richie squeezed my arm and indicated to me to keep walking. In this way, the two of us shuffled to the end of the hall, around the corner, and out the main entrance. There, in the bright overcast, we slowly made our way down the steps and to the curb, passing the police, the security people, a few nurses smoking cigarettes. Richie waved for a cab. When one pulled up, he eased me inside and got in after me.

So we escaped.

Richie drove the RAV4 back to Portland, while I lay in the backseat. As the painkillers wore off, my face began to hurt. But at least I could sit up and mumble a few words.

Eventually my head cleared enough to get out the Canon, which Richie had snagged from the emergency room. It had a big dent in the casing, but otherwise appeared fine. I pushed the power button. The battery was low but it turned on. The viewfinder, which had a thick scratch on it, came to life. I scrolled through the pictures. Had I got the girl sucking her thumb? The last picture was a dark blur. I went backward one shot: another blurry shot, of trees. I went forward: a dark blur. I went back again: a blurry shot of the trees. "Oh God," I said, letting the Canon fall into my lap. "I didn't get it."

Richie kept driving. When I recovered myself, I lifted the Canon and went through all my shots. I clicked through picture after picture. I hadn't gotten anything. Not a clear face. Not a protester. Not a cop. Not a single decent photograph. Not one.

Richie laughed when I told him. "You went through all that and you got nothing?" he said. "You'll never make that mistake again."

I looked pretty bad by the time we got home. My nose was green and swollen and I had two black eyes and the bridge of my nose had black threads from the stitches hanging out of it.

My mother and Henry Oswald were waiting at the house when I got home. Henry was talking about suing the Seattle police, but when Richie explained how we'd fled the hospital, he decided against that. My mother mostly hugged me and thanked Richie for getting me home. I'm not sure he ever knew that my mom had forbidden me to go.

I went back to school on Monday. My face was still black-and-blue. Naturally, people asked me what happened. They didn't believe it when I told them. Most people didn't know I owned a camera. I was known at our school for playing tennis and dating Grace Anderson. Nobody knew I took pictures.

When Kai saw me, though, she was speechless. And

when she heard what happened, her jaw dropped. "You were in a riot? With the cops?!" she exclaimed. "Oh my God!" So then she dragged me to Antoinette's locker, pushing people out of the way. She tapped Antoinette's shoulder and presented me to her. They both went apeshit. Antoinette kept touching my bandages and my nose. "You're my hero!" said Kai, in her slightly ironic, sarcastic way.

Several interesting things came out of the Elliot Square Riot. First, Henry Oswald called me a couple days later and told me to write my college essay about it. His brother William thought the admissions people at Cal Arts would love it. Also, his brother had liked my photos, the ones I had e-mailed before. So that was double good news.

Then Emma Van Buskirk, who was going to be the editor of our school magazine next year, asked me if I would be the photo editor. This was based mostly on the popularity of my black eyes, and the fact that nobody else wanted to do it. I said yes. That, too, would help me get into art school, I thought.

Another thing: On their first date, Richie told Nicole from Hawthorne Bakery the whole epic story. She seemed impressed and agreed to go out with him again. Richie did not tend to go on second dates, so that was pretty big.

And then, most important of all, Richie got a photo agent for his Elliot Square photos. This person—who was based in New York—sold several of his pictures to newspapers and magazines around the world. The best one ended up in the *New York Times*. It was of two African American women helping each other through a tear-gas cloud. It went viral and was soon all over Facebook and Twitter. It eventually became the main image people associated with Elliot Square.

But not for me. The image I would always associate with Elliot Square was the girl under the statue, sucking her thumb and holding her mother's arm. But of course I hadn't gotten the shot. So it was only in my mind. Clear as day. Where it will probably haunt me for the rest of my life.

So then it was summer. That was a relief. My face healed up, and soon I was back at my old job at the Garden Center with my spray hose and rubber boots. I never minded going to work there. People were always cheerful when they were at a nursery. People calm down in the presence of plants. Kai told me a bunch of stuff she had read about this: How plants are actually aware of us and communicate with us and try to help us in various ways—so that we can help them.

The other good thing was I was old enough now to do deliveries. So I would drive around and deliver stuff in the truck. It was fun going to the different neighborhoods around the city. For a couple weeks I was delivering trees every day to this one church across town. They were redoing their landscaping. It was mostly African American people who worked there. Seeing them made me think of Seattle and the church ladies and how brave they had been but also how ordinary. When I'd show up in my truck, the church people would come out and help me unload the shrubs and saplings and fertilizer. They'd offer me some lemonade if it was hot. I would never say anything, but I felt in awe of them, in a way. I'd seen church ladies in action. I knew what they were capable of.

During the week, my friends sometimes stopped by the Garden Center. Richie came by to get flowers for Nicole a couple times. He wanted to use my employee discount. Several months had passed since the success of his Elliot Square photo. His phone had rung constantly for a month or so after it appeared. But things had calmed down. "Fame is a fickle mistress," he told me, half kidding and half not.

He was still getting gigs, though. *Bon Appétit*, a food magazine, flew us down to Austin, Texas, for a big National Barbeque Sauce Competition. It was pretty ridiculous, all these overweight Texas people in big hats munching on ribs all day. But one night Richie and I drove out to the Mexican part of town where everyone spoke Spanish. We had dinner in this little place with outdoor tables, and we sat there, with the chickens and the little kids running around, listening to the crickets and the coyotes howl in the distance.

We got some other gigs too, and then Richie got an assignment from the *Portland Weekly* that he couldn't do, so he told them to send me. It was to take pictures of this vintage clothes shop that was being torn down to make room for condos. It had been there for thirty years, and the woman who ran it was this nutty, eccentric type. The SHIT WE HAVE TO HAVE list, in my mind, was the store itself, inside and outside, some clothes, some shoes. And then a couple shots of the woman herself, some of her smiling and maybe a couple looking sad, since her shop was closing down.

But things got a little complicated once I got there. For starters, the lady was being super weird and kept saying (to no one): "The photographer is here. The photographer has come." Then she insisted I address her as Lady Katrina. I was like, "Okay, whatever." Then she started ordering me around and telling me what to take pictures of, like her entire jewelry collection and some weird old bag she'd had for a hundred years.

I had to say: "Uh, ma'am . . . I mean *Lady Katrina* . . . this is for the *Portland Weekly*. They're only going to use a couple of these. They won't have room for your entire jewelry collection."

That didn't go over well. She got offended and started telling me I was a typical young person and didn't respect the past. I tried to apologize and calm her down, but she was off in her own little world by then.

Finally I said, "Uh . . . Lady Katrina . . . ? Would you mind standing over there and looking around, like you're remembering your years here?"

She totally lost it then. She started shrieking and waving her arms around. Then she told me to get out. Some of her lady friends were there by then, and they started yelling at me too. "You rude, rude boy!" they said. I tried to apologize because it *was* my fault. I should have said it differently. But I didn't know. It was my first gig! Then she started to cry. Her friends literally pushed me out the door. And then I felt terrible.

I sent the pictures in though. And the woman at the *Portland Weekly* liked them. And a couple weeks later, I got my first check.

Meanwhile, my high school friends were doing the summer-party routine. There had been talk at school about how the summer between junior and senior year was supposed to be epic. Your "last great high school summer," some of the seniors told us. "You better enjoy it." This made sense, I thought. Since everyone had driver's licenses and cars and credit cards, you could pretty much do anything. And you weren't worried about college yet, or dealing with the stresses of leaving home.

Claude and Logan took this to heart. They had regular parties at Logan's beach house. I went to a couple of these. It was the usual crowd, the rich kids from our school and the other schools, the good-looking people, the tennis-player types. It wasn't that I disliked these people. It was just so familiar. I could predict what people were going to say before they said it. The girls drank wine and the boys drank beer, and the girls talked about each other and the boys talked about sports. And everyone made fun of people who were ugly or poor or who weren't like them, laughing at them with their perfect teeth and their highlighted hair and their expensive sunglasses. Still, they were my people, the people I grew up with. So I rolled with it, like I always had, sitting with the guys, watching the girls parade around the pool in their bathing suits.

It was much more interesting to hang out with Antoinette and Kai. Agenda had half-price dance parties on Tuesday nights in June, so we went to several of those. Bennett Schmidt and some of his buddies were sometimes there. Since Kai and Antoinette were friends with him, I had to be nice to him too. He wasn't so bad. He knew a lot about music. He was also popular with the girls.

In July, Antoinette went back to Germany to see her dad. After that, she was going to travel around Europe. So then it was me and Kai doing things. That was a little strange at first. We hadn't hung out that much, just the two of us. At first there wasn't much to do, but then we went to a party with Britney Vaughn and her friends, which was way crazier than any high school party I'd ever been to. After the first one, I made sure to always have a camera with me whenever I hung around Britney or any other Agenda people. I'd bring the old Canon, which still had a big dent in the casing but worked fine. I'd leave it on the floor or on a bookshelf somewhere and then casually pick it up occasionally and snap a few pictures of people drunkenly rolling on the floor or peeing out the window or making out with someone in the bathtub. There was an art to being inconspicuous like that. The real secret, I realized, was you couldn't judge people. You just had to be there. You couldn't be like: *Oh my God, I can't believe you're doing that!* You had to be super chill and not care about anything. And the Agenda types, they all wanted the attention anyway. They loved that someone was taking their picture. So I became part of that world in a new way.

It was also fun to be with Kai. We'd have these crazy, weird nights: fleeing Britney's parties when the police showed up and then eating french fries in the parking lot of Jack in the Box until four in the morning. I had basically zero parental supervision now, so I could do anything. One night there was a full moon and Kai and I bummed a ride with some other people to the Grayson Hot Springs. These were college students we met at a coffee shop. As soon as we got to the hot springs, Kai ran down the trail, stripped off all her clothes, and plopped down into the mud. So then the college kids did too. And then the bunch of us rolled around and lay there and soaked in the mud. Kai found this cool rock and wouldn't let me see it, so then I had to wrestle her, to try to get it, and the two of us were squishing around in the mud, trying to get the rock from each other, until we got so tired we had to stop. The college kids only had one small towel in their car, so we messed up their backseat pretty badly.

That was also the summer that Kai tried to teach me about fashion. She took me around to the various thrift stores and clothing-exchange places. At first I couldn't stand to not be dressed in Levi's and cotton shirts. But Kai got me to wear different things, Western shirts and sweaters and old-man shoes instead of Nikes. Slowly I got used to it. It was weird, though, to stand out like that. To have people look at you on the street. But as she kept saying: "Do you want to be a cool young photographer, or do you want to be another high school dork with a camera?"

For a couple weeks in August, Kai and I were together almost every day. I'd get off work and we'd meet up somewhere. At night we'd go to Agenda and dance and talk about people. Also, Kai wrote stuff. She wrote poems and kept journals. Some of her writings, which she was gradually letting me read, were hilarious. She was good at observing people, and seeing the absurdity of things.

One thing though, she still hated Claude and Hanna and those people. At one point, Logan Hewitt had this big end-of-summer party. Everyone was going. Even Hanna was supposedly going, though she'd been AWOL all summer. I thought it would be super fun. I tried to convince Kai to come.

"No," she said. We were in a booth at a coffee place downtown. She was drawing something in her journal. "Not going."

"What if I promise to stay with you?" I offered. "For the whole night?"

"No," she said.

"You wouldn't have to talk to anyone if you don't want."

She continued to draw. "I don't go places where those people are. Logan Hewitt? Barf."

I was sitting long-ways in the booth, my back against the wall, sipping the dregs of an old coffee. "But Hanna's gonna be there," I said. "And she's so funny. There's a reason she's so popular, you know. She's hilarious."

"Not to me she isn't."

"But they're my friends. Can't you just tolerate them for an hour or two? If only for my benefit?"

"No," she said, straightening up to better evaluate her drawing. "I can't tolerate them. They are intolerable. I can't believe you're actually friends with them. I can barely tolerate that."

And then a miracle happened. Richie was offered an assignment from a magazine called *Nylon*, which covered fashion and music and nightlife. They wanted us to go to Berlin and shoot photos for a travel piece about Berlin. Richie texted me immediately. Could I get off work? Could I come be his assistant?

My first thought was of course I could. I'd quit my job if I had to. My second thought was Antoinette. She was over there somewhere. I e-mailed her: *I'm going to Berlin with Richie for a magazine assignment. Can you come meet us?* A day later a reply appeared in my in-box: *Oh my God! Of course I will! What days are you there?*

Nicole gave Richie and me a ride to the airport. I knew the drill by now—checking the gear through, talking to the security people. Richie and Nicole said their good-byes. I couldn't tell how much Nicole liked him. Richie was totally in love with her. He was already talking marriage—to me, not to her. She seemed to enjoy his goofiness at least, so that was good. I sure liked her. She had that solid, whole-grain feeling about her. I think I was a little bit in love with her myself. It made me sad when she left us there at the airport. It made me sad for Richie.

We landed in Berlin twelve hours later. It was a lot of airports and a lot of flying. We stumbled out of the terminal and grabbed a cab. I immediately opened the window and let the hot afternoon air blow on my tired face. It smelled different there, in Europe, in Germany. And the sky looked bigger in a way. But the cabdriver, who was Middle Eastern, started yelling at me about something, the air-conditioning, it turned out. So I put up the window.

Berlin looked like the future to me. Everything was super new and advanced and complicated. Our hotel had unusual qualities to it, like no shower curtain on the shower, a toilet you couldn't figure out how to flush, and gooey lotions that you didn't know what part of your body they went on.

The next day Richie got out the SHIT WE HAVE TO HAVE list, and in our groggy, jet-lagged state, we began to work our way through it. We started off shooting a trendy café where all the "chic" people hung out. Then we shot a German skateboarding store, and then an art collective by the university. Berlin was very fashionable, but in an alien way. Like you'd see someone and you'd think: Is she *trying* to look like an elf? Also, everyone was very serious. Like if you asked someone a question they would get very intense and think about it a long time and give you this very careful and considered answer.

Before we left, Richie had said that dressing right was crucial on a gig for *Nylon*. So I had brought only the cool clothes Kai made me buy. I was so glad I did. With Richie and his rock-star photographer persona and me with my hipster teenager look, everyone treated us with great respect. People were constantly surprised we were American. This made everything way more fun.

That night we hit some Berlin nightclubs or "discotheques," which were also on our list. These were very high-tech dance clubs. And the music, oh my God, it was on a whole other level. Also, wherever we went, we were from *Nylon*, so everyone was super nice to us and buying us drinks and taking us into the special VIP rooms or whatever.

Antoinette arrived on our second day. I was so excited to see her. And the fact that I was there with Richie, on a photography gig: I felt like that might change the way she thought of me. She couldn't just dismiss me as a *minion* anymore. She would have to take me seriously.

I'd e-mailed her our schedule that day and she showed up at a design store we were shooting in the afternoon. Antoinette had never seen us work. She'd never seen me do anything like that. I think she was impressed by how pro we were.

I was so glad to see her! And she was so glad to see me! The minute we had a break, I ran over and hugged her. I don't think I'd ever done that before. But whatever. We were in Berlin!

• • •

Richie knew about Antoinette. He'd seen my portrait photos of her ("This is the girl you're in love with?" he'd said). So as soon as we finished the shoot, he gestured for me to go. He could pack up the rest of the equipment himself. So Antoinette and I ran off.

Antoinette's Berlin was slightly different from the stuff we were shooting for *Nylon*. She knew all the cheap restaurants and where the young people were. We went to a student café she knew about, where all these brainy-looking college students were hanging out. At another place, we sat outside, watching people stroll along the Strasse. After that we walked down an alley full of little shops and galleries. Antoinette kept bumping into me. And smiling. And touching my arm. She didn't usually do that. She had never been what you'd call demonstratively affectionate.

We ate dinner at a tiny Indian food place she knew about. It was so small it didn't have chairs. You had to stand around these upright tables to eat. A bunch of Turkish and Indian cabdrivers were there, shouting at each other in various languages. Once they found out we were Americans, they wouldn't leave us alone.

"America!" they said. "New York! California!"

Antoinette was like, "Seattle! Pennsylvania!"

They said: "Florida! Dallas Cowboys!"

It wasn't what you'd call an *in-depth* conversation. But everyone was very happy to meet us.

• • •

Unfortunately, after we ate, I suddenly got so tired I could hardly keep my eyes open. And it was only eight o'clock at night. Antoinette understood. She knew about jet lag and how the time difference caught up to you. Her youth hostel was nearby, so we went there.

She had come to Berlin by herself and had her own room. It was just a bed and a sink, but it also had a little balcony. We stood out there for a few minutes, looking at the people below and breathing in the city air. I guess I never thought of Germany as super old, but it was. It felt ancient, watching it from above, with the moon shining just over the rooftops.

Antoinette told me to lie down and try to sleep. She would read her book and wake me up in an hour, since Richie would want me back at the hotel that night and ready to work in the morning.

So that's what I did. I took off the shirt Kai had picked out for me and lay down in Antoinette's narrow youth hostel bed with the tight German sheets. Antoinette told me to take off my pants and socks, too. That I would sleep better. So I did that. When I lay down, I pretty much passed out instantly.

I don't know how long went by. But it was dark when I woke up again. I woke up because Antoinette was getting into the bed with me. I wasn't sure what she was doing. Or why she was doing it. But in the dark I could see she had taken off her pants and socks as well. When she got in, the warm skin of her legs touching mine sent a shiver through my body. My brain was still in a fog of jet lag and lack of sleep. I tried to keep it that way. I made a conscious effort to not wake up, to not think about what was happening. Or why. Or what it meant. This was the only way. If I tried to do something, or even just *think* something, the magical dream would end.

Antoinette nestled up against me. And I curled around her. And then, as easily and as naturally as an autumn leaf floats gently to the ground, we came together. Like all the way together. Like as together as you can get.

Afterward, I slipped off to sleep again, and when I woke up, it was eleven thirty. I had to get back to the hotel. Antoinette had fallen asleep too. I kissed her forehead and face and eyebrows until she woke up.

"I gotta get back," I whispered into her hair. She turned toward the clock, and when she saw how late it was, roused herself out of bed. We put on our clothes, in silence, in the dark.

We walked back toward my hotel, through the streets of Berlin. It was late now. There were fewer people, which made you more aware of the city itself, its gray stone buildings, its Gothic streetlights. Even though it was still August, fall was on its way. You could feel the chill in the air. Berlin was a winter city, a cold, formidable place; soon it would be in its natural state once again.

We crossed the big main square, Alexanderplatz. There

were still people there, young people mostly. They were in groups, laughing and running around. A tram went by. People were on bikes. Antoinette and I barely spoke. We walked and watched everything. Then, as we approached my hotel, she bumped shoulders with me again. This was her way of acknowledging what had happened. It was about as much as you were going to get from Antoinette. But I took it. I absorbed the bump and held it there, in my shoulder, where I hoped it would stay for a long time.

SENIOR YEAR

My favorite thing is to go where I've never been.
—*Diane Arbus*

My idea of a good picture is one that's in focus
and of a famous person.
—*Andy Warhol*

Four short days after I returned from Berlin, I was standing in the parking lot at Evergreen High School again. This time, though, I was a senior.

I pulled my backpack out of the RAV4 and walked across the parking lot toward the junior/senior wing. Other people from my class were standing around. They waved or said hi. *So now we're seniors*, seemed to be the feeling. It was like none of us could believe it.

Inside the building, my first thought was Antoinette. Where would her locker be? Would we have any classes together? How would she react to me when we met again? I knew her well enough to not be too hopeful. I still couldn't imagine us as a couple. To be a couple at Evergreen required an acceptance of the rules and rituals of high school relationships. I couldn't see her doing any of that.

But something must have changed between us. We'd slept in each other's arms. I'd kissed her eyes and her face and her thick eyebrows. Then again, she'd gone out with Bennett for months and she seemed to have no lingering feelings for him. So who knew? The situation was confusing and hard to think about. I decided the only reasonable strategy was to do nothing, expect nothing, be as casual as she would no doubt be. If anything further was going to happen between us, let her start it.

It was nice being back at school, anyway. It was fun being a senior. You could feel the difference right away. Walking down the hall, I felt more important, more in control. There was an authority to being a senior. Nobody knew more about high school than you did. You were the expert. And at the same time there was a lightness to it. Stuff didn't matter so much. As one guy said, "What can they do to us now?"

Of course, different people had different approaches to it. Logan and Claude saw their senior year as a well-deserved vacation. They had put up with high school bull-shit for three long years. The school owed them, in their mind. This year they would put their feet up and relax.

For other people, senior year was their last chance to get their grades up, or improve their test scores for college. If you were on a sports team, this was your final shot at a league championship. Or if you were really into some particular academic subject, you could do an independent study and focus on something you actually cared about for once.

Still others seemed eager to cash in on the privileges of being at the top of the pecking order. These were mostly the socially frustrated types, the people who had been bullied or harassed as underclassman. Now it was their turn to do the bullying and harassing, and they couldn't wait.

The more earnest types—like Emma Van Buskirk, editor in chief of the *Evergreen Owl*—were energized by the responsibility of being a senior. Emma was already hard at work changing the design of the *Owl*. Not that anyone cared about things like the magazine, or the yearbook, or the winter theater production of *Grease*. But for some people that was the point of being a senior: taking charge, treating teachers as equals, bossing people around.

Another thing about senior year, it leveled the playing field socially. Claude and Petra, who had been the most closely watched couple at our school, were suddenly not so closely watched. Nobody cared if they had a fight. Nobody was interested if their love would stand the test of time. Obviously, it wouldn't. Obviously, in eight short months every one of us would walk away from this place and our high school careers would disappear into the past, dust in the wind.

And anyway, most people had their own dramas now. They had their own boyfriends or girlfriends. Love, sex, romance: It wasn't just for the popular kids anymore. Everyone was doing it.

I managed to keep Antoinette out of my mind. But after two full days of her not making any attempt to hang out or text me or otherwise acknowledge me, I started to feel frustrated.

On Wednesday she actually ate lunch in the cafeteria, which was a rare thing indeed. She was sitting by herself and I hurried to join her, but two other girls got there first. Then Kai came, and within a minute or two the whole table was crowded with girls. I eventually had to slink off without getting any sense of what was going on. I suspected nothing was.

So I didn't text her. Or call her. Or look for her in the hall. If this was what she wanted, this was what she would get.

The hard part was Kai. She had become one of my main friends over the summer, if not my best friend. But now that Antoinette was back, Kai's loyalties were with her. I kept starting to text Kai. *What's up? Why are you guys ignoring me? What the hell is going on with you two?* But I never sent them. I had to be cool. I *had* to be. I could not make a fool of myself with Kai and Antoinette.

So I retreated back into my own crowd. This meant sitting with Claude, Logan, Petra, and the others at lunch. Where Hanna was in these first weeks, it was hard to say. Sometimes she was around. Most of the time she wasn't. She didn't seem to mind that Petra and Claude were together. She also didn't seem to want Claude back. Sometimes she'd be sitting with some random person, or talking to someone from her French class. It kind of didn't make sense. Hanna had social standards. She didn't hang out with just anyone. Now it was like, *Why is she talking to that guy?*

At the same time, Bennett Schmidt was on the rise. It didn't hurt that every year he seemed to get better looking. He was now about six foot two, with high cheekbones and a certain bad-boy scruffiness. . . . On the first day of school he pulled into the parking lot in a ten-year-old BMW with tinted windows and custom rims, which he'd bought over the summer—probably with drug money. He'd been quite the chick magnet at Agenda over the summer and he seemed destined for the same status at Evergreen, especially among the sophomore and junior girls. They didn't know his past or what a creep he had once been. They just knew he was a hot senior with a BMW and cocaine if you wanted it. And a lot of them did.

Not that I was going to be friends with him. I still remembered him chopping up ants in science class. But being seniors made anything possible. It wasn't as important who your friends were anymore. There were no rules. You could hang out with anyone.

For that reason, when Bennett stopped me in the parking lot one day and asked if we could talk, I did something I never would have done as a junior: I said yes.

We walked to his car. One of the other reasons Bennett had become so popular was because he didn't make stupid mistakes socially. For instance, with me, he never assumed we were friends. Even when we saw each other at Agenda over the summer, he never tried to talk to me. He stayed within his limits. Maybe it was a drug-dealer thing. He never came to you. You had to go to him.

He unlocked the BMW and we got inside. Unlike Claude's BMW, Bennett's car was old and not in the best shape. The passenger seat had a rip in it. And the interior had the lingering aroma of pot smoke.

"I only have a few minutes," I said to him, as I spotted some old french fries that had fallen down between the seat and the door.

We both shut our doors. Bennett settled his tall frame in his seat. For a moment we just sat there.

"So what did you want to talk about?" I asked.

Bennett didn't move. His hands rested in his lap. "Hanna," he said finally.

"*Hanna*?" I said, almost laughing at the thought of it.

Bennett was not affected by my reaction. He reached into his coat and brought out a small pipe. From somewhere else came some weed. He filled the bowl and offered it to me. I declined.

He held the pipe in his lap. "I'm in love with her," he said.

"Yeah?" I said, grinning at the absurdity of this. "And when did this happen?"

"Over the summer. The last month or so."

"You saw Hanna over the summer?"

"She wanted some weed. She called me."

I watched Bennett more closely. He wasn't kidding.

"She came over. Got what she needed. We hung out." He looked down at the pipe. "We kinda hooked up."

"What do you mean, *kinda*?" I asked.

"We hooked up."

"Like *hooked up*, hooked up?" I asked.

Bennett nodded.

"Like you guys had sex?" I said, to further clarify.

Bennett didn't say anything. He was still holding the pipe and a lighter in his lap, staring out the front of his BMW like a sea captain facing a great storm.

"Wait," I said, to make absolutely sure I was understanding this. "So you. Had sex. With Hanna Sloan?"

"Yeah."

"Wow," I said.

"The thing is, I love her," he said. "But I don't know how to deal with a person like that."

"Have you told her you love her?"

"No," he said.

"Good," I said. "Don't."

"I didn't think I better."

"So you and Hanna," I said, because I still wasn't absolutely 100 percent sure I had it straight. "You guys had sex. Together. Like in a bed."

Bennett stared out his window. "It was incredible. Like nothing I've ever—"

"Okay, okay," I said. I didn't want to hear the details. "So what do you want from me?"

"Could she actually like me?" asked Bennett, turning in my direction. "Could I be with her? I mean, I feel like I could. But I don't know. She's so tricky."

"Oh yeah, she's tricky," I agreed.

"The way she talks. You can't tell if she's serious or not. Sometimes I think the whole thing's a joke. And the joke's on me."

"It might be a joke," I said. "And it might be on you."

"I can take it. I mean, who cares, right? She's worth it."

"Yes. She is."

"But if there's something real there, how do I tell?"

"I don't know how you tell."

"But you know those people," said Bennett. "They're your friends."

"They are my friends. But that doesn't mean I can read Hanna."

For a long moment we both stared out the windshield of the BMW like two sea captains.

"I really like her," said Bennett. "I think about her all the time. She has this hold on me. . . ."

"I know."

I began to feel a need to not be sitting there anymore. I looked at my watch. "I gotta go," I said. "I'm sorry. I wish I could help you more." I reached for the door handle. But before I pulled it, I turned back toward Bennett. "Can I ask *you* something?"

"What's that?"

"How did you get with Antoinette?"

He shrugged. "I sold her weed."

"And then what?"

"And then we hooked up."

"But like . . . ," I started. But I probably didn't want to hear the rest of the story. And he didn't seem eager to tell it. I pulled the door latch and got out.

"Good luck with Hanna," I said. And to myself I thought: *You're gonna need it.*

Henry Oswald arranged for me to meet his brother, William, who'd gone to Cal Arts twenty years before. William Oswald lived in Tacoma, outside Seattle, so I had to drive up there. I spent the night before the trip with Richie at Passport Photos. He'd changed his attitude about art school now that he'd had some success. He thought it would be fun for me, and helpful for my career. "You'll make contacts. You'll know the right people," he said. "And you'll learn to speak all that mumbo jumbo. You'll be able to explain your *artistic vision*."

To meet William Oswald, I went for a relatively normal look: a new shirt, my cleanest jeans, and Nikes. I even got a haircut the day before. I drove to Tacoma on Saturday. I had a dozen of my best prints in a leather portfolio Richie had lent me.

William Oswald's house was on a wooded hill, next to a small creek. I'd been to Henry Oswald's house many times over the years, for Christmas and birthday parties. They were our closest family friends. William Oswald's house wasn't half as big as Henry's. It didn't have a pool. The driveway was gravel. He didn't have a Mercedes. He had a Nissan Pathfinder.

Inside though, things got a lot more interesting. For starters, it was totally open space. The main room had a ceiling that went all the way up to the roof. There were big windows and expensive lighting and huge posters high up on the walls, some from movies, some from commercials. One poster had a giant eye, with something about Swedish TV written underneath it.

William offered me something to drink. I could see the resemblance between the two brothers. William had that same intelligence in his face. But he looked more childlike and more fun. His hair was mostly gray. His glasses had a little chain around them and rested on his chest. It was hard to imagine him naked, on peyote, running among the cacti at Cal Arts.

His wife might have been older than him. She had long silver hair and beautiful dark eyes. She was very warm and welcoming. She seemed smart and was probably very good at whatever she did in her own career. I had the random thought: *That's what Antoinette will look like when she gets old.*

I had come for dinner, so that's what we did; we ate dinner. At first it felt pretty awkward. I didn't know what to say or how to be. I'd never met a real artist before. They got me to tell the story of Elliot Square, which they seemed to enjoy. I showed them the scar on the side of my nose, which was still pretty noticeable, though everyone told me it would go away.

After dinner I got out the prints. William brought them

into his office, which had special lights and drafting tables and every kind of tool or gadget you could imagine. Along the walls, books and files were stored on shelves that went up ten feet. I noticed an old paint-splattered boombox sitting on the windowsill. I wondered if that was from his days at Cal Arts. It probably was.

William placed my prints on a worktable and turned the light on them. He studied them closely. I stood beside him. He looked for several minutes, pointing out a few things, telling me aspects of the printing process I didn't know. Then he turned off the light. He said they showed promise. But he didn't gush over them like Richie did. William Oswald was a pro in a different way. Richie was about attitude and excitement. William Oswald was more about details and getting things exactly right.

We talked a little about what I wanted to do, photojournalism or fine-art photography. I told him I didn't know. He showed me a book by a contemporary photographer I didn't know. These were very ordinary-looking photographs of suburban streets or department stores or people walking in an airport with their rolling suitcases. They weren't like Robert Frank. They didn't capture the sadness of an old man or the bored life of a waitress. They didn't seem to capture anything. They were blank and sort of empty in a way.

"I don't understand these," I told William Oswald, flipping through the book. For a second I wondered if I'd blown it by being too honest.

"Well, of course you don't," he said, smiling. "You haven't been to art school!"

On the drive home I called Kai. We still hadn't had a real conversation since school started, but now that seemed ridiculous. She must have been thinking the same thing because she picked up after one ring.

"Guess who I just had dinner with?" I said.

"Who?"

"The guy who's going to recommend me to Cal Arts."

"Oh my God! What was he like?"

"He was a serious dude," I said. It was a relief to be talking to her again.

"Well, you gotta be serious to make a living as an artist, don't you?"

"Yeah. I guess so. He was so pro. His office, it was like, the best stuff, the best of everything."

"What did he say about Cal Arts?"

"He seemed to think I would like it there. I guess he did."

"Did he like your photographs?"

"He didn't really say."

"Wow, how scary!"

Kai was also deciding which colleges to apply to that fall. She had confessed over the summer her secret life of being a good student. She had a 3.5 grade-point average. And good test scores. Also, she had been sending her writing to different websites over the summer. One place wanted her to write a weekly column about being a senior in high school.

"What about you?" I asked. "Are you writing that column?"

"No. They wanted it to be about the party scene," she told me. "Since they thought I was such a wild girl."

"And you didn't want to do it?"

"No. It was too weird. These thirty-year-old dudes wanting me to write about high school make-out parties? And anyway, no college wants to see that. They wanna hear about volunteering at the senior center or digging up arti-facts in Mexico."

"Yeah, you kinda have to play the game," I said. This was a strange sentence to hear coming out of my mouth.

"I know," said Kai. "It's lame, but it's true. You have to tell them what they want to hear."

After my conversation with Bennett, I felt a new urgency about my situation with Antoinette. If guys like Bennett were getting with girls like Hanna, it was time for me to do something about Antoinette. *I deserve to know where things stand*, I told myself.

She was, as usual, elusive at school. So I texted her, asking if we could talk. She didn't reply. So I called her. Her phone was turned off. So I drove over to her house. I knocked on the front door. Her mother answered.

I said hi and did the polite-friend routine. I asked if Antoinette was there. Her mother said yes and called up the stairs. We both waited. A minute later, Antoinette appeared in sweatpants and a hoodie.

"Hey," she said. She seemed surprised to see me. "What's up?"

"Can I talk to you?" I said.

She seemed a little worried by this request. But she walked outside with me and shut the door. It was a warm night, still September, so we walked across her front yard to the street and sat on the curb.

"So what's going on?" I said, I still hadn't quite caught my breath.

"Nothing," she said. "What's going on with you?"

"I called you, but you never called me back."

"I know. I keep forgetting to charge my phone. Sorry."

So she had an excuse for that. But now what was I supposed to say? I had promised myself I wouldn't bring up Berlin. But what else was there to talk about?

"It seems like I've barely seen you since school started," I said.

"I've been really busy."

"It's almost like you're avoiding me."

"I'm not avoiding you."

We sat there. Crickets chirped in the grass around us.

"How was the rest of your time in Germany?" I asked.

"Fine. I was only there another day or two. And then my dad got mad, because he thought I was leaving the next week, and so then he was complaining that he barely got to see me."

I nodded. She was staring at the house across the street with a faraway look. That wasn't good.

It occurred to me there wasn't any good way to do this. And anyway, it wasn't going to matter what strategy I used. So I said the exact line I had vowed not to say. "Are we going to continue what we started in Berlin?"

She exhaled softly. She looked down at her shoes. "I thought that was more of a friends thing," she said quietly.

I swallowed. I took a long breath. I gathered myself and then said with a steady voice: "Could we at least try?"

"Try what?"

"Being together."

"We have tried," she said.

"When have we tried?"

"This whole time we've been trying," she said.

"This whole time? Like starting when?"

"Starting when you came here the night my brother died." She pointed across the street at the spot I had stood with my bike.

This was a blow. "I didn't know that," I said, my voice faltering again. "You should have told me that. If I'd known we were trying, I would have tried harder!"

Antoinette sighed. "Gavin. C'mon. I like you so much."

"No. Please. Don't start with the 'friends' thing."

Antoinette let a few seconds pass. "I'm sorry," she said. "I didn't mean to mislead you. I thought since we were in Berlin . . . and it was so fun to see each other. . . . It was like a perfect moment."

"And that's all it was?" I said. "Just that one moment?"

"That's what summer is for. To do things you might not normally do."

That was it. The answer to all my questions. I looked down at my feet.

Antoinette didn't say anything for a long time. I kept my face down. Tears came into my eyes, which I tried to wipe away without her seeing.

Antoinette handled the situation perfectly. She said

nothing. She let more time pass. She let me sink down into the depths of despair. And then waited for me to float back up.

Eventually I did. I lifted my head. I stared across the street.

"Kai said you guys hung out a lot," she said.

"Yeah, we did."

"And you read some of her writing?"

"Yeah."

"What did you think?"

"About her writing? I dunno. It was good, I guess."

Antoinette smiled at that. Eventually we talked about other stuff. The conversation petered out.

Back in my car I cried a little more. None of this was a surprise. Never once had I believed, in my realistic mind, that Antoinette and I could be together. It was just a dream that followed me around, like a ghost, the ghost of Antoinette loving me, or rather, the ghost of Antoinette letting me love her.

47

I hadn't taken my photo editor job very seriously, but when our first issue came out and the photographs were terrible, I started to pay closer attention. I began stopping in at the *Owl* office after last period, partly for quality control and partly because I didn't have anything better to do.

One day, after school, I was there with Emma Van Buskirk. We were putting the final touches on the next issue. We didn't really know each other, but that night we talked for hours. We talked about the magazine, college, what kind of jobs we hoped to have someday. Eventually the janitor came and kicked us out. So then we went across the street to Wendy's.

At Wendy's we talked about less lofty things.

"You know what I heard?" Emma said, munching on her Wendy's Caesar salad. "I heard Bennett and Hanna had a thing over the summer."

"Oh yeah?" I said, playing dumb.

"You know those people. Is it true?"

"It could be." I shrugged. "They seem pretty different though. On a social level."

"Really?" said Emma. "I think they're perfect. She's a coke whore. And he's got the coke."

I looked at Emma. "Hanna's not a coke whore," I said.

She scoffed. "That's not what I heard."

"Who did you hear it from?"

"Are you kidding?" she said. "Everyone. She's always done coke. Her and Claude used to do it every day in the parking lot."

This wasn't even remotely true. But I wasn't going to argue with Emma Van Buskirk. One thing about a big public high school, the people who weren't popular, who'd never gone to a real party, who'd never had a girl or boyfriend: They had some pretty weird ideas about the people who did.

In October, my mother came to my room one night and asked if we could talk. I was like *uh-oh*. She sat on my bed in this certain way, like she had a big announcement. I thought: *We're going to have to move*. That seemed inevitable. The two of us in that huge house, it didn't make sense. But that wasn't it. It was my father's new girlfriend. She was pregnant. I was going to have a baby sister, or a half sister, or a stepsister, or whatever the proper terminology was.

Alexis Colby was the name of my father's girlfriend. I found this out two weeks later when I met the two of them at one of my father's downtown restaurants. That was where my dad lived now, in one of the brand-new high-rise apartment buildings in the center of downtown.

"It's very convenient," he was saying, while we waited

for Alexis. "I can walk to the courthouse from my front door. It takes five minutes. And if it's raining, the streetcar is right there."

I nodded and studied my menu. It was hard to stay focused. Alexis Colby was *twenty-eight*. I hadn't heard this detail before. My dad was fifty-one.

"The parking is not the best," my father continued. "The spaces are quite small. Mine is marked compact, and though the Mercedes Coupe might technically be considered a compact . . ." He was babbling. He was nervous too, more nervous than I was. Which I found alarming. I wanted the waiter to come talk to us.

Alexis finally appeared. She had light brown hair, a pretty face. She was slim, athletic looking. Her pregnancy was not visible, not that I could see. She was dressed up, with makeup and lipstick—not slutty, just like you would be if you worked in a lawyer's office.

My father stood up when she arrived. I had never seen him stand up for my mother. The situation was so strange, so surreal, I did nothing. I sat there. I watched my father kiss her cheek. He held her wrist for a moment. He was in love with her, I could see. Which was *so weird*.

Alexis took her seat. I averted my eyes. My father continued to smile and gush. When I dared to look up, Alexis smiled at me. It was a complicated smile. Shy, but also a little bit superior, I thought.

Alexis had attended the University of Arizona. That's where she was from: Scottsdale, Arizona. It was very hot there. There were scorpions in her backyard, growing up. Once she graduated from college, she had trained briefly in homeopathic medicine. Then she was going to be a lifestyle counselor. Eventually she began working in her uncle's law offices part-time. She liked the law. That's how she ended up in my dad's office. Now, though, she wasn't so worried about work. She was thinking more about the pregnancy. She was overwhelmed by it. She was not like some of her friends, who had planned their entire lives around motherhood. She wasn't sure she was ready for it. But she would manage. She was thinking of it as a journey, as one of life's great adventures. When she said that, she reached over and held my father's hand, which made me almost spit out the food in my mouth.

A couple nights later, I was in my room when I got a call from Claude. "Is this for real?" he blurted. "Hanna was with Bennett Schmidt? Is this a joke?"

I was surprised it had taken him so long to hear about it.

"How did I not know about this?" he said.

It made sense. Petra wasn't going to tell him. And none of his friends were going to tell him. I hadn't told him.

"And who does this dick-weed think he is? He's a frickin' dope dealer!"

"Yeah," I said. "It's weird how he's risen up."

"*What*?" said Claude. "Are you friends with him now too?"

"No. No. But I've noticed how he's changed."

"People are like, 'Oh, Bennett's cool now,'" sputtered Claude. "How do they figure that? And that stupid piece-of-shit car he drives!?"

"Yeah, it's pretty weird."

"I'm gonna kill that freak!"

"What for?" I said.

"For fucking with Hanna! For making her look bad. This is bad for a million reasons. Why would she even do that?"

"Girls think he's cute. He's got the bad-boy thing."

"He's a fucking fence post! Bennett Schmidt? Has everyone gone insane? What girl wants to be associated with a guy like that?"

"Yeah, well . . . ," I said.

"This is Hanna we're talking about," said Claude. "This isn't some parking-lot chick. This is Hanna Sloan! And Bennett Schmidt thinks he can put his hands on her!?"

And where was Hanna during this period when she was being attacked and slagged and insulted?

She was at school. She came every morning and left every afternoon. I sometimes saw her after third period when our paths crossed outside history class. I would smile. She would smile back. But something was definitely up. I mean, physically she still looked okay. Any objective person would consider her an extremely attractive high school senior. But there was a *worn* quality to her face. She looked tired. And unfocused. And she just seemed *off* somehow. Nobody said anything. It was possible nobody noticed. But I noticed.

One night I was driving home from the *Owl* office after dark, and I saw this girl or woman walking along Harper's Ferry Road, pretty far away from school. I watched this person as I came up behind her. It looked like Hanna, about the same height, the same length hair. But it couldn't be her. For one thing, Harper's Ferry was not a road anyone would choose to walk on. There were no streetlights and the shoulder was loose gravel sloping down to a mud ditch. After I passed, I looked in my rearview mirror to see the person's face. But I couldn't see it. I decided it couldn't be Hanna. She wouldn't be walking alone like that. At night. On the side of the road.

I told Kai and Antoinette about this incident the next day. We were driving downtown in Kai's Subaru.

"That sounds like a ghost story someone would tell around a campfire," said Antoinette.

"The ghost of the mean girl walking along the road at night!" said Kai.

"She's hitchhiking," said Antoinette. "And when you pick her up, she criticizes your clothes and your friends."

"Ha-ha." Kai laughed. "And then when you tell the old guy at the gas station, he's like, sometimes when the wind blows just right you can hear a voice saying, *Ah ma gawd, you guys!*"

"Very funny," I said, frowning at the two of them.

"Oh, come on," said Kai. "What do you care what happens to Hanna Sloan? Do you think she cares what happens to you?"

I didn't answer.

"No," said Antoinette. "She doesn't care at all. Look what she did to you last summer."

"That wasn't personal. She wasn't doing that to me."

"Oh my God, look how you defend her!" said Kai. "The woman who used you to get revenge on her boyfriend!"

"She didn't *use* me," I insisted.

"Well, what did she do, then?" said Kai.

"You are in serious denial about certain things," said Antoinette.

"Hey," I said. "You don't think I know her? Trust me, I know her. If anyone knows her, it's me."

"Well," admitted Kai. "*That* might be true. Unfortunately for you."

Senior year continued. There were lots of parties. Even people who never had parties had parties. I went to an *Owl* party one Friday night with Emma Van Buskirk. It was magazine and yearbook people mostly. I had grown to like this crowd. And they liked me. I was a bit of a celebrity, having been beaten up by the Seattle police in the line of journalistic duty.

Grace was there too. She was one of the main people on yearbook. I hadn't seen her at all over the summer. I went over to her.

"Hey," I said.

"Hey," she said back. She smiled. She drank some of her beer.

"So how's things?" I said. "How's Austin?"

"He's great. He's coming down tomorrow."

"Down from where?"

"University of Puget Sound."

"So you guys are still together?"

She grinned that they were.

"Cool," I said.

"It's been really hard," she explained. "Being apart. I'm

going to apply there for next year. I'll have to live in a dorm, though. But then after that we can live together off campus."

"How's he like it up there?"

"Well, he's not playing football. Which is hard for him. He's played football every fall since he was twelve. He's afraid he's getting fat. But he's not."

"You've been up there?"

"Twice. And I wanted to go up this weekend but I couldn't."

"Wow, so you guys are really . . ."

"We are," she said.

"I hope you're still going to enjoy being a senior."

"I could care less about that. So we're seniors? So what?"

"But what about your friends?"

"What friends? I hardly talk to Hanna anymore. And Petra and those guys. Yuck."

"I was going to ask you . . ."

"About Hanna? She's going out with Bennett Schmidt now. Can you believe that?"

"I know. It's so weird."

"She used to make such fun of him."

"What's going on with her?" I asked. "Is she okay?"

"Who knows? I guess so. I kinda have other things to think about. I'm going to apply to Puget Sound early acceptance. I shouldn't have any problem getting in. That's what Mrs. Fogarty said. . . ."

I nodded my encouragement. But I was worried a little.

Grace seemed to have everything figured out. I hoped she knew what she was doing.

In November, when it got cold, my mother turned off the heat in certain parts of the house, since it was just the two of us. But this made the house seem drafty and never quite warm. And then you'd forget and go in one of the unheated rooms and it would be freezing all of a sudden, as if someone had died.

I spent most of my time upstairs, on my computer, working on my college essay or looking at photos. In bed I would lie awake while the rain pattered on my window. I'd think about my mother, about Alexis Colby, about my future half sibling. Would I actually know her as she grew up? Would I be expected to be an older brother in some way? Talk about "older brother." I'd be eighteen years older than her.

The main thing was: I hoped to God I got into Cal Arts. Or any other art school that would take me. I had to get out of that house.

And then one night I got another late-night call from Claude. I was in my room. This time his voice was less angry, more scared.

"Hey," he said. "We got a serious problem." He was in his car. I could hear him shifting the BMW in the background.

I pushed my chair back from my desk. "What is it?"

"It's Hanna."

"Okay," I said, my chest tightening.

"Can you be outside your house in about thirty seconds?"

"Yes."

"Meet me outside. Dress warm."

I grabbed my parka and a ski hat. My mother was upstairs somewhere. She wouldn't notice I was gone.

I opened the front door and walked down the driveway in the rain. Claude's BMW came tearing around the corner and stopped abruptly at the curb.

I got in.

Hanna was missing. Claude told me what he knew: She had written a strange note and left it on her parents' kitchen island after school. Then she left and hadn't come back. At ten thirty p.m., her car had been found in the parking lot at Silver Falls State Park, thirty-five miles south of Portland, near Silverton. Her car door was open and the lights were still on. Someone had seen it and called the cops. The cops had checked the registration and called the Sloans. The police thought the note might be a suicide note. And they couldn't find Hanna. They assumed she was somewhere on the two-mile hiking trail that went from the parking lot to Silver Falls. They hoped she was.

I told Claude that I thought I'd seen her walking along

Harper's Ferry at night. He didn't think it could be her. Why would she have been walking on Harper's Ferry?

"That's what I thought," I said.

Claude was passing everyone on the freeway as we drove toward Silver Falls. He sped along the wet county roads and pulled into the state park, almost hitting a police car that was pulling out.

He steered deeper into the parking lot. There were three police cars bunched at the trailhead, one with its red and blue lights flashing. There was another car as well: the Sloan family's Chevy Tahoe. Mrs. Sloan was sitting inside, with the light on, talking urgently on her phone. Hanna's little sister was in the backseat, holding the family dog, a blank, frightened look on her face. The thought came to me: *If I only had my camera.*

Claude shut off the car and jumped out. That's when he saw Hanna's car, parked to one side. It hadn't been touched. The driver's door was open. The headlights were still on. You could see the rain falling in the beams. The car was cordoned off by yellow police tape, as if someone had been murdered in it. I could see the shock on Claude's face at the sight of it. I felt my own heart skip a beat.

Claude hurried toward the Sloans but was intercepted by a cop and a park ranger. I was right behind Claude. More cops gathered around us.

"Who are you?" said the main cop.

"I'm Claude. I'm a friend. I went out with Hanna . . . ," he stammered. He was looking over at the Sloans. "Mr. Sloan!" he yelled out.

Mr. Sloan looked up but continued his interview with the other cop.

The big main cop put his hand on Claude's shoulder. "We need you to calm down, Claude. We might need your help."

Claude was about as agitated and flustered as I'd ever seen him. He kept glancing back at Hanna's car.

"Claude," said the main cop. "Look at me. Look at me."

Claude got a grip on himself. "Have you been here before? Have you been to Silver Falls?"

"Yes, yes I have."

"Have you been here with Hanna?"

"Yes," said Claude. He was calming down. He took a deep breath.

"What did you do here? Where did you go?"

"We walked up the trail. To the falls. We came here a couple times. In the summer."

"We've got some men on the trail. They're not seeing anything. Did you and Hanna ever go off the trail? Are there any other places she might be?"

"No. We just walked to the falls. That's all. And waded in the pool. In the summer."

"Did she ever talk about this place at other times? Was it a special place for her for some reason?"

"No. It was just a hangout. We'd come with other people. It wasn't a big thing."

"Is there anything else you know or can tell us about this situation? Is she experienced in the outdoors? Does she camp?"

"No," said Claude. "She's not like that. This is weird. I don't know why she'd come here. It's raining. It's cold. It's not like her. None of this is like her."

"How about you?" said the cop. He shined the light on me for a moment. "What do you know about Hanna?"

I didn't know what to say. I couldn't think. "She used to be popular," I blurted. "But then something happened."

Behind us a large police van rumbled into the parking lot. It had the words K9 UNIT printed on the side. Several men got out, with big boots and heavy coats. The words SEARCH AND RESCUE were printed across their backs in big letters. They opened the back of the van and out poured the dogs.

The Sloans gave the policemen Hanna's ski jacket for the dogs to smell. They immediately began to bark and yowl and sniff at everything.

"Jesus Christ," murmured Claude, blinking in the darkness. *"Search dogs."*

Claude went over to the Sloans. Mrs. Sloan gave him a hug. She was crying. Mr. Sloan, who was tall and formidable, stood with the policeman, watching the dog team disappear up the trail. Hanna's little sister got out and stood in the rain, in the dark, wiping the tears off her face.

Again the thought came: *my camera*. It was a terrible thing to think at that moment. But there it was.

"Can we go up the trail?" Claude asked the main cop.

"It would be better if you didn't," he said. "We'll let the dogs go first. If we don't find her that way, we'll call in the troops and search the park."

Claude and the Sloans nodded their understanding.

"Maybe you folks want to get in your car," said the policeman. "To avoid getting too wet."

The Sloans turned back toward their SUV. Claude still wanted to do something. He wanted to help. The policemen continued to talk on their radios. More units were coming. An ambulance from Silverton County Hospital was on its way.

And that's when Bennett's gangster BMW pulled into the parking lot.

"What is he doing here?" said Claude, when he realized who it was. He began striding toward Bennett's car. Then he started to run.

I ran after him. The cops came too. Bennett's long, lean body stepped out of the car. Claude tried to hit him. It was a half punch, half shove. Bennett staggered backward. But he had four inches on Claude and was able to straighten up and fend him off. I grabbed Claude from behind. Two of the cops helped me pull him back. The main cop approached Bennett. "Who are you?"

"I'm . . . Bennett."

"He's a drug dealer!" said Claude. "He is. Search his car!"

The cops looked at each other. The main cop said, "Let's focus on finding the girl."

Bennett looked scared. Everyone could see the fear in his face.

"Do you know Hanna?" asked the head cop.

"Yeah . . . ," said Bennett carefully.

"What is your relation to her?"

He looked around at the different people surrounding him. "I'm her boyfriend."

The main cop turned to Claude. "I thought *you* were her boyfriend?"

"Fuck him!" snarled Claude.

"He used to be," said Bennett, swallowing as he said it. "Now I am."

Mr. Sloan appeared, with Mrs. Sloan right behind him. Mrs. Sloan walked right through the cops and stood in front Bennett. She didn't like him, you could tell, but Bennett was now her best hope for finding Hanna. She pulled a piece of paper out of her coat pocket. "Bennett," she said, controlling her voice. "Do you know anything about this note?"

Bennett took it from her. One of the cops shone his light on it. Bennett read it with the raindrops falling around him. He squinted and struggled to make out parts of it. Then he handed it back. "I don't know what that means," he said.

The main cop moved in again. "Do you know anything about these falls? Have you ever been here with Hanna?"

"Yes," he said.

Everyone went quiet. The main cop said, "Was there any special places here she liked to go? Anywhere other than the trail or the falls she might be?"

Bennett hesitated for a second.

"Son, we need your help here," said the cop.

Bennett spoke: "There's a place above the falls. Maybe a quarter mile. Along the stream. There's an old shelter up there."

The cops looked at each other again. One of the local

282

Silverton cops spoke up and said, "It's quite a ways up there. It's an old shack. The local kids hang out there sometimes."

"I took her there once," said Bennett. "She liked it. She liked that nobody else went up there."

I heard Mr. Sloan make a guttural noise.

Bennett continued, struggling with the words. "She said . . . that it was a good place to go . . . if you'd had enough of things."

Mrs. Sloan turned to her husband and buried her face in his chest.

The main cop stepped away from the group of us and radioed the men with the dogs.

"Apparently there's a small shack," he said loudly. "If you go up the creek past the falls. A quarter mile. She might be there."

"Okay," said the heavy-breathing voice on the other end. "We'll check it out."

Everyone went back to their cars. I sat with Claude in his BMW. Bennett Schmidt sat alone in his gangster BMW. The Sloans returned to their SUV with their family dog. The cops remained in their police cars with their computers and their radios and their shotguns.

It took about forty-five minutes for the dog team to radio back. Everyone immediately ran to the main police car and gathered around. The cop rolled down his window so we could hear. "We got her," said the crackling voice from deep inside the dark forest. "She's cold . . . she's wet . . . but she's alive."

Bennett immediately separated from the rest of us. He went and stood by his own car. I thought he was going to leave, but he didn't.

Then Mrs. Sloan walked over to him. She hugged him. Bennett started to cry. And then he said something to Mrs. Sloan. I didn't hear all of it. But I heard him say, "I don't know what happened to her. I swear, I don't . . ."

Hanna was taken by ambulance to the Silverton County Hospital where she was treated for hypothermia. The next day they moved her to a bigger hospital in Portland, where she was placed in a psychiatric ward for observation.

The rest of us went back to school. Claude alternated between stomping around angrily and sitting silently, staring into space. Petra stayed far away. Bennett I saw only once, his tall head visible over the other kids in the hallway, that scarlet flush in his cheeks as bright as ever.

I found my way to Antoinette's locker at one point, and when she wasn't there, I found Kai. She wasn't terribly sympathetic. But she ate lunch with me, and when Logan and Olivia Goldstein sat with us, she didn't get up and leave.

People quietly spread the news around throughout the day: Hanna's suicide attempt, or whatever it was, and the strange note that Mrs. Sloan had not let anyone read except for Bennett.

In general the feeling was: *Hanna deserves whatever she gets*. That's what it seemed like to me. I was shocked by how little people cared. I had thought they appreciated Hanna in a way. She was so funny and such a prominent figure at our school. She had entertained us all these years. But maybe not. Emma Van Buskirk said not one word about it in the *Owl* office. If anything, she seemed to be more cheerful and upbeat than usual.

For the next couple days Mrs. Sloan and Claude were on the phone a lot. It was like Mrs. Sloan had decided that Claude was Hanna's boyfriend again, and not Bennett. She checked in with Claude daily and eventually arranged for him to visit Hanna in the psych ward. Claude wanted me to go with him, to lend moral support.

We pulled into the big hospital parking garage and walked across the skyway with the other hospital people, some of whom were injured or sick or old. *My camera*, I thought, when I saw a wrinkled little man with a walker, shuffling step by tiny step into the elevator.

We asked at the main desk and eventually found the psych ward. It had a thick metal door and a small hard-plastic window. Claude said nothing. But the prison-style entrance made an impression on him. It made an impression on me.

We went in. They made us fill out release forms that said we wouldn't sue the hospital if someone killed us or caused us bodily harm, which creeped us out even more.

I looked around as we waited. It smelled funny in there. Like piss and chemicals. Hanna had been there three days already. How much observation were they going to do?

• • •

We were led into a lounge, a large open room with couches and chairs along the walls. Hanna was already there, sitting on one of the chairs, flipping through a magazine. She wore her own pajamas underneath a hospital robe that didn't look very comfortable. Her long brown hair was clean but mussed and frizzy, like maybe they didn't let her have her normal hair products.

When she saw us she stood up and hugged Claude, then me. I felt tears come into my eyes when I felt her warmness press against me. What a terrible spot she was in.

Claude cleared his throat. He had brought her a copy of *Us Weekly* and some other magazines, as Mrs. Sloan had advised. You couldn't have a phone in there, I guess. Claude gave her the magazines.

We pulled up some chairs. "So," said Claude. "How's it going?"

Hanna shrugged. She had a weird smile on her face. "It's like this, pretty much," she said, indicating the large room. There were a few other people there. They too were wearing bathrobes. It looked like people sitting in a dentist's waiting room. Except that you couldn't leave. And everyone had to wear crappy bathrobes and slippers.

I looked at Hanna's feet. She had the same hospital slippers. They were paper and cardboard basically. I wondered if we could get her better slippers, if her parents could. But if they could, they would have. You probably had to wear what they gave you.

I sat back slightly in my chair, trying to let Claude and Hanna have a moment, if that was possible. In one corner of the room, a woman about my mother's age—with a big diamond ring on her finger—was sitting with her legs crossed. She was watching us. When she saw me watching her, she looked away.

Hanna was eighteen, I remembered. Was that why she was in here with the adults?

"Where do you sleep?" Claude asked Hanna.

"I have a little room," she said.

"What do you do all day?" asked Claude, his voice straining.

Hanna shrugged. "Go see doctors. Take my meds. They let us watch TV, but people argue about which shows to watch."

Claude nodded, trying to be encouraging. But this was not a good situation for him. I felt like I should be talking. I would be more diplomatic. But maybe it didn't matter.

"We'll get you out of here," said Claude suddenly. "This is ridiculous. You don't belong in here. This is bullshit."

Hanna looked at him. The woman in the corner also looked at him.

"What did you write in that note?" asked Claude.

"I don't know," she said. "Everyone asks me that. It wasn't a suicide note. I don't think it was. I don't even remember what I wrote."

"And why did you go to Silver Falls?"

Hanna pursed her lips to one side, like a little girl. It was a new gesture for her; I had never seen it before. Hanna was, in general, a significantly different person, I was noticing. How had that happened? How had she changed so much, so fast?

Claude was seeing it too. He was really having trouble with this. His knee bounced in place. He wanted to do something. He wanted to yell at someone. He sat back in his chair.

Hanna looked at me. I tried to smile in a hopeful way. "How are you doing, Gavin?" she asked me.

"Fine," I said.

"I don't get this," snapped Claude. "What are these people doing?" He waved his hand toward the nurse's station in the hall. "You have school. You have stuff to do. You can't sit in here. What's the point of this?"

Hanna also looked back toward the nurse's station. Then she leaned forward and said in a quiet voice: "Can I give you guys some advice?"

We scooted closer.

"Whatever you do," whispered Hanna, "don't end up in here. I'm serious. This is not a good place. The things that happen. The things you hear at night . . ."

Afterward, we walked back over the skyway. Claude couldn't talk. He was so angry and upset, I thought he might punch someone. In the BMW, he pressed his forehead against the steering wheel and cried. I actually saw the tears dropping into his lap.

Ten minutes later he lifted his head again. "Sorry about that," he said, wiping his face with his wrist.

"No problem," I said back.

Claude took a long, deep breath. He checked himself once in the mirror. Then he started the car, revved the engine hard, and got us out of there.

It wasn't until I got home later that I felt the shock of the Hanna visit in my own body. I had been too busy worrying about Claude, and Hanna, and even Bennett, to think about myself or to *feel* anything myself. But once I was home, in my house, in my own shower, with the hot water beating on my back, it finally sank in what was happening. Hanna was in serious trouble. We were *all* in trouble, in a way. We were about to graduate from high school. We were all going to be thrown out into the real world, where God knows what would happen to us. The days of Claude and me being best friends, the days of our gang, our popular friends, being the untouchable, superior people, all that stuff was over. Real life had caught up with us. There was no protection anymore. Not for any of us. If Hanna could go down, anyone could.

I was curious what Antoinette would make of all this. The next day I grabbed her after school and we drove to Burrito Express. "It was so weird," I said, describing the psych ward. "We got there, and she was acting pretty normal, and I was like, okay, this isn't too bad. But then I started to see this change. At first I thought it was an act. Like she was pretending."

"Doesn't sound like an act," said Antoinette.

"No," I said. "That's what I realized. Definitely not an act."

"Have her doctors said anything?"

I shook my head. "Not that I know of."

"There's stuff that happens to people our age," said Antoinette. "Different things. Mental illness."

"Is that what happened to your brother?" I asked Antoinette.

She shrugged. "Possibly."

"You ever talk to Bennett?" I asked her.

She shook her head no.

"He seemed pretty shook up about it."

"I'm sure," said Antoinette. "He adores her."

We sat there in silence. "I wish I'd taken pictures of her," I said, almost to myself.

"What for?"

"Just to have. Just to remember what she looked like."

"Does she really look that different?" said Antoinette.

"She kinda does," I said, nodding slowly. "She's kind of a whole different person."

Claude and Petra broke up not long after that. This was a short week, before Thanksgiving. I think Petra couldn't handle that Claude was so worried about Hanna. Poor Claude and his girlfriends, he was always caught in some bind.

And speaking of binds: My own Thanksgiving got very

complicated very fast. My father wanted me to come to his new apartment downtown and have dinner with Alexis and her brother from Arizona. I was like, *Thanks but no thanks*. My mother had said we could go to the Oswalds for Thanksgiving, which is what I wanted to do. But at the last minute she decided to have Thanksgiving in San Francisco, with her sister, who had a man-friend she wanted my mom to meet. That was awkward. And then my mom said, "You should have Thanksgiving with your dad. You need to be nice to him. He's going to pay for your school. You have to think about that now."

I did think about it. And it made my stomach hurt.

I convinced Kai to come with me to my dad's. We developed a plan where we'd have dinner with her family first and then we'd drive downtown and go to my dad's. It was Kai's idea, actually. It gave us an excuse to not stay anywhere too long.

I showed up at her house about one. They had a full house, with Kai's family and an aunt and some cousins and some grandparents. Her aunt thought I was Kai's boyfriend. When we explained we were just friends, she looked hard at the two of us and said, "I don't think so."

It was okay though. I liked Kai's mom. She was funny and said interesting things. Her dad, the dermatologist, was a jolly guy and smart, too. You could see where Kai got her "secret good student" thing. Everyone in her family was smart.

By the end of the dinner, Kai's dad was looking at me in an odd way. Not bad, but with a little extra attention. He knew about Kai's many escapades and the places she hung out. She was a father's worst nightmare. (She was at that moment wearing a very short skirt, black tights, and pink underwear, which you could see occasionally.) I think I might have been the first boy Kai hung out with who he could have an actual conversation with.

After that we got in Kai's Subaru and headed downtown to my dad's. On the drive, I said something about Hanna, who was never far from my mind. Kai continued to insist she was a terrible person, which seemed kind of mean, considering. At one point I hinted that Kai was jealous. That really pissed her off. She got so mad she pulled the car over.

"Gavin," she said, slamming the transmission into park. "I wasn't going to tell you this before, but I'm going to tell you now."

"What," I said, sulking in my seat.

She took a long breath. "When I was in sixth grade, I wore glasses. Big, stupid, embarrassing glasses that my mom bought me. One day in gym class, Hanna walked up to me, took them off my face, dropped them on the floor, and stepped on them. She said, 'Someday you'll thank me for this,' and everyone laughed. Then she walked away, with all her little friends trailing off behind her."

I sat waiting for the rest.

"And do you know what I did?"

"No."

"I went home and made up some story about how I sat on my glasses. Because I didn't want *Princess Hanna* to not like me because I had told on her. That's right. I protected her. I actually *helped* her humiliate me. Because she was Hanna Sloan. She was the golden girl. You couldn't go against Hanna. Nobody would dare go against Hanna."

I said nothing.

"And you know the worst part? Hanna didn't even *remember* me after that. Freshman year at Evergreen, I had her in one of my classes. She started talking to me one day and I realized she didn't know who I was. She didn't even remember stomping on my glasses!"

"Okay," I grumbled. "So she's horrible sometimes."

"Yes she is," said Kai. "And not just sometimes. If you're capable of doing things like that, there's something wrong with you."

"You've been cruel to people."

"Not like that I haven't. I wouldn't know how to be that cruel. I'm not capable of being that cruel."

"Well, you got your revenge, then," I said. "Now that she's locked up in the psych ward."

"I don't want revenge! Don't you understand!? I don't want to hate her! I don't want to hate anyone! I just want you to stop talking about her! *Gawd!*"

"Okay, okay," I said. "Jesus."

• • •

We didn't talk again for the rest of the drive. We pulled into the underground parking garage and walked up the stairs to the lobby. We stood at the elevator and continued our silence. I pushed the up button a couple extra times. Kai looked at herself in the reflection of the elevator door.

"I'm sorry," I said, finally breaking the silence. "I'm sorry about your glasses."

"It doesn't matter. I'm over it."

We stood there looking at ourselves. You could hear the elevator making faint noises as it made its way down to us.

"Is this skirt too short?" she said, looking at herself.

"It's pretty short."

"Can you see my underwear?"

"Only when you sit down. Or bend over. Or walk."

She pulled down on her skirt. Then she fluffed her hair and combed her bangs to one side with her fingers.

"I'm sorry I constantly talk about Hanna," I said.

"It's all right," she said.

"Seriously. I am."

"She's your friend," said Kai. "I get it. I understand."

"She's not my friend, though," I said as the elevator doors opened. "She's never been my friend. You're my friend. Not her."

We rode the elevator to the eighteenth floor. This was

the first time I'd seen my dad's apartment. It was big and elegant and very high up. You could see over the entire city. You could see down onto the rooftops of other people who could see over the entire city.

Kai was nervous with my dad. But she shook his hand and said all the right things. Alexis was there, with what appeared to be a slight bump in her midsection. Her brother was also there. He was visiting from Arizona, where he trained horses. His story was vague. He was good-looking, though. Like Alexis. He seemed excited about his sister being with my dad despite the bizarre age difference.

The food was very good. It was catered. When we'd finished, we sat at the table and talked. But the conversation never got any rhythm to it. My dad figured out that Kai's dad was a dermatologist and inquired about that, in his weasely way, trying to figure out who he knew socially.

After dessert Kai and I stood together at the big main window, staring down at the city below. "What do you think of Alexis?" I asked Kai.

"She's *a lot* younger than him," said Kai.

"She's not that smart."

"Maybe that doesn't matter," said Kai.

"I don't know," I said. "I have a bad feeling."

"Yeah," agreed Kai.

I stared down at Portland. "Well, it's his life," I said.

"Yeah, but it's your life too," said Kai. "He's your dad. What he does affects you."

"I guess so."

"You guess so?" said Kai. She sipped her drink. "You should know that better than anyone."

SENIOR YEAR (PART TWO)

I have a burning desire to see what things
look like photographed by me.
—*Garry Winogrand*

When I have a camera in my hand, I know no fear.
—*Alfred Eisenstaedt*

I picked up my mother at the airport on Sunday night. She was flushed and excited. The first thing she said was, "Gavin, I want you to know that nothing is going to change until after you go to college."

"Like what would change?" I asked.

She told me she had seen Peter Frohnmeyer in San Francisco. They'd had dinner. This was the advertising guy she'd been engaged to twenty years ago, in San Francisco, before my dad showed up and snatched her away.

"You went on a date?" I said.

"It wasn't a date," she said, checking herself in the visor mirror. She had lipstick on, which was unusual. "We had dinner. We talked."

It began to rain and I turned on the windshield wipers. "Is he still in advertising?"

"No," she said. "He does PR for a solar energy company. He sold his advertising agency for a lot of money."

"Well, that's good," I said.

My mom put the visor back up. "I don't need his money, Gavin."

"I'm not saying you do," I said. "I just meant, you know, good for him."

At home my mother went upstairs to her room and stayed there. Later, I could hear her talking to one of her friends. She was going to be doing that a lot, I suspected. Getting advice, discussing strategy, how best to proceed with the Peter Frohnmeyer situation. How to marry him, basically, if that was what she wanted to do, which it seemed like it was.

Back at school, in December, things had become very different. There was no Hanna. She was still in the hospital. I didn't see much of Claude. Or Petra. Logan was around and Olivia Goldstein. They had broken up but were still friends.

At lunch I often sat with Emma Van Buskirk and the other *Evergreen Owl* people. I sat with Grace occasionally too, and the yearbook people. I had been giving them photographs, which they badly needed. I had become the only reliable photographer at school, it seemed. I even took pictures for the principal and the sports teams sometimes.

I saw Krista and Ashley in the halls occasionally, since they were juniors and in our wing. But they had completely evolved away from my friends. They were still big partiers, but they had become more preppy and jock-oriented. At least Krista had. Maybe "sporty" is the correct word to describe her. She was going out with a sophomore basketball player who was one of the stars of the team. To be honest, it was always a little painful to see Krista. She had bruised my ego in some subtle way, so that every time I saw her I cringed a little. She would be a big success in life, I thought. With her cute smile and her bouncy energy. She would end up on TV, or would invent some new exercise machine, or would marry some rich guy. All of which would maintain her McMansion lifestyle. But as my father had often pointed out, I shouldn't make fun of people like that. I would be lucky to do so well.

In the midst of everything else, I finished my college applications. I sent them to a bunch of different places, but Cal Arts was the application I focused on the most. Before I pushed send on that one, I said a little prayer to the photography gods, to Robert Frank, to Richie and the little girl whose picture I had not taken in Elliot Square.

Once my applications were out, I felt like I should party it up. Kai, too, had applied to a bunch of liberal arts colleges and was feeling restless and bored. So we went out a lot, sometimes with Antoinette, sometimes just us two. There was a big dance party at Agenda right before Christmas, which the three of us went to. The DJ was from Los Angeles, according to the Facebook invite. Naturally, I was eager to check out anything that was "from L.A.," since that's where Cal Arts was. So I immediately snuck up to the front. The DJ was wearing sunglasses and shiny slacks and his hair was shaved close on the sides, with long bangs hanging in front of his face. He had a certain aura about him, a certain hardness. Watching him, you could sense what Los Angeles would be like. It would be tough and intimidating. But also very cool and stylized.

The three of us danced. It was pretty freeing, being there with the Agenda kids. Art school: It was going to be a lot like the Agenda scene, I imagined.

Bennett was there that night too. Later, when they kicked everyone out, he was standing next to his car with some people. He was still pretty shook up over Hanna, I knew. As we were leaving I veered over toward him. I was going to say something, but I couldn't think of what. So I gave him a head nod instead. He nodded back. Judging from the many girls that hovered around him these days, he would not have a problem finding a new girlfriend. But he didn't seem interested in that.

For New Year's, Logan Hewitt had a huge party that everyone went to. I managed to talk Kai and Antoinette into going, though they were complaining the whole time. Claude and Petra and a lot of our old crew were there. Krista showed up looking super hot. She had dumped her sophomore basketball player and was on the prowl. I thought people would be talking about Hanna, but nobody was. She was out of the psych ward and in a new facility, but the Sloans were not telling people what was going on. Not even Claude had a clear idea what was wrong with her. "Psychotic break" was one phrase he'd heard. We'd looked it up online and it was not good.

As Logan's party began to thin out, a girl from yearbook came and found me. She said that Grace was upstairs and would I come talk to her? I asked what it was about, but she wouldn't say. "Grace really wants to talk to you," she repeated.

This sounded suspicious, but I went, following the girl up the stairs and down the hall. She led me to Logan's bedroom, the same room where Grace had caught me making out with Hanna.

I was now even more on guard. But when I went inside, I found Grace sitting on the bed with another of her girlfriends, sobbing into a wad of toilet paper.

This was about Austin Wells. He had just broken up with Grace over the phone, from college. Grace was still clutching her glowing phone in her tiny hand.

The girl who'd brought me upstairs told me this. I felt like saying, *What do you want me to do?* I honestly didn't know what help I could be.

Grace asked the other people to leave. They obediently got up and left the room.

So then it was just Grace and me. I moved closer. She didn't do anything. She sat there on the bed, hiccupping and blowing her nose.

I cautiously took a seat on the bed. Was that what she wanted? I had no idea. But it must have been, because she lunged toward me and threw her arms around me and began crying even more.

So I went with it. I held her. And let her cry and get snot all over my shirt.

"Oh, Gavin," she said. "What happened to everyone?"

I wasn't sure who exactly she meant. But I understood the basic idea.

"I don't know, Grace," I told her, rubbing her back in a slow circular motion.

It was weird about Grace. We were nice to each other, but we weren't friends. We had almost nothing in common. I couldn't have kept up a conversation with her if my life depended on it.

But I did still love her in a way. Maybe more than I did when we were going out, since I understood her better. So I sat with her. And listened to her cry. And rubbed her back. And told her everything would be all right.

My brother, Russell, showed up briefly during that same Christmas break. He only stayed at the house a couple nights before he headed to the coast to stay with his friend David Stiller and some other Evergreen friends.

My mother was not happy with this arrangement. She wanted Russell home, like for the whole vacation, like a normal college kid. She hated that her family was scattered all over for the holidays. Russell had reasonable excuses for his short visit. But I suspected the truth was that he didn't want to hang around that big depressing house.

The first night he was home, Russell seemed subdued. He barely spoke. I assumed this was about my dad: the new girlfriend, the coming half sister. He'd had such a close relationship with my dad previously. All these sudden changes were probably more difficult for him than for me.

My mother was having her own problems. She kept acting like she'd let Russell down somehow, like she'd let the whole family down, though I didn't see how she figured that. None of this was her fault.

During dinner we managed to relax a bit. I told Russell more about my applications to different art schools. He seemed to think art school was a good place for me in general, though he mostly nodded and ate. His hair was longer than I'd ever seen it. And he had that same beard, which he'd never cut. It didn't look so goofy anymore. It looked more mature, like it belonged on him. *He's a man now*, I thought to myself. *A not very happy man.*

My mom asked him about school and he said he'd shifted his studies around. He talked for a long time about one of his teachers, Professor Friedman, who'd had a big effect on him. This Friedman guy had worked on an important social justice initiative for the president and had actually worked directly with the White House for a year on a project to help disadvantaged kids in the south. That was kind of a shock. Russell was interested in helping the poor? When had that happened? And then came an even bigger bombshell.

"I think I'm gonna take a leave of absence for a year and help run this new program he's starting in Alabama," he said into his plate.

My mother and I exchanged looks.

"Really?" said my mother. "Starting when?"

"Starting immediately."

My mom was stunned. So was I.

"Did you talk to Dad about this?" I asked.

Russell nodded that he did.

"And what did he say?" asked my mom.

"At first he tried to talk me out of it. Now he doesn't say anything."

"What do you mean?" said my mother.

"I told him to go fuck himself," said Russell without looking up.

My mother literally dropped her spoon. I sat with my mouth hanging open.

"When did this happen?" asked my mother.

"I don't know . . . last October?" said Russell.

"And why didn't you tell anyone?" said my mom.

Russell made a helpless shrug of his shoulders.

A silence fell over the table. We ate.

"Have you met Alexis?" I asked Russell.

He shook his head no. Then he looked up at me. "Have you?"

I nodded that I had.

"And?" he said.

"She's young. She's pretty."

Russell shook his head. "What a dick," he said, going back to his food.

"Oh, please don't say that . . . ," said my mother. She was nearly in tears now. She hadn't touched her food.

"It's not your fault, Mom!" I snapped.

"At least we're not little kids," said my brother in a low voice.

In January, everyone was back in school again. That's when Claude called me one night. "Do you know a girl named Rachel Lehman, from Hillsdale?"

I was at home. The house was empty. Mom had gone out to dinner with Henry Oswald, I think to talk about whether she should marry Peter Frohnmeyer.

"Yeah, I know her," I said. "I told you about her."

"You did?"

"We played tennis once. She's friends with Olivia and Logan. I went on a date with her."

"What happened?"

"Nothing. She wanted to talk about you."

"Oh yeah?" said Claude. "Well, that explains it. She's been messaging me. She says we went to summer camp together."

"Yeah, she mentioned that."

"I checked her out. She looks pretty hot."

"She's totally hot."

"She good at tennis?"

"No," I said. "Not really."

"Well, what the hell," said Claude. "She wants to hang out. And she's got a friend. You up for it?"

"What do they wanna do?"

"They want to go snowboarding. Her family's got a cabin on Mount Hood."

"No kidding."

"They want to go up the night before. So we'd spend the night."

"Wow."

"I know. Too good to be true, right? Logan said she's

cool though. You went out with her. What do you think?"

"Hard to say. She didn't really say much when I was with her."

"Hmmmm," said Claude.

"But she didn't like me. You're the one she likes. From summer camp."

"Yeah," said Claude, thinking about it. "What did she say about that?"

"She said you guys made out. When you were thirteen. You broke her heart."

"I wish I could remember. I made out with a million girls at that place."

"Well, one of those girls was her."

So Claude accepted the invitation. Rachel sent us the address, and on Friday night we packed up the RAV4 and headed out. We drove into the deep forests of Mount Hood and then pulled off the main highway and had to four-wheel it up a snow-covered side road. A bunch of cabins were clustered in this one area, all of them identical and new-looking, like mini-McMansions, but ski cabins instead.

We checked the numbers until we found Rachel's place. Then we parked and sat in the RAV4 for a moment and looked at it. Even by Claude standards this was a pretty miraculous hookup.

We got out of the car. Rachel and Ingrid were already inside from the looks of it. All the lights were on and a shiny

Lexus SUV, with a bunch of snowboarding stuff in the back, was parked in the snowy driveway.

We walked to the front door and knocked. Immediately we heard giggling and voices inside.

It took a while, but the door opened. Rachel and Ingrid were both there. Rachel was even cuter than I remembered. She wore a red ski sweater and UGGs and black yoga pants. Ingrid was cute too. She was short, with long blond hair and small, delicate features.

Claude and I stomped the snow off our boots. We went inside, and for a moment the four of us stood there in the entrance, grinning at each other. This was going to be fun. You could tell right away.

Rachel had a bottle of white wine in the fridge. Claude and Ingrid and I followed her there. We got the wine open and talked and ate cheese and crackers and grapes. Claude and Rachel did most of the talking. They figured out where and when they had met at summer camp. It was during a game called Totem Poles, in which people hid behind different trees and you had to count out a number using the trees and then kiss whoever was behind the tree your number ended on. She teased Claude for not remembering. Claude insisted he did remember, but it was obvious he didn't.

While they reminisced, Ingrid and I snuck looks at each other. Ingrid seemed pretty shy. You could tell she generally let Rachel take the lead. But that was okay.

•   •   •

The four of us attempted to cook dinner. This was a disaster, but we ended up with some pasta that was edible, more or less. Then we walked down the road, to the tiny town of Edelweiss, which was basically an intersection with a gas station and a tavern and a hotel. We went inside the tavern and watched a folk-music lady sing and play her guitar. But then they carded us and kicked us out. So we walked more, along the snowy road, through the sharp, crystal-clear mountain air. Above the treetops you could see the stars. They seemed to come alive up there, if you stayed still and quiet and stared upward long enough. For a moment the four of us did exactly that, standing in the middle of the road, our faces turned upward, nobody speaking or moving.

"Think of the thousands of years those stars have been up there," said Ingrid.

Heading back to the cabin, Claude and Rachel lagged behind, whispering and teasing each other about the Totem Pole game.

"You don't even remember!" I heard Rachel say.

"But I do remember!" Claude laughed. "I swear I do. . . . You were hiding behind a tree. . . ."

"We were all hiding behind trees! That was the point of the game!"

Ingrid and I smiled at each other as we listened to them. I didn't think anything was going to happen between us. But Claude and Rachel seemed to be on their way.

Back in the cabin we ate more of the mushy pasta. Claude and Rachel curled up together on the couch, where they alternated between talking loudly to us and having private whispery conversations with just each other.

When it was time for bed, Claude came into our room.

"I'm gonna . . . ," he whispered, pointing to the upstairs, where Rachel's loft room was.

I nodded that I understood.

He gathered his stuff and hurried up the stairs to Rachel. I could hear their low voices, whispering, teasing, giggling. Judging from the sounds that came later, everything proceeded smoothly from there. Ingrid was in a separate room downstairs. I don't know if she heard what was happening. I guess she must have. If she was Rachel's best friend she was probably used to it. Just like I was.

Our alarms went off early the next morning and off we went up the mountain. Rachel and Ingrid were both excellent snowboarders. Because we were so near the slopes, we got an entire hour when the runs were basically our own private domain. That part was fantastic: the early-morning sun, the stillness of the mountain, carving trails through the fresh snow. Claude and Rachel rode up the chairlift together every time, so Ingrid and I did too. She told me about herself. And vice versa. But mostly we watched our friends.

Later, driving home in the BMW, Claude was in a very good mood. He told me about his night with Rachel, making it funny and sexy like he does. It was classic Claude. That stuff was always happening to him.

I was happy for him, of course, but also a little surprised. I had thought that even if he did get another girlfriend, Claude would still be there for Hanna. At least until she got well enough to leave the facility. That's how close they were. At least in my mind.

But, in fact, after that weekend, Claude never mentioned Hanna again. Instead, he became totally swept up in Rachel Lehman. He wanted to be happy was the truth of it. He was selfish in that way. Rachel was super fun. Hanna was having serious problems. So what did you want him to do? Be miserable on purpose? Claude wasn't born to be miserable. Claude was born to have the best of everything. And so he would.

I still thought about Hanna, though. Even if nobody else did. I had recently begun my first real photo project, *Cars at Night*, which involved taking pictures of cars parked on the street late at night. I shot them in profile. I took a string and put a paper-clip hook on one end, which I would attach to the door handle of the car I was going to shoot. That way I was always exactly twenty feet away. This made the photos all the same, like mugshots, or passport photos.

I'd drive around in different neighborhoods looking for interesting cars. When I found one, I'd hop out and measure for distance, set up a tripod, and get the shot. Some nights I'd stay out very late. I wanted that to be part of the mood of the project. Things got very quiet on the street at three in the morning. It was just me and the raindrops and the cats. It was during those nights, driving around, looking for cars, that I would let my mind wander. I'd think about my friends, my parents, my future. And Hanna. God, poor Hanna. The golden girl. I still couldn't believe what had happened to her.

• • •

The other person who still had Hanna on his mind was Bennett Schmidt. He wanted to see her. He had tried calling her family, but they wouldn't speak to him. So then he asked me if the two of us could go. Could I work it out with the Sloans? This was probably not the best idea, but I went along with it. I called Mrs. Sloan myself, without mentioning Bennett. She gave me the number at the facility. I called and made arrangements for a visit.

So we went, Bennett and me. I drove. Her new place was different from the hospital. It was a residential treatment facility, a big house basically, with carpets and fireplaces, but with the doors locked and security people and nurses on duty 24-7. We signed in and met Hanna in a library. Another woman, a nurse, sat with us and read a magazine while we talked.

Hanna looked worse than before. Her hair was cut shorter and it looked limp and dried out. She kept sighing and breathing in a strange way, like she couldn't quite get settled. She had become a little bug-eyed, probably from the medication she was taking.

She also wasn't that happy to see us. There were probably other people she'd rather be visited by than her ex-boyfriend's tennis partner and the drug dealer she was sleeping with just before she lost her shit.

She didn't treat Bennett like a former boyfriend, that's for sure. She didn't treat me much better. She thanked us for coming and then fell silent. We ended up telling her random news from school, how the basketball team was doing and that Mrs. Jamison, the English teacher, was pregnant. Hanna began to yawn. After twenty minutes it was time to go.

On the drive back home, Bennett didn't say a word. I didn't either. It was humiliating to visit someone who was that screwed up and yet was still completely indifferent to you. It was probably worse for Bennett, being in love with her. It was interesting, too, because in the months that followed, Bennett began to wind down his drug-dealing career. Maybe it was that the Sloans were so repulsed by him. Or maybe it was how Hanna dismissed him that night. Or maybe he just grew out of it. But by the end of senior year, Bennett Schmidt was pretty much out of the drug business.

I shouldn't say *Cars at Night* was totally my idea. The beginning of the idea was mine, to take photos of cars while they were "asleep." But Richie had input too, like using the string with the hook. That was the secret to passport photos, he always claimed. Making them all exactly the same. Same distance. Same light. Same stool. Same backdrop. If you looked at discarded passport photos all day, which Richie and I did sometimes, you saw how the more standard and uniform you could make the format, the more noticeable individual peculiarities became.

I didn't see Richie very much that winter. He was trying to get better gigs now. He didn't want to lose ground after his famous Elliot Square photo, so he wouldn't take just any job. This was good for me. It meant I got all the boring assignments from *Portland Weekly*. I did something for them almost every week. Which meant I always had some extra money in my pocket.

It was funny, too, because most of the editors at *Portland Weekly* didn't know how young I was. They'd send me to some microbrew place or a new wine bar, and I'd have to bluff my way in. This wasn't that hard. Nobody turned down free publicity. And if you acted like a pro, people didn't stop to think about how old you were.

When I did see Richie, it was usually at the shop. And then, after the holidays, I started working at Passport Photos myself a couple days a week after school, helping out his uncle when Richie wasn't around. It was a pretty easy job. I'd clean lenses or do some of the basic repairs. Then at night I'd sweep up, close the cash register, and count the money, if there was any.

And then one night in February, just as I was locking up, Richie showed up at the store wearing a suit coat and a new white shirt. He pounded on the door and I let him in. He had this stunned, slightly horrified look on his face. I thought he might have been in a car accident.

But no. He slammed a bottle of champagne dramatically on the counter and stared at me with huge eyes. "I just asked Nicole to marry me," he blurted.

"What did she say?"

"She said yes."

"*Dude.*"

"I know."

So then we had to celebrate. At first we couldn't get the champagne bottle open. And when we did, it sprayed all over the place. We poured what was left into two of his uncle's dirty coffee cups from the back. We toasted and drank. And then we stood there, in the quiet shop, and laughed a little and drank champagne. Richie was basically in shock. But he was "all in," like he gets. That was Richie's best quality. When he decided to do something, he did it. Not always perfectly. Not always gracefully. But he got it done.

"Antoinette wants to go snowboarding," Kai told me one day after school. "She wants to know what all the fuss is about."

"How open-minded of her," I said.

"Will you take us?"

"Sure I'll take you."

"And Antoinette says you can't make fun of her."

"I will try not to make fun of her."

I had not seen much of Antoinette since winter vacation. She had two independent studies that term, and a study hall, so she barely came to school on some days. It was impressive how she had turned her rebelliousness and bad behavior into extra off-campus privileges.

When I did see her that spring, she was reading. Sometimes novels, but usually memoirs of famous women or artists or people you wouldn't expect, like Eleanor Roosevelt. Antoinette told Kai that for girls, reading biographies of famous women was the only way to learn how to succeed in the world. And how to get what you want. They sure weren't going to teach you that stuff in school.

The main thing I'd noticed about Antoinette as a senior:

She'd calmed down. She'd quit smoking. She was vegan for a while. She still wore her weird clothes, but she didn't do it with the same attitude. She didn't do it *at you* like when she was younger. She was more contained now, more under control. She was biding her time. Bigger things were coming for her. So she lay low and stayed out of trouble. And read biographies of Lady Gaga.

I thought that big things were coming for me, too. *Cars at Night* was turning out great. I would have liked to talk to Antoinette about it. I felt she might give me good feedback. But that was the problem with Antoinette. She was never going to take a guy like me seriously. Not after I dated Grace Anderson and Krista and was still friends with Claude and Logan. These sins were unforgiveable, I guess. Once a popular jock, always a popular jock.

But if she wanted to go snowboarding, I would take her snowboarding. Of course I would. I would have taken her anywhere.

Kai pretended she didn't know anything about snowboarding because that would have marked her as boring and suburban. But when I went to her house the next day to see what equipment she had, her garage was full of skis, boots, snowboards, and every kind of accessory you'd need. So we had plenty of gear. Kai and I then drove to Burrito Express for dinner to discuss how best to introduce Antoinette to snowboard culture, which devolved into a conversation about Antoinette in general: what books she read, what she thought about high school, what she thought about us.

"She thinks I'm an idiot," I said. "That's pretty obvious."

"No she doesn't."

"Then she thinks all my friends are idiots."

"Well, they are, kind of."

"She never gives me any credit."

"Maybe that's not her job. You have to have your own confidence. You can't get it from her."

I shrugged. It was always a little awkward, talking about Antoinette with Kai.

But now, though, for some reason, I brought it up. "Did she ever say anything to you about Berlin?"

Kai became anxious. "Just that you guys fooled around a little, because you were so jet-lagged. . . ."

That was the official story. Which was true enough.

Kai sighed. "You can't pine away for her for the rest of your life."

"I know," I said. "It's not like that anyway. I know my place with her."

"What is that, exactly?"

I thought for a moment. "I'm the guy who can teach her how to snowboard."

The three of us slept over at Kai's on Saturday night—Kai and Antoinette in Kai's large bed and me on the floor on an air mattress. At five thirty a.m. Kai's mother woke us up and had a huge delicious breakfast waiting downstairs. Then we piled into the prepacked Subaru, with the snowboards on the roof, and drove to Mount Hood.

Antoinette was somewhat athletic, but she had a terrible time with the snowboard. We started her on the bunny slope, but she couldn't figure out the balance. She faceplanted multiple times. When a bit of blood appeared on her lower lip, we decided to take a break.

So then we had lunch and sat in the lodge, watching people. I had been snowboarding my entire life, but with Antoinette there, I saw the ski-lodge crowd in a more critical light. Like how much status was being expressed by the different clothes and equipment people had. And how vain and full of themselves everyone was, tromping around in their French ski boots and thousand-dollar parkas.

"This is quite a scene," said Antoinette, with her slightly swollen lower lip, which she was dabbing at with an ice cube wrapped in a napkin.

After lunch Antoinette insisted that Kai and I go snowboard ourselves. She didn't want to hold us back any more than she already had.

So Kai and I rode the big chairlift to the top and came down together. Kai was not as good a snowboarder as Rachel and Ingrid, but she was still pretty good, and we carved gentle turns back and forth together, zoning out on the dazzling white snow, in the brisk mountain air.

At one point Kai got caught in some deep snow beside the trail and wiped out. She did a serious tumble in the snow. I skidded to a stop and hiked up to get her hat and goggles, which had fallen off above her. I then scooted downward on my butt, until I slid into her back where she was sitting. I stayed there while she rearranged her hat and scarf. I helped brush the snow out of her hair. Then, since we were off the trail and tangled up together anyway, we just sat for a while, enjoying the view of the mountains in the distance and the trees and the snow.

The last week of March was when most people found out what colleges they'd been accepted to. Wednesday was the big day for most people. Many of them got the news on their phones. You'd hear random screams or outbursts from other classrooms. And then people in the hall would be laughing and super happy and threatening to not bother going back to their afternoon classes.

After last period, people who hadn't heard were frantically checking their phones. You'd see someone beaming with joy at one locker and then, a few lockers down, someone else in tears. In the midst of the excitement, an e-mail from Cal Arts silently materialized on my phone. Staring down at it while I stood at my locker, I felt like my life was about to take its first major turn. I slipped my phone into my pocket. I couldn't look at it yet.

I drove the RAV4 home. My mother wasn't home. It was just me in the big house. I did my usual routine, opening the refrigerator and getting out the milk. I took a bowl out of the dishwasher and a box of Cheerios from the cabinet. I filled the bowl and poured in the milk.

I took out my phone and set it on the table beside me.

I looked into my bowl and began to eat. I kept my head down. Antoinette had once said if I'd been born in a different century I'd be a monk. I felt like that now. Spooning the Cheerios into my mouth, my head down, my mind empty, my eyes focused on the light brown circles floating in the white milk as I scooped up every last Cheerio.

When I was done I put the bowl in the sink and sat down at the table again. I picked up my phone. I opened the e-mail, which sent me to a link. I opened the link and found a message. I pressed on it:

We are pleased to inform you . . .

I'd been accepted. I let out a long breath. I sat back and closed my eyes for a few seconds. I waited for a feeling of great happiness to come over me. And it did. A little bit. But what I mostly felt was a growing sense of *now I'll have to go.* It had been such a pleasant daydream: *art school*, being an *artist*, me and my *camera*. But what was the reality going to be? And I had no backup plan. I'd basically thrown myself off a cliff. This was the direction I was going, whether I wanted to or not.

Kai didn't get into Oberlin, her first-choice college. She didn't get into her second or third choices either. She did get into New York University, though. She called me from in front of the supermarket where she was with her mother. I could hear the shopping carts banging together. She read me the acceptance notice. She was of course relieved that she got in somewhere. But NYU? From everything she'd read, it was huge and impersonal and there was no real campus. You were dumped in the middle of New York City, basically. She wasn't sure she wanted that. She didn't know if she could handle the stress.

"But you want to be a writer," I reminded her. "New York is great for that." She had told me this a couple months before.

"Yeah, but I'll be all alone. And the dorms are tiny. And there's no grass."

"Maybe that's a good thing," I said.

There was a pause. I heard a sniffle on her end. "I wanted to go to a real college," she said, her voice filling with emotion. "With courtyards and Frisbees and all that."

"Frisbees?" I said. "You've never thrown a Frisbee in your life."

"You know what I mean."

"Maybe they'll have other things. That are good in other ways."

"I don't want to go to New York," she said. "It's too much. It's too scary."

"But how do you know until you get there?"

Antoinette got accepted to a college called St. John's. It was a small school in New Mexico where you only read the classic books. That was the entire curriculum. You started with Plato as a freshman and then went right through the rest of civilization. It was for weirdos and geniuses, it sounded like. I imagined skinny dudes with wire-rim glasses, wearing tank tops and sandals to class.

Antoinette didn't say much about it. And then she made fun of Kai for being afraid of New York. "You're going to love it," she said one night as we drove to Burrito Express in Kai's Subaru. "Are you kidding? You're going to be so glad you're not surrounded by frat boys and football games. NYU will be perfect for you."

"I hope you're right," said Kai.

"Oh my God," said Antoinette. "I am *so* right."

By mid-April, it was mostly settled where people were going to college. Grace Anderson would not be going to Puget Sound with Austin, but instead was going to University of Oregon. So were Petra Jones and Logan Hewitt. Logan Hewitt would be living in the Hewitt-Lonsdale dormitory, which his father had donated the money for, since he'd gone to Oregon too. Claude was going to Santa Clara College near San Francisco. I didn't know anything about it but someone said everyone was preppy and good-looking, which sounded about right. Emma Van Buskirk was going to Yale. Olivia Goldstein was going to Smith College back East, which Kai wanted to go to, but didn't get in. Bennett, I found out, was going to University of Portland to study electrical engineering. Which people joked about. "If you want to have your brain rewired, who better than Bennett!"

And last but not least, I was going to Cal Arts. Which, I found, confused people. Or at least nobody really said anything about it. I was tall and blond and good at tennis. That's how most people thought of me. But nobody really cared that much. High school was almost over. We were already starting to drift away in our own directions.

Once the college stuff was settled, a new feeling of freedom set in among the seniors. People really started to flake then. The photographer who was supposed to do sports suddenly couldn't do it anymore, which left me to take pictures of Althea Jones, who was our school's best girl athlete. She was a sophomore and a sprinter and was already the district champion in the 100 and 200 meters and 100-meter hurdles. This year she was projected to be the #1 girls sprinter in the state. The yearbook people needed pictures of her, and Emma wanted to put her on the cover of the *Owl*, and the track coach actually came and found me at my locker and wanted me to take some pictures of her for the trophy case, where she would probably be for the next twenty years.

I drove to one of our rival high schools on a cloudy day and stood around at the girls track meet. When they began running the sprints, I found Althea and introduced myself and took some pictures of her warming up. She was tall, with long legs but a very young-looking face. There was a sweetness there, but also an edge, too. I remembered tennis players in the twelve and unders often had a similar appearance. They looked like children. But they were going to take you down, just the same.

They announced the 100 meters. Seven girls lined up, and I walked down the track a little ways and got a bunch of different shots of Althea and the others as they stretched and shook out their arms and adjusted their blocks. I noticed a new energy come into the crowd. Everybody stopped what they were doing. Nobody was going to miss this. When the girls got into their stances, a deathly quiet came over the stadium. You could actually hear the flag waving over the stadium for a second. The girls crouched down and then crouched a little more, and then the gun fired. They were all fast. After twenty yards they were still bunched together. But then Althea switched into another gear. She surged out ahead of the others. I blasted away and kept shooting, even after she'd won and come bouncing to a stop and then turned and fist-bumped some of the other girls, who seemed in awe of her.

I didn't say anything to her afterward, but I followed her around for several minutes, still shooting, while she waited for her next event. *She was the best.* That was the story. You kept seeing glimpses of it in her face and the way she did things. She was very nice, very polite. But then, as she looked at her hand, or fiddled with her shoe, you could see a kind of maturity in her face, a kind of firmness. *She was the best.* It sent a shiver up your spine. It was the most interesting thing I'd shot since the riot in

Seattle. And I was pretty sure I'd got something usable, since I took about two hundred pictures.

Later that week, when my father heard about my college acceptance, he did what he always did: he made a reservation for dinner.

I met him in a new restaurant near his apartment.

"So," he said, putting his napkin in his lap. "I understand congratulations are in order. You've been accepted to art school."

I smiled. I couldn't help myself. "Yes," I said. "I'm very excited."

"I understand Henry Oswald had some connections there."

"That's right," I said, nodding, trying to give Mr. Oswald the credit he deserved but not making it sound like he had overshadowed my father in any way. "His brother went there."

"It always helps to have an alum recommending you," said my dad. "Especially one who has done well."

"I went to see his brother in Tacoma," I said. "He makes movie posters. And does layouts for advertising."

"So you actually met with him? And Henry set this up for you?"

"Yeah. It wasn't a big deal or anything."

"How did Henry know you wanted to go to Cal Arts?"

"I told him."

"When did you tell him?"

"I don't know. In the fall."

"He came to the house?"

"Yeah. He came over a couple times . . . to check on us."

"To check on you."

"Yeah," I said. "To see how we were doing. What do you care?"

"I don't care," said my father with perfect calm. "I don't care at all. Except that if someone takes an interest in my son to the point of getting him admitted to an expensive, out-of-state art college, it seems odd that nobody told me about it."

"Well," I said quietly. "I hadn't been accepted yet."

"You've been accepted now."

"And now you've been told," I said.

"Yes, after everything has been decided."

I looked across the table at him. "You can't blame Mom for not keeping you in the loop."

"Why can't I?"

"Because you totally fucked up her life," I said.

My father sighed. "Your mother and I will have a good relationship once the situation has normalized. Once the emotions have worked themselves out."

"And when will that happen?" I said. "Never?"

My father stared at me then, with a special look he used in certain situations. He let his eyes go dead a little, to let you see the hardness in his soul. Like if you thought you could manipulate him emotionally, you were sadly mistaken. "It will happen when she has the good sense to let it happen," he said.

During dessert, though, my father's mood improved. He wanted to hear more about Cal Arts.

"A lot of famous artists went there," I said.

"Famous like how? Like they make posters for movies?"

"No, like really famous. Like their paintings sell for millions of dollars."

"Does the school guarantee that? The millions of dollars?"

I knew what he was referring to. He had once explained to Russell and me that if you went to the right law school, you would average an income of a million dollars a year for the rest of your life. It was practically guaranteed.

"No, of course it's not *guaranteed*," I said. "It's *art*."

"How much does your friend the photographer make?"

"You mean Richie? He does pretty well at times. And other times he works at his uncle's photography shop."

"I see," said my father, adjusting his napkin. "I'm not trying to be critical. I just don't know how one makes a living as an artist. I'm sure that some people make a very good living at it. But I would guess that the percentage of those people would be very small. And that the vast majority . . . well, they would be grateful to have a job making movie posters or whatnot."

I didn't like the direction this was going.

"And then one wonders," he continued. "What makes an artist popular? How do you make a success of it? I would imagine you would need some sort of gimmick. And it would probably be useful to appear mentally deranged to some extent. That seems to be something people associate with great art. Someone like van Gogh, where would he be if he hadn't cut off his ear? And mailed it to his girlfriend! I mean, people like his paintings, sure. But it's all about marketing when you get right down to it. Who has the craziest backstory."

My father was mocking me with these comments. I was used to this. He had said worse to me. But at that moment, some part of me could not let these insults stand. I had the thought that I could ram the table into him. Or throw the butter bowl at his head. Instead, I lifted my head and stared at him across the table, letting *my* eyes go dead a little, letting the hardness of *my* soul show through.

When I escaped the restaurant, I drove straight to Kai's. I didn't text first, so I didn't know if she was home, but I rang the doorbell anyway. Her mother, who knew me by then, sent me up to her room.

Kai was in the shower. So I flopped on her bed. Her laptop was open. She had been writing something. I read a little of it. It was about a girl who was moving to New York to go to college, and how scared she was.

The shower turned off. I could hear Kai pushing the shower curtain back. I heard her say something. She was talking to herself, not a lot, just a few quiet things.

"Hey, Kai, it's me," I said loudly toward the door.

"Oh my God, what are you doing here?"

"I just had dinner with my dad."

"Oh. Poor you."

I heard bathroom drawers opening and closing. The hair dryer came on for a minute. Eventually the door opened. She came out with a towel wrapped around her.

"I'm reading your story," I said. I was on my stomach, on her bed, with her laptop.

"Don't read that. It's terrible."

"No it's not."

"Don't look. I have to put my clothes on."

I didn't look.

"What did your dad say?" she asked me.

"Nothing. He was being his usual dickish self."

"My mom doesn't want me to go to NYU," said Kai.

"Why not?"

"It's too far away."

"Maybe you shouldn't go."

"Now I want to go."

I turned back toward her. She was still in her underwear, looking for her pants.

"Don't look! I'm not dressed yet."

But I did look. Not in a sexual way. I just wanted to watch her. Kai would not be around forever. Time was ticking away.

Meanwhile, spring had snuck up on us. We were seniors, of course, so what did we care if the air got warmer, if the flowers bloomed? Our whole lives were about to change. We didn't care about spring. We *were* spring.

I found myself hanging around the *Owl* office. The staff had thinned out by then. I was taking all the pictures. Emma was writing all the articles. The two of us would stay late and fiddle around with the layout. It had become a two-man operation. Emma didn't mind. She liked to do everything herself, which was probably how she got straight As and was going to Yale. She paid great attention to detail.

We would hang out in the office until six or seven some nights, drinking coffee and feeling very responsible and adult. Mr. Hull, the faculty adviser never stayed after school anymore. Emma had convinced him to leave it to her, which he happily did. It wasn't like Emma was going to do something edgy or controversial. She wasn't capable of that.

One night we locked up the office and walked across campus to the parking lot and I noticed Emma seemed especially chatty, in a different way than usual. As we crossed the parking lot, Emma continued to talk in a rushed, nervous voice. We came to my car.

"All right," I said. "See you tomorrow."

"Oh, uh, Gavin?" she said.

Her voice ran out of air as she said this. I could see her chest heave. Her eyes bounced around in their sockets.

"Yeah?" I said.

"Would you, uh, want to go to a play with me on Saturday?"

"A play?" I said. I wasn't sure what she meant. "Like a school play?"

"No, a real play. My parents have tickets they're not going to use."

"Oh," I said. "So not for the magazine?"

"No. Not for the magazine."

I was confused. Why would she think I wanted to go to a play? "What's it about?" I said.

"I'm not sure," she said, her chest heaved again. "But it'll be good. It's at the Civic. They only have good plays there."

I almost said, *Why are you asking me?* But then I understood. She was asking me out. On a date.

"Oh," I said, my confusion about the play turning into confusion about how to respond to Emma.

She could see I was unsure. She probably thought since we hung out so much, and talked a lot, that maybe something was happening between us. And being the studious, nonsocial person she was, she didn't know how to tell if a person actually liked you or not.

"Uh . . . ," I said. I had never been in this situation before. A girl was asking me out. A girl I was not attracted to. All I could think to do was not hurt her feelings. "Uh. Yeah. Okay . . . ," I said. "I mean, if you need someone to go with."

"You would have to drive, though. I can't use my mom's car that night."

"Okay," I said. "I can drive."

At home that night, I got an e-mail from Emma with her address. I looked it up. Her house was in a neighborhood I didn't know, which was surprising. I thought I knew every nook and cranny of our high school boundary. But this was on a road I'd never heard of.

That Saturday, before the play, I watched tennis on TV. Then I took a shower and went through my ritual of getting ready for a date. This time was different, though. Usually I went out with girls who I liked and wanted to impress. Girls like Rachel Lehman, who I would put on extra deodorant for, since I would be nervous in their presence, since they had been on lots of dates, usually with guys who were as cool or cooler than me. But Emma? Had she even been on a date before? Probably not.

I drove the RAV4 to the Van Buskirk house. It wasn't that nice. I mean, it was fine, but it was small and on a dead-end cul-de-sac. It seemed odd that Emma was going to Yale.

But she did have a 4.0 grade-point average. And she was the editor of the *Owl*.

I parked and rang the bell at her front door. Her mother answered. She was very excited to meet me. She invited me into the small entrance area and told me about the play: who wrote it, who directed it, how great the local theater productions were. Then she yelled—too loudly—up the stairs for Emma, which I was sure Emma didn't appreciate. And then Mr. Van Buskirk showed up, taking off his reading glasses to shake my hand. He also told me about the play and how great it was. I felt like saying, *If it's so great, why aren't you going?*

It was all very weird. Emma was still upstairs. "So Emma tells us you're going to art school in California," said her mom. "You're a very talented photographer."

"Yeah," I said, looking up the stairs.

"That's wonderful. Your parents must be very proud."

"They're sort of occupied with other things."

"What do your folks do?" asked Mr. Van Buskirk.

"My dad's a lawyer."

"Oh," said Mrs. Van Buskirk. "A lawyer!"

Finally, Emma came downstairs. She was wearing a dress. She looked pretty good. She had cute shoes on and a bit of lip gloss. But she also had a small orange scarf tied around her head. I'd never seen her wear anything like that before. We were going downtown, to the big theater, so I guess that's why she went for the scarf. Her parents were still talking and asking me questions about myself. But the scarf had thrown me off, and with everyone talking at once, it was hard to focus.

When we finally got outside, I found myself opening Emma's door for her, so she could climb into the RAV4. When she was in, I closed it for her. Everything was going to be very formal tonight.

We drove downtown, making small talk on the way. Emma directed me to park in a parking garage, so I did, even though it cost twelve bucks. Then we walked up Broadway to the theater. There was a pretty big crowd, older people mostly, people who looked like Emma's parents.

I made a joke about the old ladies, but Emma was too nervous to laugh. And she never liked my jokes anyway. She always got touchy whenever I joked around at the *Owl* office. Like high school journalism was not supposed to be funny.

Anyway, we made it through the play and then walked to the frozen yogurt place across the street. Several other people from the play were there, dressed-up middle-aged people. It was all very polite and civilized.

Emma finally seemed to relax once she had the frozen yogurt in her hands. It gave her something to focus on. I ate mine too, and we sat there and tried to talk about the play, which I totally didn't understand. It was about people living in a New York apartment building. Kai might have liked it. She might have understood the jokes.

As I drove Emma home, I suddenly felt sorry for her. When she got inside, her parents were going to grill her. What happened? Did he like you? Will he ask you out again? That was Emma's problem. She had been dominated all her life by her parents. They had pushed her to excel at high school and then pushed her to go to Yale. Now they were pushing her to go on dates, because it was getting to be "that time." She needed to learn about boys so she could eventually meet her husband and start her family.

One good thing though, halfway through the play she took off the scarf. And she did look good in the dress. She would eventually get a husband, at Yale or whatever.

I wasn't the only one going on awkward dates. In May, Peter Frohnmeyer flew up to Portland from San Francisco. This was a business trip supposedly, but his real purpose was to see my mother.

Naturally, she was a wreck about it. I wasn't supposed to know what was happening, but it wasn't hard to figure out. My mother would walk around talking on the phone and getting advice from various friends. Should she marry Peter Frohnmeyer? Had too much time passed? Were they too different as people? After a couple glasses of wine, she'd forget to keep her voice down. Or she wouldn't notice I was there. Or she was too worked up to care.

The day she was to meet Peter Frohnmeyer for dinner, I came home from school and found the kitchen a mess. My mother was upstairs. I cleaned up a little. I was nervous too, for some reason. I had found Peter Frohnmeyer on Facebook and looked him over. He was old now. He was thin at least, unlike my dad, who remained heavy and out of shape, even with his twenty-eight-year-old girlfriend. Frohnmeyer had a runner's body: gaunt, a bit skeletal. His sharp nineties clothing style had morphed into fleece and khakis and lame caps that said PUERTO VALLARTA on them. His hair was mostly gray and there wasn't much of it left on top. He looked much more corporate in general. There were glossy headshots of him on his Facebook page. He was a senior vice president at a big solar energy company. I clicked through to their site, which was super slick and full of eco-friendly philosophies and grassy fields and babies. Which probably meant they were evil.

The night of their date arrived. My mother came down the stairs looking better than I'd seen her in years. She looked *sexy*, which was good for her, I guess, but wasn't something I wanted to see or think about.

I made my own dinner that night, but I couldn't eat it. Then I didn't feel like sitting around the house, so I drove over to Claude's, which I hadn't done spontaneously like that in probably a year. He was playing *Assassin's Creed* while he texted back and forth with Rachel, who was out to dinner somewhere with her parents. I texted Kai and then checked to see if anyone was liking the two *Cars at Night* pictures I had posted on Instagram. It was a strange night of nobody paying attention to anything or anyone. Claude and I barely said a word to each other.

So then Rachel came over to Claude's, which was my cue to leave. As I stood up to go, Rachel gave me an update on Ingrid, like she always did, as if Ingrid and I might get together. I left and drove around in the RAV4. I thought about my mother and Peter Frohnmeyer. I didn't want her to make a mistake based on desperation. I felt like that was a possibility.

My mother's car was in the driveway when I got home. Inside, she was sitting at the kitchen table, a glass of wine in front of her, disappointment weighing on her face.

"You okay?" I said as I closed the door behind me.

She nodded that she was.

"How did it go?"

She shrugged. "Not that good."

"I'm sorry."

"I tried at least. And he tried. So at least we know." She took a slow sip of her wine.

I did what I always did when I got home late. Got the milk out. Got out a bowl and the box of Cheerios, only this time it was Special K, because we'd run out of Cheerios. We had Special K because my mom was trying to lose weight now that she was single.

"Does he like Portland?" I asked.

"Not particularly. He said he could never live anywhere but San Francisco."

"Well, that's where they do the tech stuff nowadays," I said.

"He's like that about a lot of things," said my mother, with a blank look on her face. "He's very clear about what he can and cannot do." She put down her wineglass. "I guess I've become set in my ways too."

I nodded and poured the milk into the bowl. Then I tried

to make my escape, through the dining room to the stairs. Special K got soggy fast; you had to eat it immediately.

"Wait a minute," said my mom.

I stopped.

"There's something I need to talk to you about."

"What's that?"

"It's about Henry Oswald."

I looked down at my bowl. I had not moved quickly enough. The Special K was already turning to mush.

"Henry and his wife . . . ," said my mother. "They're going through a transition."

"What does that mean?"

"They're not living together anymore."

This I did not want to hear. My feelings about Mr. Oswald were very simple. He had helped me get into Cal Arts. And I was grateful. And whatever else he was up to, with or without my mother, was none of my business. I didn't need to know. I didn't want to know.

"This might affect us," said my mother.

"Not us, *you*," I said.

"No. All of us. A lot of people are involved. His family. Our family. It's a very complicated situation."

"Are you and Mr. Oswald going to be together?"

My mother looked at her wineglass. "That's what he wants. I haven't decided yet."

"Couldn't you at least wait until I leave for college?"

"Hey, this isn't easy for me. Why do you think I went

out with Peter? Believe me, if there were an easy way out of this, I would take it."

I looked down at my bowl of mush. "Could we talk about this in the morning?" I said. "I'm sorta tired."

My mother looked at me. "You're tired?" she said. "How do you think I feel?"

June 12 was graduation day. It was one of those days, like a
wedding or a funeral, where you feel like you're not quite
in your body, at least not in the usual way. You kind of float
through things. As I walked through Evergreen's halls that
day, I could already feel a distance forming. I was already
separating from it. And the sports fields, and the breezeway,
and the picnic benches, even the courtyard where I used to
watch the fog during geometry class: It was already getting
smaller, turning into something juvenile and in the past.
Like whatever happened here, however important it had
seemed at the time, it was already fading. Nothing lasted.

Emma Van Buskirk gave the big speech, the same one
my brother gave two years before. It was the usual stuff,
about looking toward the future, not compromising our
ideals, and contributing to society. Everyone stopped listening after the first thirty seconds. When it was over, we threw
our hats in the air.

Logan had a big party that night. He had the pool going
and the hot tub. Kai and Antoinette even came: I guess
they figured since we were graduated, it was safe to come
mingle with these people. Claude and Rachel were there,

and Ingrid, who I talked to a bit. Then Emma Van Buskirk showed up. That was interesting. After having her opinions about the popular people, here she finally was, seeing them in their natural environment. The funny thing was, she got a little drunk and then started talking about Hanna in this loud voice. Like how some people thought she was a bitch, but how she, Emma, had always liked and respected her as a strong woman and how sad it was, what had happened. And then a bunch of other people who never knew Hanna also chimed in about it. Nobody who actually knew Hanna said a word. And then, just in time, someone started pushing people into the pool. Emma screamed and ran away.

In July we had to start packing up my parents' house. My mother was going to be moving at the end of August. This was a pain in the ass, but inevitable. I was still working at the Garden Center, so I could only help with the packing after work and on the weekends. It was quite a job, sorting through everything, trying to figure out what to save and what to throw in the big Dumpster in the driveway. My eighteen tennis racquets? A book I wrote about space aliens in fourth grade? An old skateboard I never rode? Kai came over during this, which was nice of her. One night she sat at my brother's desk while Russell gave me detailed instructions on the phone of what to do with his stuff. I was all in favor of the new Russell, who cared about the poor and loved his new professor who personally knew the president, but when he started telling me how exactly to pack up his things, I saw that he was still basically the same old Russell, wanting everything done very meticulously and thinking his time was much more valuable than anybody else's.

Since it was summer, and warm, Kai and I would sometimes take a bottle of wine from my dad's collection and drink it outside in the backyard late at night. This was super fun, doing nothing, being there together.

"Do you ever think of how totally different we might be when we're older?" said Kai one night. I was on my side, pulling on the grass. Kai was on her stomach beside me, watching a ladybug crawl up her finger.

"Different like how?" I said.

"Just like, all the different directions there are. That we don't even know about yet."

"I guess so."

"Like people go to college and figure out they really love molecular biology. And then they go off and do that."

"I don't think I'm going to love molecular biology," I said.

She watched the ladybug. "I feel like there's going to be this moment in the future when we'll have to choose."

"Yeah," I said.

"I wonder what I'll choose."

"I think you'll choose something cool."

"But you don't know," she said. "Because my mom? She was going to do all these things. But then she got pregnant, and now she's a housewife, driving a minivan."

"I can't see you as a housewife."

Kai blew gently on the ladybug. "If I become super boring, will you come find me?" she said.

"Yeah, if you want."

"Maybe you and I could get married," she said.

"I'd marry you."

"You would?"

"Yeah," I said. "I'll have my little molecular biology job and I'll need a wife, so I'll hit you up."

"Thanks a lot!"

"No, but seriously," I said. "There's probably a time in your life when the minivan makes sense. There must be. Since so many people have them."

"Why would you marry me?"

"Why?" I said. I put a piece of grass in my mouth. "Because it would be fun. You wouldn't take it too seriously. And I could be myself."

"I could write things and you could take pictures."

"Exactly."

She sighed. "God, life is going to be so strange."

"Yeah, but it'll be fun. I think it will be. I hope it will be."

She rolled onto her back and stared up at the stars. "Would you really marry me?"

"I think I would."

She thought about this. "That's good to know," she said.

Antoinette was the first to leave. She flew to Germany the first week of August to be with her dad. Then she was going to fly directly to her college in New Mexico. Her mom and Bald Mike were going to drive down with her stuff and help her get situated in her dorm.

Antoinette didn't want to make a big deal of saying good-bye. She didn't want us to come to the airport. But Kai and I insisted we do something, so we all went to the downtown Jamba Juice the night before. Kai drove us in the Subaru. Once we got there, we mostly checked out the other Jamba Juice customers and made fun of some of them and also said which ones were cool. This led to us wondering what music people would be listening to at our various colleges and what they would dress like and be like in general. Antoinette thought her college would be super nerdy but would probably have some geniuses hidden among them. Kai thought everyone at New York University would be chewing gum and have designer clothes that cost a fortune. I didn't know what the people at Cal Arts would be like except that supposedly people took mushrooms and walked around naked. Antoinette said she couldn't see me doing that, I was too conservative, but Kai said she could see it. And I could see it too, since my brother had changed so much at college. I was pretty adaptable, I thought.

Then Antoinette's mom called to remind her she wasn't done packing, so then we all got back in Kai's car and drove back to Antoinette's. And then we really did have to say good-bye, which was kind of shocking and terrible in a way. I guess I hadn't prepared myself for that part, actually hugging Antoinette and then standing there while Kai hugged her. Everyone started crying. Even Antoinette cried a little. And then Kai and I stood there like idiots while Antoinette went back in her house and did a final wave before she went in the door.

Kai drove us back in silence, wiping the tears off her face the whole way.

Kai left next. She left in the third week of August. She said you had to go early to NYU because the housing there was so impossible, and dorm space was so limited, and if you screwed up you might end up living on the street or under a bridge. She was pretty worried about the city in general. Her neighbor had recently visited New York and lost her wallet, or had it stolen, or something. Kai was pretty sure she would get robbed by someone or kidnapped by a taxi driver. "What's to keep them from just driving off with you?" she said. "Who would ever know?"

It didn't help that nobody in her family had ever lived

anywhere east of the Mississippi. Her dad knew one guy who he'd gone to dental school with who lived outside New York, so they'd looked him up on Facebook and gotten in touch, in case Kai needed to be rescued. Richie laughed at all this. He said New York was "five million rich assholes walking their dogs at night" and that Manhattan was probably the safest place on earth. I told Kai this, and her dad, who I was seeing a lot of, since Kai was constantly wanting me to come over during that last week while she was packing and getting ready.

At least she had great clothes. By this point, Kai was the best dresser of any high school person I knew. All summer she had been on fashion blogs studying what people were wearing. The couple times we went to Agenda, she would wear weird colors and combinations and the other girls would be super jealous. Still, she thought she would look like a hick in New York. I'd been in Berlin, which was probably similar to New York, so I kept telling her: You're hot. You look great. Everyone is going to think you're amazing. But she never believed it.

Finally, her day came and I rode to the airport with her and her family. Kai cried during much of the drive. She was really scared. She'd apologize and fix her makeup in the mirror and then start crying again. Her mother was pretty upset too, and her dad was getting a little annoyed with everyone for being so emotional. He kept reminding everyone she was coming home for Thanksgiving—they'd already bought the plane ticket—which was only twelve weeks away.

When we got to the airport, we got out, and Kai suddenly remembered something she needed out of her big suitcase. She pushed it over and unzipped it, right there on the ground in front of the airport with all the cars and the people crowding by. Nobody knew what she was doing. She took out her folded clothes and stacked them on the dirty cement. She was panicking, basically. She finally found whatever she was looking for, but now she was sweating and her makeup was all a mess again. I knelt down on the ground to help her repack the suitcase, and then we all started laughing. Even Kai laughed. Then her dad took her in his arms and really squeezed her hard until she went limp for a minute to calm her down. We had plenty of time. We were two hours early.

So then she gave me a long hug, and I kissed her forehead, and she said in my ear, "Oh, Gavin, why am I so scared?"

"Because you're doing something amazing," I said back.

Then she got all her crap together and tromped off, all red-faced and crying but also with her determined Kai energy. I had tears in my eyes too, and her mom was crying, and Kai went into the big revolving door, and that was it. She was gone. She was gone away to New York. And we were all standing there, getting yelled at by a traffic cop. . . .

• • •

My flight was a week later. I didn't do much for those days. I packed. I drove around. I kept my camera with me, since I was having all these different feelings about everything, and Richie always told me, whenever you're going through something, that's the best time to take photos.

I'd drive to the mall, the same one I'd been going to my whole life, and I'd buy some new socks or some underwear. I'd walk around looking at the people and thinking how different Los Angeles was going to be. No matter what adventures I had, or where I ended up, this mall would always be here. With these same people, eating their ice-cream cones and being content to live in the suburbs, where nothing ever happened.

My mom drove me to the airport. I mostly sat beside her, staring out the window. But it was good for my mom. She hadn't been able to totally focus on my leaving with everything else that was happening. Now, though, for the half hour it took to get there, we talked. She said how she was proud of me for sticking to my guns. And not letting my dad push me around. And doing what I wanted to do. Which, even if it didn't work out, she at least respected me for trying. She had loved the arts, in her way, which had led her to Echo Advertising. And here I was, doing it.

When we got to the airport, I got out and pulled my bags out of the car. My mom came around and gave me a long hug and I hugged her back and wished her luck with Henry Oswald or whatever. She told me not to think about her. And to have a wonderful time. And that I had a whole great life ahead of me. She said a few other motherly things that made me sad. I teared up a little.

But I got through that. And I went inside the airport. It was pretty busy in there, which forced me to focus. I got my boarding pass and checked my big bags, keeping my trusty Canon with me, and my carry bag. And then the security people got paranoid about the camera stuff. So they searched me again before they finally let me through.

I walked to my gate. I paced around a little bit, then settled myself by the big window and stared out at the tarmac. When they started loading the passengers, I hung back, like Richie used to do. *I'm not sitting in some over-crowded plane any longer than I have to*, he would say. So I let the other people go first.

When everyone else was on board, I went to the gate and handed the woman my boarding pass. She smiled and wished me a good flight. I slung my Canon over my shoulder and strode into the empty Jetway. It felt natural, that motion, that walk through the tunnel, to the waiting plane. I felt like I was in the right place. I heard a voice, my own voice say: *Welcome to your life.*

ACKNOWLEDGMENTS

Big thanks: Liesa Abrams Mignogna, Jodi Reamer, Alec Shane, Bethany Strout, Jennifer Altshuler, Laura Locker, Melissa Locker, Jason Etemad-Lehmer, David Colton, Chelsea Hogan, Kevin Samuels, Celina Burns, and Mother Foucault's Bookshop.